Summer Constellations

Summer Constellations

ALISHA SEVIGNY

KCP Loft is an imprint of Kids Can Press

Kids Can Press gratefully acknowledges the financial support of the Government of Ontario, through the Ontario Media Development Corporation; the Ontario Arts Council; the Canada Council for the Arts; and the Government of Canada, through the CBF, for our publishing activity.

Published in Canada and the U.S. by Kids Can Press Ltd.
25 Dockside Drive, Toronto, ON M5A 0B5

Kids Can Press is a Corus Entertainment Inc. company

www.kidscanpress.com
www.kcploft.com

The text is set in Minion Pro and Hickory Jack

Edited by Kate Egan
Designed by Emma Dolan
Cover photo courtesy of Cribb Visuals / iStock

Printed and bound in Altona, Manitoba, Canada in 1/2018 by Friesens Corp.

CM 18 0 9 8 7 6 5 4 3 2 1
CM PA 18 0 9 8 7 6 5 4 3 2 1

Library and Archives Canada Cataloguing in Publication

Sevigny, Alisha, author
Summer constellations / written by Alisha Sevigny.

ISBN 978-1-77138-929-7 (hardcover)
ISBN 978-1-5253-0043-1 (softcover)

I. Title.

PS8637.E897S86 2018 jC813'.6 C2017-903196-1

For my parents, who camped us all over the countryside.
And for the stars, which inspire the dreamers, the artists
and those who wish to change the world.

"We are all connected. To each other, biologically. To the earth, chemically. To the rest of the universe atomically."

— Neil deGrasse Tyson

"A starry sky is something that touches your soul. Our civilization's religion, philosophy, science, art and literature all have roots with our views of the heavens, and we are now losing this with consequences we cannot fully know. What happens when we cannot be inspired by the night sky?"

— Fabio Falchi (on light pollution)

Chapter One

"I can't believe you're leaving me."

Wind whips through the cab of the ancient Chevy, stirring my hair across my face. I gather frenzied strands into a high ponytail using the elastic around my wrist. Hot sun beats down on the chipped windshield.

Paige looks over at me, expression pained, hands fixed at ten and two. "It's not like I really have a choice."

"But for the whole summer?" I fiddle with the volume knob. Old Blue only gets the oldies station, and some doo-wop song warbles through tinny speakers.

"I know." She sighs, then makes a face at spending the next two months with her philandering father and his new girlfriend. Her words, not mine. "It's all so tragically cliché."

"On the bright side, you get to go to Japan and see all your relatives. How cool is that?" I inject false cheer into my voice; it sucks seeing her so down. The truck huffs its way up a hill as the sun starts to set on the mountains, casting a tangerine glow over the surrounding forest.

"Yeah." She gives the steering wheel an encouraging pat. "I feel bad for my mom, though."

"She'll survive." I lean my head against the rusty window frame, flecks of copper blending in with my hair. "Just like me." Though not entirely sure how I'm going to cope without my best friend for the next few months, I don't want to add to her guilt.

"At least you have dreamy Dan Schaeffer to look forward to," Paige says as we finally reach the summit, lake sparkling in the distance below. The truck shudders with relief.

"True." I've been trying to rein in the excitement at seeing him, but now that the day has actually come, something in my chest swells, finally breaking free of its bindings. We begin our descent, my heart racing along with the vehicle, down the steep slope.

"When's he arriving, anyway?" Paige says over the roar of the wind.

"Tomorrow. At least that's what the reservation says."

Paige pumps Blue's brakes, which seem to be working decently this week, anticipating the right-hand turn around the bend. A weathered wooden sign in fading white paint reads "Charming Pines Campground."

Home.

The paved road turns to gravel, crackling and crunching under tires as we drive through the entrance.

"I wonder if it'll be weird seeing him in person after all this time," I say. Dan Schaeffer and his family have been coming to our campground every summer for the last five years; I've been falling for him since the first one, when I was twelve. Last July things heated up and some intense make-out sessions … transpired. Though we never really talked about our status then or in any online chats since, I'm hoping — make that determined (Paige is always reminding me to think positively) — that this summer it's going to be more than just a seasonal romance.

"So, you gonna lock it down this time, or what?" One of her big brown eyes winks. "I want to get a text that Julia Ducharme is officially off the market." She turns the wheel to the left. "Preferably while I'm eating mind-blowing sushi and belting out karaoke with my cousins. Hopefully, Shinto and Haru have some cute friends," she muses.

"I'll do my best," I vow. Paige has been helping me dial back the tomboy while turning up the femme fatale all year. Judging by the reactions of a few boys at school, she says it's working, but I have my doubts. More likely it's just that skirt of hers I borrowed, but I'm crossing fingers that her lessons in Flirting 101 and Being Irresistible in Real Life 102 will pay off. There's only so much charm a girl can exude onscreen and by text.

We pull up in front of my house, and Paige puts the truck into park as my little brother ambles up our driveway.

Paige leans out the window and waves. "Hey, Caleb."

He gives a shy wave back, then pulls his ball cap farther down, slowly climbing the porch steps. His limp is getting slightly better, for sure.

"How's he doing?" Paige murmurs as the screen door closes after him.

"Pretty good," I say, voice soft, as I slip on my sandals. It's been a tough year. Not only have I been pining for Dan, but infinitely worse is that my little brother's been sick. Like, really sick. Paralyzed for months after contracting some rare disease called Guillain-Barré syndrome. Unable to breathe on his own, hooked up to all sorts of freaky machines. But then last month, thank goodness, he slowly started getting better. "Though he's pretty self-conscious about his face." The paralysis hasn't completely released his left side, resulting in the limp and a crooked smile that appears once in a lunar eclipse.

"Is physio helping?" Paige taps her fingers on the wheel.

"Yeah, but he still spends most of his time alone in the basement playing video games." The old Caleb used to play outside all day, climbing trees, swimming and generally raising hell around the campground. "And he's not happy about having to repeat fourth grade."

"But the doctors say he's going to make a full recovery?"

"That's what they say." I feel grateful that after such a crappy year, things are finally turning a corner. A light breeze rushes through the trees.

"Well." Paige sighs, pushing back smooth straight hair that never looks less than perfect. Mine usually resembles a red squirrel's nest, complete with leaf pieces and the odd twig. "Guess I better get going."

Hopping out of the truck, I dart around to the other side and jump up on the oxidized running board, flinging my arms around my best friend. "Have a great time."

She gives a wistful laugh. "We'll see. But I meant what I said about texting me. I'll be waiting."

"Who knows what kind of texts you might get." I wiggle my eyebrows up and down suggestively, holding on to Blue's battered flank.

"Why? What?" Paige's voice rises. "Jules! You're not seriously considering losing your V-card, are you?"

I shrug as nonchalantly as I can manage, given that my heart's pounding at the mere thought. I repeat her words back to her. "We'll see." Though Dan and I never went all the way, it wasn't for his lack of trying. But I hadn't been quite ready. Then.

She smacks my arm.

"Ow!"

"Every detail. Got it?"

Jumping onto the gravel, I rub my bicep. "Every detail," I promise.

*

After heaving an ATV wheel out of the back of the truck and waving Paige off, I roll the wheel up to the big shed at the side of the house.

Red, maintenance man for the Pines, strolls out, his paint-splattered overalls so worn the blue denim's almost white. Along with Mom and me, this guy basically keeps the place running.

"Hey, Red," I say, as he holds the door open for me.

"Hey, Jules, thanks for grabbing that for me. How was the last day of school?" he asks.

"Good, especially now that it's over." I duck under his arm, rolling the tire inside. It's weird to think that high school is over. Done. Finished. I'm not really sure how to feel. But I have to admit I'm looking forward to spending all day and night outdoors and under the stars, swimming in crystal-clear lake water and breathing in the sweet mountain air.

And seeing Dan, of course.

"So, you're officially on summer vacation, hey?" Rubbing a hand over his gray beard, he reminds me of a rugged Santa Claus.

My eyes narrow. "Yeah, but don't get any ideas. I don't 'officially' start full-time around here until tomorrow."

"I was just gonna get you to check out some boards at the dock." His tone is cajoling. "Some campers mentioned that there's a couple o' loose ones."

"A woman's work is never done." Sighing, I lean the wheel against the wall. "I'm headed down there tonight. I'll take a look. Supposed to be a killer meteor shower later on."

"Thanks, girl." Red's worked at the campground for as long as I can remember and is pretty much family. He was a good friend of my grandfather's and took over mentoring me in the ways of the handyman, or handyperson, I should say, after Gramps passed. They both felt that girls should be able to do things like change a tire, frame a cabin and manage basic plumbing. The latter being extremely gross. Useful. But gross. Thanks to Red, I can do all three.

"No problem," I say, wiping my hands on my shorts and exiting the shed after him.

I inhale the comforting smells of fresh cut wood and campfire. The campground's been open to the public for more than a month, but now that school's out and summer holidays have officially begun, we're gearing up for our busiest season. It's mostly just been retirees and weekenders, so far, but soon we'll be booked full. Which is good. Though Mom doesn't like to let on, I know money's been super tight this year with all the recent medical bills. I walk into the house, where the fragrance of baking supplants the campfire smoke.

Weird. Mom doesn't usually bake unless it's one of our birthdays or something.

"Mom?" I yell. "I'm home."

"In here," she calls from the kitchen.

I walk into a war zone. Our refrigerator has exploded.

"Been busy?" I survey the mess and the undomestic goddess that is my mother.

Her apron reads, "Get your Asana in Gear!" Aside from running the campground with Red, she also teaches hot yoga and is a bit of a fanatic about it. You'd think a hard-core health nut would love to cook, but she prefers we eat mostly raw whole foods from the organic market. At least that's the story she's selling. "Just wanted to make you and Caleb a special dinner tonight," she says, slightly out of breath. My mom has a pretty rocking bod for someone in her mid-forties, but I notice a few more fine lines around her eyes. Caleb's illness was rough on us all, and Mom pretty much lived at the hospital when he was in there. "Red's joining us."

I inhale deeply as another uncommon smell drifts under my nostrils. "Is that meat?"

"Pot roast," she says, pride tinged with regret.

"Seriously?" Mom's a vegan, though the rest of us are carnivores.

"Free range, grain-fed and hormone-free." She opens the oven door and takes a peek. "Poor thing."

"Yummy." I look at her. "What's the occasion?"

"Can't I cook a nice dinner for my family?" she says, the tautness of her shoulders belying her innocent tone.

I look at her more carefully. "No, really, what's up?

"We'll talk about it at dinner."

Okaaay. My heart drops into my stomach, thoughts automatically going to Caleb, though he looked fine when I saw him a few minutes ago.

"Where's the C-man?" I ask.

"He's fine, Julia." Our semi-telepathy goes both ways.

Despite her reassurance, I want to check for myself. Most girls my age find their little brothers annoying, but Caleb is a pretty awesome kid. And I thought that *before* he got sick. I head for the stairs to the basement, leaving Mom to put the final touches on dinner.

I descend into near darkness. The glow from the fifty-inch television illuminates Caleb's white face. He's wearing a headset and talking to one of his gaming friends, playing the latest Minecraft installment.

"Hey, Cale." I pronounce it like the leafy green vegetable.

"Hey," he says, staring at the screen.

"How you feeling?" I examine him closely.

"Fine." Despite his overall pallor from too much time spent in the hospital and down here, it does look like he's added a couple of pounds to his too-skinny frame.

"Are you winning?" I ask, flopping down beside him on the worn olive couch.

"Yup." Such a dazzling conversationalist.

"Did you notice anything up with our dear mother?" One of my legs bounces up and down.

Pressing the pause button, he looks at me with the clear blue eyes he got from Mom. I've inherited my dad's algae green ones, one of the few things I have to remember him by. "What?"

"She's making pot roast. And baking."

"Sweet." He goes back to his game.

"Aren't you the tiniest bit curious?" I am not the most patient person. My brother, on the other hand, could give a Buddhist monk a run for his prayer beads. I wonder if all the lying around in a hospital taught him to accept things as they come. It had the complete opposite effect on me. Now I get super anxious, super fast.

"Nope," he says, still staring at the screen.

I sit there for a few more minutes, watching his fingers fly around the controller. The sound of a screen door slamming has me jumping to my feet.

"Red's here," I say, adrenaline thrumming. Caleb's fine, but I have a lingering sense of foreboding. I seriously need to find out what's going on. Then I can get back to daydreaming about reuniting with Dan. I've been imagining the scene in my head for weeks. Will it be down at the lake? Will he come up to the house looking for me? What am I going to wear? You can't really dress up in a campground. Well, you can, but you'd look like an idiot. Did I give Paige back her skirt?

"Dinner!" Mom calls down the stairs.

Caleb mumbles a few words into his headset then removes it. He gets up stiffly and turns the game off.

"It's probably just something to do with the grounds," he says, as we head for the stairs. I love that, my little brother trying to calm *me*. "Maybe we're getting new fire pits installed down at the beach and they need our help."

His small hands grip the railings. His right leg lifts, comes down on a step, the weak left dragging up after it. The right one leads again, followed by the left.

"Maybe." I watch his progress.

"Or maybe we're canceling Wakestock this year," he adds, turning his head with one of his rare half smiles.

"Don't even joke about that." I've been practicing my 560 for the annual wakeboarding festival for the last two months, despite the subarctic temperature of the water. I can't wait to show Dan.

"Kids!" Mom calls again, voice strained and over-cheery, just as we walk into the kitchen.

"How you doing, bud?" Red walks over and ruffles Caleb's hair. I wonder why he didn't mention he was coming for dinner.

"Happy to be done school, Jules?" Mom asks. "I'm so proud of you!" Then, without waiting for an answer, she winks. "And the Schaeffers arrive tomorrow." I blush. Everyone kinda knows that Dan and I have a thing. His parents are good friends with Mom, and I'm sure they've talked about it. Not humiliating at all.

Mom has the picnic table in the backyard set up, so we head outside. The good china rests innocuously on Grandma's fancy tablecloth.

"Are we celebrating anything?" I ask, folding my hands and placing my chin on top of them. Maybe my instincts are all wrong.

Mom and Red look at each other as we sit down to eat. "Actually, we're having someone come by tomorrow to assess the property," she says without preamble.

What? "Why?"

"Well." She clears her throat. "I'm thinking of possibly selling it."

I pick up my fork and knife, looking at both of them. "Like, part of the land?" The campground is situated on a lake with tons of undeveloped forest stretching for miles in almost every direction.

"Like the whole campground." Mom's voice is calm. She glances at Red, who remains silent, then from my brother to me.

Boom.

Chapter Two

I sit there, gobsmacked.

Caleb looks at his empty dinner plate.

"Why?" I croak out, clutching my cutlery like it's the last American Girl® doll in the store on Christmas Eve.

"Well, I think it might be nice to have a change." Red — who apparently is there for moral support, though he doesn't look happy either — gives Mom a nod. She continues: "Running the campground is expensive, sweetie. It takes a lot of upkeep and maintenance and ..."

"It's because of me." Caleb's voice trembles, a 7.5 on the Richter scale. "Because I was sick."

"No, sweetheart," she says quickly. "It's just a lot to manage."

"We've never had a problem managing before." My voice is as shaky as Caleb's. She cannot be serious. Selling our home? This is so completely out of left field.

"It's the money," Caleb croaks. A few tears roll down his face, and he wipes them away angrily. "With all we spent on medical bills this year, we can't afford it, right?"

"Don't be silly, Cale."

I know he's probably right but I don't want to make him feel worse. Neither does Mom. She doesn't want to lie to us, but, by the look on her face, I'm guessing we don't know the half of the money problems. Our insurance coverage isn't the best because we run our own business. I've heard her worrying about this on the phone with Aunt Cheryl when she thinks I'm not listening. And now, after months of Caleb in the hospital, medications, physio, missed work, maybe it's just all too much.

I put down my cutlery. "May I be excused?"

"Julia," Mom begins. I don't wait for an answer.

I start walking. Around the side of the house, down the driveway, out to the road; one foot in front of the other. My cheeks are wet. This isn't happening. I trudge past several campsites — on autopilot — in no particular direction. It's Friday and people are getting all set up. Tents are being put together, RVs backed in, firewood collected, tarps hung. Music blares from docking stations, and bursts of laughter clash with my agony. Mom can't be serious. The campground is our home. Where would we go? What would we do? The overwhelming urge to vomit isn't going away. Like the time I slept over at Paige's house and mistakenly drank the glass of water on the bedside table that she uses to soak her night guard. I walk for what feels like hours, up and down the rows of campsites. When I finally look up from my dazed wandering, I'm approaching site 33.

Dan's site. His family books the same spot every year when they come from the city for their month-long stay. Three's his favorite number, he explained that first summer, so double threes is extra good luck. But an enormous RV that looks like it sleeps twenty comfortably is parked in the spot. It's not the Schaeffers'.

Idiots, I think. Didn't they see the Reserved sign on the site's post? Marching up to the RV, I wipe the tear tracks off my face and take a deep breath, eager to unleash my frustration on the unsuspecting campers. The RV door swings open and a pretty blonde descends the steps, laughing. A tall guy with brown hair styled to the side follows behind her.

"Excuse me," I say. "This spot is actually reserved. You're going to have to move your ..."

"Jules?" the boy says.

My mouth drops. "Dan?"

Racing the remaining distance, I fling myself at him, burying my face in his chest. He smells so good. His arms wrap around me, feeling so familiar that more tears start to form. "It's so good to see you," I blubber. "I can't believe you're here, I have so much to tell you ..." This is not quite how I pictured our grand reunion, but I am too upset to care.

"Um, Jules." Dan awkwardly untangles himself from my clutches. "I want you to meet someone."

I've totally forgotten about the blonde model standing beside us. I manage to wipe most of the snot off my face before facing her.

"Hi," she chirps, perfect and mucus-free.

"Hi." My voice is unsure.

"Jules, this is Taylor."

I look from Taylor to Dan, confused.

"My girlfriend."

Wow, I can't believe he's introducing me as his girlfriend. I mean it's what I was hoping for, but we never even talked about ... Then I pick up on the body language between them.

Oh.

Taylor is Dan's girlfriend.

I force myself to smile. "Nice to meet you."

"Jules's family owns and runs the campground," Dan explains to Taylor.

She nods politely. An uncomfortable silence settles around us.

"So ... you guys bought a new RV, hey?" A maniacal grin takes my face hostage.

"Yeah," Dan says. "Want a tour?"

Um, no.

"Actually, I promised Red I'd check on something down at the dock." I need to get out of here. "But say hi to your parents for me." I catch a glimpse of two dark shapes moving around in the RV.

"Sure," he says, voice hesitant. "Jules ..."

"Bye!" Turning around, I walk away as quickly as possible, almost tripping over the fire pit I shoveled out yesterday to prepare for his arrival.

"Nice meeting you," Taylor calls after me.

"Same." I wave over my shoulder. I can't think. I can't breathe. All I can do is walk.

Dan has a girlfriend. He brought her here. Why didn't he tell me? Ten minutes later, I'm down at the lake. The sun has disappeared and the first few stars are out. I aim straight for the shed behind the bathrooms, where we keep supplies like toilet paper and soap. I open the padlock, navigate my way around two hundred rolls of paper towels and heft a long black bag over my shoulder. The meteor shower won't be at its peak for a few hours, but I head over to the dock to set up anyway. For some reason, looking up at the night sky and contemplating the vastness of our universe and our insignificance in it somehow calms me. Maybe it's like, if none of it matters, then none of it *actually* matters. And my heart, just hit with the one-two punch, could use some Zenning out.

Soft guitar music floats on the breeze. Ugh. Someone's out there already. I approach the pier. At least they're not singing. It's so awkward when they're singing. Whoever it is, they're good, at least. Making out a faint silhouette at the end of the dock, I step onto boards that groan gently as they sink slightly into the water. The playing pauses for a minute, then resumes. As I get closer my foot catches one of the loose planks Red mentioned, and I stumble forward, sprawling face-first onto splintered wood, clutching the telescope to my chest to keep it from landing in the lake.

The guitar stops. It clatters to the dock as its owner jumps up and rushes toward me.

"Are you all right?" the low voice asks.

"Fine," I mumble, getting to my knees.

Best day ever.

A hand extends toward me. Still clutching the telescope with my left arm, I take the offered palm with my right and wonder how a pirate came to be on my dock. Eyes like midnight, jet-black hair and olive skin: he is the absolute definition of tall, dark and handsome. Like a picture on the cover of one of Mom's romance novels. Complete with no shirt. Or is that "incomplete"? My palm burns in his.

"Somebody should fix that plank." He grins, letting go of my hand. There's a blinding flash of gleaming white teeth.

"Somebody is planning on it," I say, mouth dry, unnerved to find a half-naked man on my dock. I can only imagine the picture I must present. Scratch that. I don't want to imagine. "Thanks," I add lamely.

Dan bringing his girlfriend and me falling at a handsome stranger's feet? Paige's words echo in my head, *It's all so tragically cliché.* I stifle an urge to laugh.

"No problem." He flashes that devastating smile again and walks back to the guitar. Dangling his feet in the water, he starts strumming again while I stand there, unsure of what to do. Handsome pirate or not, this is *my* dock. I stick with my plan and set up my scope.

"Nice night for stargazing," he says, still strumming.

"Yes," I respond, adjusting the height.

"So, who's planning to fix the dock?" he asks.

"Me." My tone is clipped. "Why do you ask?" *Don't look at him and he'll leave you alone.* I'm not in the mood to make small talk with pirates.

I feel his eyes on me. "Need a hand with that?"

"Got it under control, thanks." I peer into the scope and fiddle with the lens. "My family owns this place."

But for how long?

He stops strumming the guitar. "Really?" He turns around on his butt to face me, drops of water flying from his feet.

"Hey!" I say. "Watch the equipment." I examine Astra for any damage. She's dry.

"Sorry." His tone is sincere, and I forget to not look at him. His dark hair is mussed as if he's just returned from a long, windblown voyage at sea. "What are you looking at?"

"The sky," I say, pointing up.

"I can see that," he says. "Anything in particular?"

My cheeks flush. "There's a meteor shower tonight."

"Nice. Can you see it with the naked eye?"

Something about hearing the word "naked" makes the flush spread down my body. Good thing it's dark.

"If the clouds cooperate." Turning my back to him, I busy myself with the telescope.

He doesn't take the hint. "You have a beautiful property here," he says.

"Thanks." My voice cracks as a few residual tears well up and spill over. Oh, God. I still can't believe what Mom's considering. This is our home. My home. Are we going to move to some cookie-cutter house with a tiny backyard? I need fresh air, the trees, the lake, the freedom that comes from wide-open spaces and all that other stuff Mom's beloved Dixie Chicks sing about.

"Are you okay?" he asks.

Great. Now I'm crying in front of strangers.

"Fine." I sniffle. Unfortunately, getting sympathy when crying always makes things a million times worse. It's like dousing flames with kerosene. Tears fall down my cheeks faster than I can wipe them away. You'd think I'd have none left by now. "I'm fine," I blubber again. I squat down on the dock and scoop up some fresh lake water to splash on my face. "I just wish that life wasn't, you know, so … unfair." The words fly out as I think of Caleb and the campground. Dan and Taylor.

The pirate crouches beside me. "Why don't you wish that on one of those stars up there?" His voice is soothing, like how you'd talk to a wounded animal.

I rattle off an old astronomy joke. "When you wish upon a star you're a few million years too late. That star is dead, just like your dreams." It's lame, not to mention inaccurate, but it fits my mood.

He bursts out laughing, the sound echoing over the lake. "Well. That's uplifting."

I kick off my flip-flops and submerge my feet in the lake. The cool water caresses my shins.

The stranger sits next to me. "Do you want to talk about it?"

"No offense, but I don't really know you," I say, not about to bare my soul to some random guy. With no shirt on. And very hairy legs. You'd think I'd be used to it around here, but they don't usually make them as, um … Chiseled? Ripped? Perfect? … as this guy.

"Sometimes it helps to unburden yourself to a complete stranger," he says, all reasonable. "Like confession. Think of it as a free therapy session."

"And you're the therapist?" I give him a sidelong glance. Definitely not a priest. "What qualifications do you have?"

"I've been told I'm a great listener." His smile is the only light in the dark. "I also happen to be free of charge and currently available." Something about his gentle tone gets to me. He's trying really hard to be nice.

I hesitate. "It's hard to even know where to begin." But I do.

Chapter Three

A fish jumps to my left. There's a soft splash, then an expanding ring of circles. "My little brother was pretty sick this past year," I finally say, the urge to talk outweighing propriety. "He spent a lot of time in the hospital and our family racked up some pretty big bills."

He remains silent, so I continue, staring out at the water.

"My brother's mostly better now, which is great, but my mom just told us that she's thinking of selling this." I gesture all around. "Our home." My voice breaks again on "home."

He shifts beside me, still not saying anything.

"Then this guy that I … hung out with last summer, who I thought was, you know, someone I was going to be with." I cringe, humiliation as fresh as the night air. "Anyway, I've been waiting to see him all year, and he shows up with a gorgeous girlfriend." Now I am fully indulging in this pity party. "And to top it off, my best friend left today on vacation, leaving me alone for the entire summer."

He clears his throat. "So, all in all, not a great day, hey?"

"That's an understatement."

I've completely spilled my guts to this stranger, and I don't even know his name.

He seems to read my mind. "I'm Nick." He turns to me and offers his hand.

I shake it, looking at him and his magnificent chest. "Julia."

"Well, Julia. It sucks about that dude, but he's obviously an idiot. And as for selling your campground, is that a sure thing?"

"I don't know." I look back out at the water. "My mom said someone's coming by to take a look."

"Well." Nick's thoughtful. "What if he doesn't like what he sees?"

"What do you mean?"

"I mean, what if you could convince him that it isn't a good investment?"

"How would I do that?"

Nick shrugs. "I'm sure we can come up with something."

"We?"

"Yeah, let's brainstorm. Any bad things about this place?" He slaps at his thigh, "Other than the mosquitoes?"

"Not a thing," I say, glum.

"You're going to have to do better than that," he says. "Didn't someone drown here a few years ago?"

"No," I say, horrified. "We have a perfect safety record. What are you talking ..."

"That's not what I've heard." He interrupts, voice lowered. "I've heard that on some nights, when the moon is high and full, a ghost haunts this place." As subtly as possible, I scoot a few inches away. Someone must have forgotten to take his medication today. He continues, "And don't you guys have a problem with bears?"

"Well, once in a while, but only if campers don't put away their food. Actually, it's usually toothpaste that's the culprit ..."

He shushes me. "What about that man-eater that they've been trying to catch for years?"

As I look at him, bewildered, it dawns that he's messing with me. A reluctant smile spreads across my face. He's being ridiculous, but I appreciate what he's trying to do.

"Right. Old Claw." I nod. "He's already made off with two campers this season."

"There you go." Nick pats me on the back. I feel the heat from his hand through my shirt. "Just get creative."

"It won't work," I say, shaking my head.

"Most developers like to bet on a sure thing," he says. "A few rumors might be enough to sow the seeds of doubt. You can always go with a good old-fashioned sinkhole."

I laugh, and some of the all-encompassing gloom of the day dissipates.

"There you go," he says. "That's better." He looks up at the sky. "So when's this shower supposed to hit?"

"It's starting now." I point. "There, look." His eyes follow my finger. A flash of light streaks across the sky. He lies back on the dock, hands going behind his head to cradle it.

"Luckily, it's only a crescent moon," I say. "Otherwise it'd be a lot harder to see." I point again. "There."

He cranes his neck. "How do you know where to look?"

Something about my confession has me feeling completely comfortable with Nick — not a feeling I get around most guys — so I lie back beside him, folding my own hands behind my head, bare feet up on the dock.

"You look toward the radiant," I say, settling in.

"The what?" I feel him turn to look at me so I turn my head to face him.

Our faces are inches from each other's.

Hastily, I turn back toward the sky. "It's the area where the shooting stars start from. The constellation the radiant is in gives its name to the meteor shower."

"What's the name of this one?" he asks. I'm hyperaware of lying beside a hot shirtless guy, who's at least a few years older than me. In the dark. With no one else around.

"Camelopardalids," I say. He probably thinks I'm a total nerd. Let's face it — astronomy is not the sexiest pastime. Definitely not mentioning that I named my telescope.

"So the meteors are coming from the Camelo-whatever constellation?"

"Yes." I smile. "Most meteor showers are at the same time every year, like the Perseids in August or the Geminids in mid-December. But this one is brand-new; it's the first time we've been able to see it."

"That's pretty cool," he says, and I feel his gaze on me. "Seeing something beautiful for the first time." We watch in silence for a few more minutes as his words echo in my head.

"It's supposed to peak between twelve and two tonight," I say.

"Not for a few more hours, hey?" The dock creaks as Nick shifts his weight, grabbing something from his pocket. Pulling out a mangled bag of M&M's, he gives it a few shakes. "Good thing I brought rations. Want some?"

I didn't eat dinner and lunch feels like eons ago.

"Sure." I hold out my hand. He rolls onto his side and tilts the box into my outstretched palm. "Thanks." We munch in companionable silence until I think to ask him, "Do you know what time it is?" In my dazed departure, I'd left my phone at home — not that the reception is any good down at the lake, anyway.

"Think it's around ten," he says. "How long until your people send out a search party?"

I shrug. Usually I'm pretty free to roam, but Mom's probably worried about my abrupt exit. Serves her right, I think, as resentment floods my body.

"Julia?" A voice calls out from the beach, tentative.

"There's the search party now," I say, sitting up to wave. "Over here, Cale." He walks unevenly to the dock.

"Watch out, there's some loose boards over here," Nick says.

"Oh, yeah?" He eyes Nick with a curious expression. "How's the shower?"

"Doesn't hit full stride for a few hours," I say.

"Are you coming home?" He looks directly at me, and I feel a pang of guilt. However crappy I'm feeling, Caleb's probably feeling worse.

"Yeah, just let me pack up," I say, taking down Astra and putting her away.

"Do you want me to walk you guys home?" Nick offers. "Wouldn't want you to run into Old Claw on your own."

"Who?" Caleb asks.

"The local man-eating bear." I can't help smiling. "Nick had this bright idea that we come up with a few stories to make the property seem less appealing to the developer," I tell my brother.

"Oh. Right." Caleb looks down into the water.

"Cale." My voice is soft as I shift Astra over my shoulder. "It's not your fault, you know."

He swallows hard, still looking at the water. I sigh and turn to Nick, who is illuminated against the starlight, watching me. My stomach pitches with the dock.

"Well, it was nice meeting you." I feel awkward, not sure whether to shake his hand or hug him. I settle for neither.

"You as well." He puts his hands in his pockets. "You guys sure you can make it back all right?"

"We'll be fine." I follow Caleb to the end of the dock and step onto the soft sand. "We live here, remember?"

"Right," he calls. "Watch out for that sinkhole."

I look back over my shoulder, getting a final look at the pirate. I have a tingling feeling that I may have already fallen in.

*

Spitting in the sink, I turn on the faucet to rinse the toothpaste down. Caleb and I share a bathroom on the second floor of our house. He's already washed up, and I poke my head into his room.

"Cale?"

"Yeah?" He looks up over his book, light brown cowlick out in full force with no ball cap to tame it down. I'm struck by how young he looks.

"Can I talk to you for a sec?"

He sighs. "I did enough talking with Mom."

"Sorry I left you to deal with her on your own."

She tried to talk to me when I got home, but I pled exhaustion, asking if we could discuss things in the morning instead. I guess she didn't really feel like getting into it either because she let me go upstairs.

"That's okay."

I enter his room and sit on the end of his bed. "Is it? Are you?"

"I'm fine." He goes back to reading his book. I grab it from his hands and toss it on the blue comforter.

"Hey!" he exclaims.

"I know when you're lying."

"So what?"

"Don't worry, we're not selling." I've already decided to do everything in my power to keep our home.

Caleb's small chin juts out. "You have some money saved up that you're not telling the rest of us about?" For only nine he has some pretty snappy retorts. Must be from all the books he reads. God knows, the video games don't do much for his verbal skills.

"No," I say. "But talking to that Nick guy got me thinking." And feeling. And thinking some more.

"Come on," he scoffs. "You really think a few dumb stories about killer bears will stop someone from buying this place?"

"Well, maybe not bears." We sit in silence for a minute. Caleb looks so down; I rack my brain for something to distract him. In the hospital, when he couldn't even hold his book because of the paralysis, I used to read to him. He loves adventure stories the best. "I do remember this one tale Gramps used to tell …"

"What about?" Too young to remember much of our grandfather, who'd built the campground on the land his father left him, Caleb loves it when I talk about him. He was a big man with a quick smile, flashing blue eyes and a story for everything.

I lower my voice. "About something really valuable hidden on the property." Hook.

Caleb is skeptical. "What, like a treasure or something?"

"I'm not sure," I admit. "All I know is that he used to say there's something here, buried or hidden on the grounds." Line.

He picks at the fluff on his blanket. "Oh, yeah?" Sinker.

"Yeah. I don't really remember all the details, but maybe we could go take a look at the old cabin, see if we can find anything." The cabin was where my grandfather lived while he built the campground. A ramshackle bachelor pad, it still has quite a few of his things in it. After he met my grandmother, he built her a proper house — this house. When Paige and I were little, the cabin was our clubhouse. Then Paige stepped on a rusty nail one summer and had to get a tetanus shot. After that, Dad and Mom said it was off-limits until they got it cleaned up, but that never ended up happening. When Dad left, a lot of things never ended up happening.

"Doesn't Dan get in tomorrow?" Caleb says. "Won't you be spending all your time with him?" Ouch. Hanging out with my little brother wasn't high on my list of priorities last summer, but that's all changed now.

"He's already here," I say, getting off the bed and handing the book back to Caleb. "And I think he has other plans." My voice catches.

"Jules?" he says as I'm leaving.

"Yeah?"

"What do you think the developer wants to do with the land?"

I pause at the door. "Guess we'll find out tomorrow." I flick off his light and he turns on the bedside table lamp as he settles in to read a little longer. "Night, Cale."

"Night."

I pad down the hallway to my bedroom and am greeted by soothing lilac walls. Changing into a ratty gray T-shirt and boxers, I turn out the light and flop onto my bed. What I told Caleb about our grandfather is true. He did used to talk about something being hidden on the property. But he always told such wild stories — we'd always have to confirm with Grandma whether they were real or not. Now neither of them is around to ask. Both would be gutted to hear Mom's thinking of selling.

Rolling over onto my side, I look at the corkboard above the antique oak desk that was my grandfather's. The board is full of pictures. Even though it's dark, I know each one by heart. Paige and me up in a tree, my brother and me balancing a canoe on our heads, shots of us with random kids we played with over the summers. My eyes go to the picture in the center and I scowl. It's of Dan and me sitting on a picnic table, his arm around me, giant grins on our faces. I walk over to the corkboard and rip it down, leaving the pushpin stuck there. How could he bring his girlfriend here? I feel like such an idiot. Did I completely hallucinate that there was something between us? I stare at the photo in my hand, searching for clues. We look like a couple.

A couple of what? Gramps's cheesy crack rings in my ear. Not quite able to crumple the photo, I throw it on the desk and collapse back on my bed, staring up at glow-in-the-dark stars that no longer glow. The meteor shower should be in full force about now. I wonder if Nick's still out there. Some of the tension leaves my body. He'd been nice. I flush, thinking of his perfectly sculpted body, like one of those anatomy drawings, every muscle outlined. And hot. How long is he here for? I wonder. That's the one crappy thing about living in a campground. You make friends pretty quickly, but people are always leaving. Some you see again; most you don't. Even sharing the same DNA doesn't guarantee people will stick around. Though I suppose you don't have to live in a campground for that to happen.

I never asked what site Nick is in. I'll take a peek at the registration records tomorrow and swing by to see if he needs anything. Make sure he's stocked up on firewood. Or that Old Claw hasn't gotten him.

Chapter Four

I come down for breakfast the next morning, restless from dreaming about betrayals, buried treasures and handsome pirates.

"Morning," Mom says, sipping from a mug Caleb and I got her a few years ago with a picture of the two of us on Halloween, the year we'd gone as Ewoks. Brown hair curls down around her shoulders, and she's wearing a flowery dress, buttercup yellow.

"Morning." I keep my voice neutral. "Any chai left?"

"Just made a fresh pot."

I pour myself a cup and sit at the kitchen table with her.

"Sorry I took off yesterday." Adding an extra stick of cinnamon and a sprinkle of nutmeg, I take a sip.

"Sweetie, don't apologize," Mom says. "I know it's a big shock."

"So, it's a for-sure thing?" I ask. I don't really want to hear the answer.

"Is anything in life?" she says. "It's an option. We're just going to hear what this guy has to say. He might not even make an offer."

Not if I have anything to do with it.

Mom continues: "And even if he does, we might not accept it. It's still in the early stages."

"So when do we meet him?" I ask, adding more cinnamon.

"He's coming by this morning." She glances at the clock on the wall. "In about half an hour."

"And you're showing him around?"

"I thought we could do that together. As a family. But I understand if you don't want to," she adds hastily.

Hmm. Maybe I could get this guy alone and casually mention the whole sinkhole thing. I think of Nick. I want to find him today to thank him for his idea. And his M&M's. And his broad shoulders.

"How did this guy hear about the campground in the first place?" Caleb says, yawning as he walks into the kitchen.

Good question. I look at Mom. "Yeah, were you, like, advertising?"

"Actually, it's a funny story." She shifts in her seat. "I was put in touch with him by the Schaeffers."

Chai sprays from my mouth all over the table. Choking and coughing, I manage to get out a strangled "What?" Caleb walks over and pounds me on the back.

"He's Dan's mom's brother." Mom hands me a glass of water.

"So Dan knew about this?" Somehow that hurts almost as much as him bringing Taylor. I think of the pretty blonde. Not quite, but almost.

"His parents might've mentioned it to him," Mom says. "Though it's all happened pretty quickly."

"You're telling me. It feels so surreal."

"For me, too." Her blue eyes beg me to understand. "I just want what's best for all of us."

My stomach grumbles so I get up from the table to pour myself some granola. I pour a bowl for Caleb, too, then walk over to the fridge for the milk. Grabbing some organic blueberries, I toss a couple in each of our bowls and deposit the granola in front of my brother.

"Thanks." He looks up in surprise as I hand him a spoon.

"And you think what's best for us is selling the campground?"

"I don't know yet," Mom says, sighing. "Right now I'm just looking at our options."

There's that word again. Options. What about my and Caleb's options? Red pops his head in the back door just as there's a knock at the front. He's wearing his one button-up plaid shirt and his best jeans.

"They're here," he says.

Caleb and I look at each other.

"They're a bit early." Mom forces a smile, running her hands down her dress, adjusting it and brushing an invisible speck off. "Shall we?" She offers her arm to Red and they walk out into the hallway. "Be nice, guys," she calls over her shoulder, as he leads her out of the kitchen. I grunt something noncommittal.

Caleb looks up from his cereal. "They?"

Voices murmur, then the screen door slams shut. *They* must be outside. I leave my uneaten bowl of granola on the counter. Caleb follows me to the front door.

We walk into the warm sunshine and down the porch steps. Then I realize that I'm still in my pajamas, and I'm about to turn around when a deep voice reaches my ears. Looking up, my mouth drops.

"Julia," Mom says. "Come meet Mr. Constantine." She gestures to a tall, dark and handsome man who, despite the informal setting of the campground, manages to look completely at home in a jacket and tie. But that's not who I'm staring at.

"And this is his son, Nick," she goes on, unaware my jaw is grazing the gravel.

Nick turns to look at me. Gone are all traces of last night's scruffy pirate. A polished businessman stands before me in an extremely nice suit. "Hey, Julia," he says. Charcoal eyes implore mine, and there's a wry smile on his lips as if this is all just some amusing coincidence.

I'm speechless.

Caleb's not. "You." His voice is accusing. "From the dock."

Mom and Red look back and forth between us, picking up on the weird vibes.

"Sorry I didn't say anything last night," he apologizes. "It just didn't seem like a good time."

"You met last night?" Mom's uncertain.

"Let me guess," I say, words finally returning. "You're staying in campsite thirty-three?" With Dan.

Nick's dad clears his throat, interrupting. "Nice place you've got here."

The shock of discovering Nick was playing me all along makes me forget to be nice. Not that I agreed to in the first place. "Isn't it?" I whip around, unable to keep the aspartame from lacing my words, all artificial sweetness. "It's too bad you won't be getting your greedy hands on it."

"Julia!" Mom says.

Feeling at a slight disadvantage in my sleepwear, I turn around, tears swimming in my eyes, and head for the house.

"Sorry," I hear her apologizing. "This has been a bit rough on her."

Mr. Constantine murmurs something in response. His traitorous son keeps quiet. I feel his eyes on my back, watching me stomp up the porch steps to wrench open the door. I don't give him the satisfaction of turning around, plans already forming in my mind. Rough on me?

Things are about to get a whole lot rougher for Mr. Constantine and Junior. Big time.

*

Betrayed emotions are quickly replaced by cold calculations as I change out of my pajamas into jean shorts and a turquoise tank.

"I'll show Nick and his dad around the campground all right," I mutter. "Right into a patch of poison ivy." A severe case might even land them in the hospital. Or maybe devil's club. Now *that* is a nasty plant to get tangled up in. Nick's creativity is catching.

Caleb pokes his head into the room. "Are you coming?"

"Yup," I say, putting my hair up in a messy bun. "What's the plan?"

"Starting down at the lake," he says. "They seem pretty interested in the beachfront."

"I guess Nick didn't get a good enough look at it in the dark," I say.

"Did you know?" Caleb asks.

"No," I say. I never would've eaten his M&M's otherwise.

Grabbing my sunglasses, I follow Caleb back downstairs. The day is already warm; it's going to be a scorcher. Mom and Red are chatting with Nick and his dad. Nick sees me first.

"Julia," he says, infusing his voice with warmth. "Glad you're joining us."

"Can't say the same," I say under my breath. Mom gives me a warning look, then turns to catch up to Red and Mr. Constantine.

"I'm staying here," Caleb says.

"Are you sure?" I say.

I can't exactly blame him. It's my turn to deal. Nick and I walk after our respective parents.

"So did you know who I was before or after I fell flat on my face?" I ask, the morning's revelation causing me to feel particularly combative.

"That's one of the things I like about you," Nick says. He pulls a pair of pricey-looking aviators from his jacket pocket and puts them on.

"Me being a total spaz?"

"No, your lack of filter." The sun glinting off gold rims. "You're an open book. It's refreshing."

"Just because I spilled my guts to you last night doesn't mean you know me," I say.

"It was after." He goes back to my original question. "When you said it was your family's place, I wanted to tell you, but you got upset and it seemed like you needed someone to talk to."

"Yeah. Preferably someone who isn't trying to steal my family's campground out from under our noses."

"Who said anything about stealing?" he says, voice smooth. "If any deal were to go down, we'd pay your family fair market value."

I snort. "We? Don't you mean your dad?"

An expression crosses his face, but he doesn't say anything.

"So what exactly were you trying to do, giving me all those ideas about sabotaging things? You must have been laughing to yourself."

"No," he says, shoving his hands into his pockets. He has to be hot in that gray blazer. He is hot. *Stop it.*

Another thought dawns. "And did you know I was referring to your cousin?" Oh, God. He, Dan and Taylor must have had a good laugh after he got back to the campsite, seeing as how they're all sharing an RV.

"Actually, no." He pauses. "Dan never mentioned you." Which is even worse. "Not that he's really had a chance," Nick hastens, seeing my face. "Yesterday's the first time we've seen each other since ..."

"Since when?" My tone is as blistering as the sun. "Since you evicted another nice family off their property?"

He gives me a sidelong glance. "Since my mom's funeral," he says.

I sigh. "Sorry to hear that." The words sound stiff to my ears.

"It's okay." Nick clears his throat. "It's been a while."

I feel bad for him but don't want to let his vulnerability sneak through my defenses. "So you're having a family reunion while carving up our homestead at the same time? Multitasker." The minute the words tumble out of my mouth, I feel like a jerk. Must. Control. Temper.

"It's not like that." Nick's voice is patient, despite my barb. "Your mom asked us to come."

I suck in a breath. She neglected to mention that.

"So you're doing us a favor?"

"She must have discussed your situation with my aunt and uncle, who obviously told her what my dad and I do." I don't say anything. I take one of the trails that lead down to the water. "And we wouldn't be 'carving up your homestead,'" he says with air quotes. "We'd be taking something and making it better."

We reach the top of the beach, sunlight sparkling on the water. The lake is nestled into the base of the surrounding mountains and lush forest. Fluffy white clouds dot the blue sky, so soft and pillowy you could almost imagine a few Care Bears bouncing around up there. "You think it gets any better than this?" Incredulous, I gesture around me.

Nick stares out at the lake. "Maybe 'better' isn't the right word."

I look at him. "So what's the right word?"

"*Different*, I guess."

"What is it you plan on doing, exactly?"

"It's up to my dad." I can't see his eyes behind the sunglasses, but I get the feeling he knows more than he's telling.

"You owe me," I challenge. "For not being honest last night."

He lifts the sunglasses off his face onto his head. "I told you, I never meant to be dishonest. You just looked so sad; I wanted to make you feel better, not worse." He looks at me. "I couldn't sleep last night."

"Guilty conscience?" I arch a brow then walk toward the dock. There are a few boats tied up to it this morning.

"Yes," he responds, following me. "Julia, I'm sorry."

I step onto the wooden slats, careful to avoid the loose ones, and walk to the end, looking down into the water. Anywhere but at him. It's bizarre that only a few hours ago we were lying here together, sharing M&M's and secrets. I truly am clueless when it comes to guys.

"Fine," he says, coming to stand beside me. "I want you to trust me, so I'm going to be completely honest." I wait, listening to the gentle lapping of the waves. "You really want to know what the plans for the property are?"

"Yes."

"There's been some talk about a resort and casino." His words hit me like a tsunami.

"What!?" My yelp startles a few birds out from the trees behind us. "You want to build a casino?" I motion all around us. "On beautiful natural lakefront?" From the corner of my eye I see my mom and Nick's dad talking, Red pointing out various features of the lake.

"It *is* prime real estate," Nick says.

"Over my dead body."

"A place like that would make a killing." Nick turns to face me, grabbing my hands, holding them tightly. "Think of what you guys could do with the money. Maybe we could even work something out where you stay on to run the place."

Does he not realize what he's saying? He'd let *my* family stay on our *own* freaking property to run a disgusting casino? He's still holding my hands, dark eyes begging me to understand. Black spots appear in my vision. Firmly placing both palms on his flawless chest, I push with all my might.

Chapter Five

Nick flies backward off the dock, rueful eyes meeting mine just before he hits the water. A giant SPLASH catches the attention of everyone on the lakeshore. I hear my mom scream, "Julia!"

Ohmygodohmygodohmygod. What did I just do? I stand there, frozen, hands at my mouth. He comes up spluttering and coughing. Oh, God. What if he can't swim? I mean, of course he can swim. Everyone can swim, right? He goes under and comes up again gasping for air, arms more frantic. He sinks under a second time. This time he doesn't resurface.

Shit. Without stopping to think, I jump off the dock.

The water is cool and quiet, as I sink down, down, hands outstretched, searching for a piece of Nick.

Nothing.

Sunlight filters through the green lake water, illuminating a billion fizzing bubbles, but still no Nick. Kicking down, I swim around, trying to find him. Something grabs me from behind and I scream, which doesn't work so well under water. I ingest half the lake as strong hands lift me to the surface. It's my turn to choke and cough.

"You jerk!" I splutter, turning around, treading water.

"Me? Um, I believe you just pushed me off a dock." His broad arms move beneath the surface. "Fully clothed, I might add."

"You deserved it." Splashing water at him, I make for the shore. He follows behind me, strokes strong despite his soaked gray jacket.

I stand up when my bare feet touch the bottom and walk to shore, dripping. Our parents stand ten feet away, mouths wide open. Nick's father has his chin resting in one hand, half covering his mouth. Is he trying not to laugh?

"Julia Meadow Skye Ducharme, what on earth has gotten into you?" my mother demands.

"Meadow Skye?" Nick murmurs as he sloshes up beside me.

The way Mom and Red are looking makes me want to slink back into the water.

"It's my fault," Nick says. I look at him. Hands go up to his sunglasses, no longer there of course. Mine are gone, too. Along with my flip-flops. I feel a brief spurt of satisfaction. His shades were much more expensive.

"It didn't look that way from where we were standing." Mom's eyes are narrow.

"No, really, I tripped on a loose board on the dock. Jules here came to my rescue."

Jules?

"Maybe you'd better dry off," Nick's father suggests.

Red hands me a set of keys. "Julia, why don't you take Nick back to his site with the golf cart."

"But …" I protest.

"Now." His voice is firm, for Red. Meekly, I take the keys then stomp off as best I can in bare feet, toward the golf cart locked up down by the boathouse. I hear Nick squelching behind me.

"Nice ride," Nick says as we reach the cart.

Stabbing the key into the ignition, I reverse the cart. It beeps annoyingly. Putting it into drive, I stare stonily ahead, clothes plastered to my body, toes on the gas.

"Are we even now?" he asks.

"Are you kidding me?" slips out before I can stop it. "You want to poach my family's home, demolish it, then put a stinking casino on it and you think we're even?" I crank the wheel sharply to the left and the cart veers up on two wheels as we go around the corner.

"I thought we'd been through this." Nick grabs on to the small dashboard. "We won't be poaching anything." The cart thumps back down onto four wheels. "This could set your family up nicely for the rest of your lives. More than nicely."

"We're doing just fine, thank you."

"That's not what you were saying last night," Nick says.

Note to self: do not tell handsome strangers life story within minutes of meeting them.

I turn onto the road with campsites 30 to 45, catching a glimpse of myself in the tiny rearview mirror. Strands of limp hair fall out of my bun, resembling strawberry-colored seaweed. I pull up to site 33 and brake. Dan and Taylor are sitting at the picnic table, playing cards. Both look up, taking in our soggy state. Awesome.

Dan lifts an eyebrow. "If you need to borrow a bathing suit, Cuz, all you have to do is ask," he calls.

Taylor looks at us, confused. "Why are you all wet?"

"Freak rainstorm," I say. "Very isolated shower."

She tilts her head back to look up at the sky.

"Jules wanted to show me her lifeguarding skills," Nick says, pushing curling dark hair out of his eyes. What is with this "Jules" all of a sudden?

A smile creeps across Dan's face. "From what I remember, she's pretty good at mouth-to-mouth."

He. Did. Not. Just. Say. That.

Nick stiffens beside me. Taylor stops scanning the horizon for errant clouds and frowns at Dan, who realizes what he's just said and rushes to change the subject. "So, how's the tour going?" he asks, two bright red spots appearing high on his cheeks.

"It's over," I say, looking at Nick. "Can you please get out?"

He doesn't.

"I really don't think I've seen everything yet," he says, crossing his arms.

"Oh, I think you have." I am not spending one more minute in his company. Or Dan's. Or Taylor's. "Now are you going to get out, or am I going to have to push you again?"

Maybe he hears the tremor in my voice because he does what I ask.

I release the brake and he jumps back as the cart lurches forward.

"Julia ..." he calls.

I keep driving and don't look back.

*

I park the golf cart as Caleb comes out of the house.

"What happened to you?" he asks as I get out.

"Felt like a swim."

"With your clothes on?"

"If you must know, I pushed Nick off the dock. Then jumped in to save him."

"Seriously?" Mischief lights up his face, reminding me again how young he is. It feels like we've both aged a lot this past year. "Does Mom know?"

"She saw the whole thing." I grab a towel from the laundry line and wrap it around my shoulders, going to sit on the rusty three-seater swing in the front yard. "And is pissed." Not that I blame her.

"I bet." He comes and sits beside me. I push my feet against the ground and the chair creaks as it swings back then forward. I'd always found the swinging motion comforting. "Did you give them the full tour?"

"Not really. All they saw was the lake." Nick a little closer up than his dad. "I did find out something, though," I add.

"What?" Caleb fidgets with the hem on his shorts.

"*If* they buy the property, they plan on building some kind of hideous casino and resort." I shudder.

"Does it even matter?"

"What? Of course it matters!"

"I mean, whatever they do with it, it won't be ours anymore." He looks so sad.

"Don't worry, Cale, it's not going to come to that." He nods, but I can tell he's still pretty distraught. "They might not even want it, remember?" I try to sound upbeat.

"When do you think we'll find out?"

"Can't see it taking more than a few days to make an assessment," I say. "They'll probably look around a bit more, go through the hiking trails to get a sense of the property, then maybe check out the cabins, though I'd imagine they'll just tear them down …" I wince, thinking of all the work that went into building them. Picturing them as flattened heaps has me feeling physically ill.

Caleb puts his feet down on the ground and the swing stops abruptly.

"Hey! Mid-conversation here." I stare after him. "Where are you going?"

"Gotta check something out," he calls back.

"What?" What on earth is he up to?

He waves. "Tell you later."

I'm tempted to go after him but decide to give him space. Maybe he just needs to get away for a bit. He hasn't gone off by himself too much since we've been home from the hospital. Other than being holed up in the basement with his games, he hasn't done much of anything lately. When we were younger, we used to roam the woods for hours, exploring, climbing trees, building forts, though I kinda stopped doing that stuff with him a while ago. Maybe he spotted a cutie in one of the campsites and is doing a stakeout mission? Red calls it "going trolling." I used to do it all the time with Dan's campsite, but Caleb is still a little young. I walk up the porch steps to change out of my wet clothes, shaking my head. Things are so messed up. This summer is not turning out at all how I expected. And I'm only one day in.

*

After pulling on some dry cut-offs and a black tank, I email Paige, telling her everything that's gone down in the last twenty-four hours. Then I make myself a grilled-cheese sandwich, and here is Nick, walking up the driveway. His timing is the worst for interrupting meals — first breakfast, now lunch. He stands there staring at me, hands in the pockets of dry pants. How many suits did this guy bring to a campground? Powerless to stop myself, I leave the half-buttered bread on the counter and walk outside to meet him.

"Hey," he says.

"Hey."

"Can we start over?" He squints against the sun.

"No."

Mom and Mr. Constantine are walking toward the house. Mr. Constantine's phone rings as they reach the bottom of the driveway. He talks in a low voice as Mom continues toward me, pretty agitated.

Nick sees the expression on her face and tactfully goes off to stand by his father. There goes my buffer.

"What were you thinking?" she hisses when she gets close. "*Pushing* Mr. Constantine's son off the dock?"

I decide to stick with Nick's story. "Um, he tripped on the boards, remember?"

"I saw you, Julia," Mom says. Her look of disapproval cuts me. "We're supposed to be trying to make a good impression, *remember*?"

I glance over at Nick and his dad. Mr. Constantine's voice is getting louder as he paces.

"He doesn't look any the worse for wear," I mutter. In fact, he looks pretty damn good.

Stop it.

"You're lucky he seems like a nice guy," she says.

"Oh, yeah, robbing us of our home, real nice," I retort. *Remember that.* Gorgeous or not, he's still the enemy.

Mom sighs. "It's not his fault."

Then whose fault is it? Caleb's, for getting sick? Hers, for not having stellar insurance? I'd rather blame the pirates. Nick's father hangs up the phone, swearing softly. The two talk for a few minutes, voices low, faces serious. They turn and walk toward us.

"Sorry about that," Nick's father says, flashing a grin as lethal as his son's. "Some issues with another deal."

"Sorry to hear that, Tom," Mom says. "Nothing serious, I hope?"

Tom?

"Actually, yes." He doesn't elaborate. "I'm afraid I need to leave." Mom looks taken aback. "I've spoken with Nick. He's going to stay on to make a full assessment of the property. I'll be back in a few days."

I'm shocked at the relief that flashes across her face. She *wants* this deal to happen. Crap. Things must be really bad. "Sure," she says warmly. "We'll set him up in one of the cabins."

"Appreciate that, Mrs. Ducharme," Nick says, all businesslike. "The RV's great, but it'd be nice to have my own space."

Sheesh. Mom may as well just roll out the red carpet and present the keys to the campground over my bikini-clad body. Nick and his father confer for a few minutes. "Tom" is most likely imparting some last-minute tips on how to rob us blind.

I feel another spurt of rage, swirled with despair. "Well, I'm supposed to be opening the canteen in twenty minutes." I start across the lawn, needing to get out of there. "See you guys later."

"Why don't you take Nick with you?" Mom calls. I freeze. Wait? What? She folds her arms in a way that makes the question seem less suggestion, more command. "You can show him around the rest of the campground."

"Great idea," Tom echoes, coming up and clapping his son on the shoulder. "In fact, why doesn't Nick shadow Julia for the next few days? That will get him acquainted with the place, while not inconveniencing either of you too much." He looks at Mom, lifting an eyebrow. "Seems like it takes a lot to keep things up and running."

"Works for us." Mom's eyes drill holes into me. "Nick, consider Jules your personal guide to the area."

You've *got* to be kidding me.

I turn and start toward the golf cart, not looking to see if Nick's following me.

"Watch out for loose boards," Tom calls to his son.

Very funny.

Chapter Six

We drive in silence. Birds chirp as sunlight streams through the trees.

"Sorry about Dan's mouth-to-mouth comment," Nick says.

Startled at the random apology, I look at him. "Why are you sorry? You're not the one who said it."

"He can be kind of a dick sometimes."

"That's not the impression I've had of him," I say, not sure why I'm defending Dan. Nick snorts. But it's true. Dan's always been sweet and thoughtful, right up until he showed up with his new girlfriend. I'll never understand guys. I sneak a quick look at Nick. That's why I need to keep this one at arm's length.

Red is headed for the registration office, where campers check in when they first arrive.

"Hey, Red!" I wave, slowing down. He glances up and sees my passenger, looking like he's trying to keep his expression neutral. I wonder what he really thinks about having these developers sniffing around. What will happen to Red if we sell Pines? This is as much his home as ours.

"Hey, girl," he says, walking over to the idling cart, giving Nick a courteous nod. "You get around to fixing that dock yet?"

"Um, been kinda busy, with the evil land developers and all that." I nod at Nick, who laughs. Glad this is all one big joke.

"No excuse for letting things get run down around here," he says.

"Don't worry," I say. "I'll get to it."

"Good. Now if you'll excuse me," Red says. "The money doesn't collect itself. Though it'd be a heck of a lot easier if it did."

Nick is silent for a few minutes as we continue driving.

"Evil?" he says finally. "Is that really how you see me?"

We pass campers headed for the water, loaded down with coolers, towels and inner tubes. "You're right," I agree. "*Dastardly* suits you much better."

He just shakes his head.

Reaching the beach, I pull up beside the Sugar Shack, the little canteen we open for a few hours each day where people can buy cold drinks, ice cream and other non-nutritional snacks like chips, chocolate bars and penny candy. It's a constant battle not to completely pig out, though you'd think living in a bathing suit all summer would make me put that second Mars bar back. Unlocking the door, I step into tight quarters that smell like chocolate-covered sawdust, Nick close behind me. I heave up the metal awning that reaches down to the counter, opening it like a mini garage door.

"This is cozy." Nick looks around. "How long are you open for each day?"

"One to three." I check the little cashbox to make sure I have enough change. "Usually my friend Paige helps out, but she's away in Osaka." Why did I tell him that? For some reason, I find him incredibly easy to talk to. I'm going to have to get better at reining that in.

"Cool. Fun city." Huh, he's been to Osaka? "Here come your first customers," Nick says, nodding.

Dan and Taylor are walking up to the counter. A pang hits me right in the solar plexus.

"Hey, Jules, thought I might find you here," Dan says, rubbing his hands together. "Can we get two ice-cream cones?" Both are in their swimsuits, perfect specimens of the human race. Taylor's pink bikini hugs her perfectly tanned body. She has a diamond belly ring, and golden blond hair flows over her shoulders in tousled beachy waves that probably took a few hours and a bottle of forty-dollar spray to perfect. Dan, too, is tanned and toned, sporting his familiar six-pack that never seems to have any problems with the treats I sneak him every summer.

Used to sneak.

If he thinks he can sweet-talk me into free Cookies 'n' Cream for him and his girlfriend, he's seriously mistaken.

"No problem," I say with a smile, serving them each a miniscule scoop. "That'll be five dollars please."

Dan's face falls. "Really? I, uh, don't have my wallet on me." He looks at Taylor, who shrugs and licks her ice cream.

"Guess you'll just have to give them back," I say, still smiling. But not nicely.

He laughs, but stops when he sees my face. "Um, maybe you can swing by the campsite later to grab the cash?" He flashes a grin that used to get my heart pounding. As a matter of fact, it still does. Except it's not hormones making it race, it's rage. He seriously thinks he can just walk up to my shack and demand free ice cream for him and his girlfriend? I open my mouth to tell him what he can do with the pointy end of his cone, but Nick interrupts me.

"I got it," he says and hands me a five. I deposit it in the cashbox with a loud clang.

"Hey, man, didn't see you in there." Dan peers in. "So you two best buddies now, or what?"

"Julia's just showing me around," Nick says, crossing his arms.

"Is that right?" Dan says. There's a weird edge to his voice.

"Let's go swimming," Taylor says to him, nibbling at her cone. Dan doesn't move, looking from Nick to me. There's definitely some "negative vibes" floating around, as Mom would say. They practically shimmer in the air. "I'll pay you back later," Dan says to Nick, crossing his own arms, cone grazing the outside of his left bicep.

"Don't worry about it," Nick says.

"I can't always be taking charity from my big cousin." Dan still hasn't licked his ice cream, which is beginning to drip onto his clenched fingers.

"What are cousins for?" Nick replies.

"Daaannn," Taylor whines. "I'm hot, and I want to go swimming."

"Coming." Dan turns, then stops, looking back at us. "Hey, why don't we all go out in the boat later?" He gives me a look. "We can show them the island, Jules."

The island is a little piece of land covered in bushes and shrubs out around the bend in the middle of the lake. Technically, no one's really allowed on it; it's protected for the loons that nest there. That doesn't really stop people from going there when they want a little privacy. My cheeks grow warm, thinking of the times Dan and I spent there last summer. It's where we had our first kiss.

"Can't. Promised Caleb we'd go out in the ATVs," I lie. Spending time together as a fabulous foursome doesn't sound all that fabulous to me.

"That sounds like a great way to see the rest of the property." Nick looks at me then back at Dan. "Besides, I'm sure you don't want Julia and me crashing your party." He nods at Taylor, who's cavorting in the water, much to the enjoyment of every male on the beach.

"Maybe tomorrow, then." Dan looks at me intently. "It's a pretty special place." Blushing, I drop my gaze. What is up with all his not-so-subtle comments? He pitches his untouched ice cream into the garbage can and joins Taylor in the water, splashing, causing her to shriek as she tries to protect her hair.

I take a breath and turn to Nick. "I didn't invite you to come quadding," I say.

"I know," he says. "I just wanted to give you an out. It didn't look like you were up for a boat cruise with Barbie and Ken."

"Oh," I say, reorganizing a tray of Aero bars. It's oppressively warm in the canteen and I'm feeling faint, whether from the heat, the claustrophobic conditions or a combination of both. I open the ice-cream cooler and stick my head in.

"What are you doing?" Nick asks.

"I think we're out of Cherry Chip." I stand back up, black spots appearing in my vision.

"Are you okay?" His voice sounds fuzzy.

"Fine." I fan myself. "Low blood pressure."

"Come here." He puts an arm around me, leading me out of the canteen into sunshine and fresh air. He sits me down on the sand. "Put your head between your knees and breathe."

I oblige. Little by little my vision clears and the dizziness recedes.

"Have you eaten anything today?" he asks, concerned.

"Does chai count?"

"No." He goes into the canteen and comes out with a Kit Kat. "Here, try this."

Now that I think about it, the last thing I ate was his M&M's.

"Thanks," I say, biting into the chocolate bar and looking out at the water. Dan and Taylor are coming in from their swim. He's piggybacking her, her arms wrapped tightly around his neck. I feel another pang in my stomach and try to convince myself it's hunger.

"You weren't expecting Taylor, hey?" Nick says.

"That obvious?" I swallow, staring at the No Lifeguard on Duty sign. The beach is starting to fill up, as people stake out their real estate. The scents of coconut tanning oil and inflatable plastic mattresses lie heavy in the air.

"That, and you told me last night." Oh. Right. "Do you want to go for a swim to clear your head?" Nick changes the subject.

"Had one this morning, thanks," I say, recalling his expression as he flew backward off the dock. "Sorry about that, by the way," I say, semi-grudgingly. Despite everything, he's been nothing but … kind … since we met last night. Not counting his being here to take my home away and all.

His smile is teasing. "Nothing like a quick dip in the lake to clear out the cobwebs."

I think of him groomed and serious in his suit. "You don't seem very … webby."

"I was a bit out of it this morning," he admits. "Up all night watching stars."

"You stayed up for the whole thing?" I'm surprised, and envious I missed it.

"Yup, pretty sweet show. Hey, I was thinking," he says, "maybe you can give me a few lessons?"

"In astronomy?" I look to see if he's kidding.

"No, in swimming." He laughs. "Yes, in astronomy."

"Why?" I ask, suspicious.

"Just thought it might be a cool thing to get into." He looks up at the sky, shielding his eyes with his hand.

"I don't really know that much," I admit. "I only started getting into it this past year."

"Well, identifying the Big Dipper is about the extent of my knowledge." Nick stands up, brushing sand off his shorts. "That and the North Star is the brightest."

"Actually, it's not," I tell him. "More like the fiftieth."

"See." Nick offers his hand to help me up for the second time in twenty-four hours. I hesitate, then grab it and stand. "You obviously know a lot more than me."

I somehow doubt that. "You're seriously interested in astronomy?"

"Well, there is another reason," he says, standing there with his hands in his pockets.

"What's that?"

He takes a step toward me, his mass entering my orbit. "I had a good time with you last night." His eyes lock with mine. "Before ... everything."

His closeness is making me dizzy again. "You mean before I found out the truth about who you really are and why you're here?" I try to look somewhere other than his face and settle for his chest, which happens to be at eye level and three inches from my nose.

"There are many truths." He looks regretful. "That is but one version, little grasshopper."

What the heck is that supposed to mean? "I'm going to lock up the canteen," I say.

"So is that a yes for the astronomy lessons?" he asks.

I yank on the padlock to make sure it's shut. "Fine, whatever." Keeping an eye on him is not the worst idea.

"Great." A light dances in his dark eyes, like the sun off the water. "Now, how about those ATVs?"

*

"Cale?" I shout down to the basement. No answer.

Hmm. I haven't seen him since he took off this morning. I go outside, where Nick is sitting on the chair swing.

"He's not here."

"Is that unusual?"

"Since coming home from the hospital, he practically never leaves the basement." Despite nonstop encouragement from Mom and me. I walk to the shed and come out with two helmets. "Try this." I toss one at him.

He slides it over his head. "Fits like a glove."

"It's parked out back," I say, strapping on my own helmet. Nick follows me around the side of the house. The ATVs, or quads as we affectionately call them, sit under a red aluminum roof supported by four wooden posts. I stop short. One of the vehicles is missing. Nick notices me looking at the empty spot.

"What's up?" he asks.

"Nothing," I say. "Looks like my brother already took one of them out."

"The kid's allowed to take out these bad boys by himself?"

"He's been riding them since before he could walk." I haul myself up into the driver's seat. Just not since he'd been sick. I feel hopeful, but also slightly worried. Not to mention extremely curious.

"I'm not used to being in the passenger seat," Nick says, climbing up behind me.

I rev the engine, mask hiding my grin. "You'll get over it."

Chapter Seven

Thirty minutes later we've driven all around the campground, down to the beach and over to the cabins. Still no Caleb.

"Guess we're going off-roading," I shout over the rumbling quad and feel Nick nod. Taking one of the trails, I make sure to drive slowly in case any hikers are out enjoying the scenery. Nick's thighs wrap snugly around mine. Not quite bringing himself to entwine his arms around my waist, he settles for holding on to the side grips of the quad.

"Where exactly do all these trails go?" he shouts in my ear.

"All over the property." Tall trees stand sentinel on both sides of the trail. It's looking wild and unkempt, and I make a mental note to come back with shears.

"How far back does the property go?" he asks.

"Far," I reply, distracted. Fresh quad tracks appear in the dirt. Caleb's been out this way. I follow them. They turn off onto an overgrown trail, and I slow as leafy branches bar our path. It hits me that I know where Caleb is. No one's been down this way in a long time.

"Taking the scenic route?" Nick shouts, letting go of the handles to push sticks and leaves out of our way as we crawl along.

"I would've thought you'd like to get off the beaten path," I say, hunched over. The quad hits a divot and Nick lurches, grabbing on to me automatically. "Better hold on." We bump along for a few more minutes until I spot the other ATV, park beside it and turn off the engine. There's another small trail leading from it, even more overgrown than the one we're on. "We walk from here," I say, hopping off the quad.

"You and your brother haven't worked out some elaborate scheme to murder me and leave my body in the woods, have you?" He takes his helmet off and shakes his head, dark tendrils framing his face.

"Not at all," I say, taking my own helmet off and hanging it on the handle. He does the same. When I start off through the bush, Nick follows. I glance back. "We already decided that a boating accident will seem way more plausible."

"Can I ask where we're going?" he says.

"You wanted to see the property," I say. "Look around."

"Where?" He looks around; we're surrounded by trees, rocks and birds.

"There." I point.

He peers around trunks the size of Smartcars, and I wait until he sees what I'm pointing at.

"A ramshackle old cabin," he says. "Not creepy at all."

I ignore him and cup my hands at my mouth. "Cale?" I shout. No answer. We pick our way over fallen tree limbs and rocky earth, approaching the decrepit cabin. "Cale?" I call again, voice uncertain. A chipmunk darts over a fallen log that is dripping with lime moss. The door of the cabin hangs haphazardly, knots in the wooden boards creating small whorls of darkness. There's an air of desertion about the place. A sense we're disturbing something.

What if he hurt himself coming out here? Spooky stories told around campfires come to mind, and I shiver. One in particular that always terrifies me: a serial killer, hiding out in an abandoned cabin just like this one, waiting for unsuspecting campers to wander by ...

A face pops up at the glass-free window and I jump back with a screech.

"Julia?" Caleb says, as I crash backward into Nick. He steadies me, and I give both males a dirty look, embarrassed to be caught daydreaming.

"How did you know I was here?" Caleb asks.

"Psychic," I mutter.

"Why is he here?" Caleb looks at Nick.

"She got stuck with me," he answers.

Caleb looks at me. "Babysitting?"

"I guess you could call it that."

"Careful," Caleb says. "Last time she babysat we had to call the fire department."

"Well, if you hadn't climbed that tree and gotten stuck, it wouldn't have been necessary."

"Weren't you supposed to be watching me?" The right half of his face curves up the slightest fraction, teasing.

"I was making you lunch," I protest, but am secretly pleased to see the smile.

"Oh, right, you were in the kitchen." He shrugs. "It was probably a good thing we had the fire department on hand."

Nick laughs. "Ouch."

I shoot him a look. "For your information, I've never burned anything in my life."

"That's because you've never cooked anything in your life," Caleb says.

"I have so!" I say. "Who made you breakfast this morning?"

"Granola and fruit doesn't exactly count as cooking," he points out. "And that's not true about not burning anything."

"What did I burn?" I rack my brain, but Caleb's right, I don't cook too often. I take after Mom in that department.

"The old outhouse." Caleb smirks again. "When we were renovating the bathroom."

Oh, right.

"You burned down an outhouse?" Nick asks, eyes crinkling in amusement. "How does that happen?"

Caleb is unable to resist. "She lit a match." Nick snorts along with Caleb, who doesn't seem to mind him joining in at my expense.

"If you must know, it was in the middle of the night, and I knocked over a candle." My face is getting warm.

"Couldn't you just blow it out?" Nick says between chuckles.

"I was otherwise occupied," I say, looking at my fingernails. The candle flame had caught the toilet paper, and WHOOSH! I freaked and ran — or, rather, hastily waddled — from the wooden outhouse as fast as one can with PJ bottoms around their ankles.

Both boys are in hysterics now, tears streaming down Nick's face. I roll my eyes. Apparently all it takes is a little toilet humor to bond members of the opposite sex. "Hilarious." I attempt to change their focus. "Why are you here?" I say to Caleb, who's still doubled over the window frame.

"I ... came ... here ... to ... look for clues, about the ... thing," he manages to get out between giggles.

"What thing?" I push open the creaking door and stride into the cabin, my eyes adjusting to the dim interior. Dust motes swirl through the air where the sun's rays stream in and old papers lie strewn about. I used to love playing in here, a secret hideaway from the world.

"What you told me last night," Caleb says.

What I told him last ...? Oh. Gramps's story. Widening my eyes meaningfully at him, I jerk my head back at Nick, who's followed me in.

"Cool place," he enthuses, looking around at antiquated bookshelves and rickety stairs leading up to a loft.

"It was our grandfather's," Caleb informs him.

"You know we're not supposed to be here," I say. "Remember what happened to Paige? It's not exactly safe." Especially for someone in his condition, I want to add, but bite my tongue.

"I can take care of myself," he says, with a challenging glance at Nick. "*I* don't need a babysitter."

It's quiet for a minute.

"It doesn't look too bad," Nick says, dispelling some of the tension. "It could use a bit of TLC, but overall the structure seems sound." He walks around knocking on different areas of the log walls. "This would actually make a pretty cool clubhouse," he adds.

"It was when we were kids," I say. "Then my friend stepped on a nail. It went right through her foot." I shudder. "There was a lot of blood."

"So you sweep and take out any old nails," Nick says, gesturing.

"You really think we could fix this place up?" Cautious excitement filters through Caleb's voice, like the sunlight through the tattered curtains.

"Construction stuff is kind of part of my job," Nick confides, and I stiffen.

"I happen to know a little about it myself," I say, crossing my arms, thinking of all I've learned from Gramps and Red.

"Then between us both we should be able to fix it up, no problem, over the next few days," Nick says easily.

"That would be awesome." The last of Caleb's suspicion melts away as he looks at Nick, face lit like a lantern.

"Why would you want to help fix this place up when you're just here to tear everything down?" I ask Nick.

He's looking at Caleb, who's moving slowly around the cabin, musing to himself, "… and my comics could go here …"

"Could be a fun side project," Nick says. "Let's be honest, it's not going to take three full days for you to show me around the campground. Plus, carpentry happens to be a hobby of mine."

Along with charming little brothers, I almost add. Though I can kind of see what Caleb sees. I saw it last night. God, was it only last night? There's an easygoing affability about Nick. And that kindness that causes you to — mistakenly? — want to trust him. Profession notwithstanding.

"Can we, Julia?" Caleb looks up from his inspection, from Nick to me, hope and eagerness radiating from his entire body.

I haven't seen him this animated about anything in a long time. Definitely not since he was sick. And it would get him out of the house, into fresh air and away from the basement. It would give him a purpose. I wish Nick hadn't put me on the spot, but feel myself relenting.

"We'll just do a bare-bones job," Nick says. "Make it safe and then your bro can have a place to hang." He walks over to Caleb. "Every man needs a place to get away from it all," he says, offering his fist out for Caleb to bump back. I don't fully understand or trust what Nick might be up to, but I find myself unable to refuse my little brother.

"Fine." I hold my hands up in mock surrender.

"Sweet!" Caleb fist pumps the air.

"But I'm lead contractor on this," I say to both of them.

"Sure thing, boss." Nick grins and folds his arms over his chest. "I'm starting to enjoy the view from the passenger's seat anyway."

"Good," I say tartly, "because that's where you're headed right now. We have to get back."

Nick looks over at Caleb. "She always this bossy?"

"Always," Caleb says to his co-conspirator.

Traitor.

*

I decide to confront Nick on our way back home. Caleb's in the quad behind us.

"What was all that about?" I yell, glancing over my shoulder, words partially muffled by the helmet and engine.

"What?"

I gear down. "The whole 'Let's build a fort' buddy-buddy thing with my brother."

"From what you were telling me last night, it sounds like your brother could use a buddy."

"So you're just giving him something else to be disappointed about when you and your dad take it all away?"

"I thought you said that's not going to happen," he says.

"It's not," I say.

"Then what's your issue?"

"My issue is you getting Caleb excited about something that you'd like to destroy."

"Believe it or not, Julia, I don't like destroying things." There's an edge to his voice.

"What else do you call putting up a casino and mega resort on pristine lakefront?"

"My dad's idea, not mine," he says. "And we are two very different people."

Something about his tone has me holding back my next dig. We reach my house, and I park the quad, taking my helmet off and shaking out my hair. My mom comes out of the house, balancing drinks on a tray.

"Iced tea?" she calls, as Caleb pulls in behind us.

"Thanks, Mrs. Ducharme, appreciate that." Nick flashes his dashing smile and takes a glass. *Ugh. Did I just think his smile was "dashing"?*

She turns to me. "Julia?"

"No thanks." I'm thirsty, but I know what her organic kombucha tastes like. Dirt.

I watch Nick swallow the drink down in one gulp, without making a face. Points to him.

"Delicious." He wipes his mouth with the back of his hand.

"Thank you," Mom says. "It's my own brew."

"Really?" he replies. "You should start your own line of health drinks."

"I'd love to, but things are just so busy around here …" She looks around, and for the first time I wonder if there are other things she'd rather be doing than running a campground. A lump in my throat has me turning away. Caleb's parked the quad and is walking toward us.

"Thanks, Mom," he says, grabbing a glass.

"Just a few sips, Caleb, the caffeine content's high in this batch," she cautions, then turns to me. "Hon, I've prepared one of the cabins down at the lake for Nick. Would you mind taking him down there?"

What am I, a chauffeur? I open my mouth to protest, but Nick gets there first.

"That's okay, Mrs. Ducharme …"

"Anna," she says.

"Anna." He smiles at her again. "I'm sure Julia has enough to do without escorting me everywhere."

"I can show you," Caleb offers. Okay, enough's enough.

"Excuse me one second," I say through gritted teeth, pulling Caleb behind me. "I just need Caleb to show me where he left the gas."

"Try the outhouse," Nick murmurs, and Caleb guffaws. As I march away, brother in tow, I hear her invite Nick to dinner.

"What is going on?" I demand once we're behind the shed. "Since when is Nick your BFF?"

"Ever heard of catching more flies with honey than vinegar?" Caleb looks me square in the eye. Grandma always used to say that.

"You think just because you're nice to him, he's going to leave us alone?" I say.

"He might if we can convince him Pines isn't a good investment," Caleb says.

I sigh. "That was his idea; he's not going to fall for that."

Caleb's lower lip trembles. "Being mean to him isn't going to help either."

"I'm not being mean," I protest.

"You're not being very nice."

"Didn't I just agree to reno the old cabin with him?"

"That reminds me." Caleb brightens. "I didn't get a chance to tell you what I found before you two showed up."

"What?" I say.

"Some old papers of Gramps's." He lowers his voice. "I think you're right, and there's something hidden on the property. Maybe if we found whatever it was, we wouldn't have to sell."

"That's a pretty big 'if.'" Not to mention, I'm pretty sure that particular yarn may have been laced with a little bullcrap.

"Julia?" Mom calls. "Caleb?"

"Coming," we yell at the same time.

"Let's talk more about this later," I say to him. "You can show me the papers."

"Deal. But maybe you should try to be a little friendlier to Nick."

I don't mention that things might have been headed in that direction last night. Until I found out who he is and what he's doing here.

"Please, Julia?" Caleb begs. "Maybe if he gets to know us, we can get him to stop his dad from buying the place."

As far as plans go, I don't really have a better one.

I relent. "I'll try to be nice. But I'm only doing it because you asked me to."

"So I hear you're staying for dinner?" I say to Nick when I'm back inside.

"I was just telling your mom I should check with my aunt and uncle back at the campsite to make sure they weren't planning anything special."

"Why don't you invite them as well?" Mom asks. "We're just having veggie burgers, and I can throw together a quinoa salad. It would be great to catch up with them."

"Will do," Nick says. "I'm sure they'll appreciate the invite."

Which means I'll have to endure Dan and Taylor all lovey-dovey at dinner. I have enough trouble getting Mom's veggie burgers down without gagging as it is.

Chapter Eight

"So this is where you'll be staying." I nod at the cabins ahead, clustered at the other end of the long beach, far from the noisy boats along the dock.

Nick gives a low whistle. "Sweet A-frames."

I feel a flash of pride, but keep my "Thanks" nonchalant.

"You built these?" he asks.

"Some. Well, helped build," I amend, bringing the golf cart to a stop and hopping out. "Red, my father and I." If he wonders where my dad is, he's too polite to ask. I point to a few at the back, closer to the water. "Gramps put those ones up with Red." There are half a dozen in all.

Nick hefts up his tan guitar case and luggage from the back of the cart. Louis Vuitton. Really?

Nick follows my gaze. "A bit much, right?" I stay silent, remembering my promise to Caleb. "It was a birthday gift from my dad."

"How old are you?" I ask.

"Twenty."

"Really?" My eyebrows go up. "You seem a lot older." And look it.

"I feel older," he says, a shadow crossing his face, but leaves it at that.

We walk up to the closest cabin. Each one has a small porch out front, overlooking the lake. Some are two-story with lofts, some just one; all have solar panels and floor-to-ceiling windows in front to maximize the view. They are tiny triangles of awesomeness.

"Nice wood." He drops his bags and knocks on a beam, rubbing his hand over it, sniffing. "Cedar?"

"Yup, locally sourced from a family sawmill about half an hour from here," I say. He strokes the wood, almost lovingly. "Careful. Wouldn't want to get a splinter."

He laughs, saying, "No chance of that," and holds up two calloused palms. For a brief second I imagine what those palms would feel like on my skin. Trailing from my shoulders, skimming down my arms and ... I shiver. Giving my head a shake, I turn so Nick can't see the crimson bloom in my cheeks. Where did that come from?

"You're staying in Aquarius," I say, annoyed at myself and him and his calloused palms.

"Aquarius?" Nick asks, looking around.

I point to the farthest cabin, nestled back into the trees, where the bay curves around and forms a tip, like a crescent moon. Gramps had built that one, but we'd renovated it a few years ago. "Yes. That one's Lyra. Aquila and Cygnus are over there and Pegasus and Sagittarius are there." I point to each.

"Horoscopes?" he muses, picking up his bags again and following me.

"Constellations."

He carries his guitar in one hand and suitcase in the other, biceps round and hard. I walk up the cottage steps, bypassing two wooden rocking chairs on the deck, and open the door. "I hope this isn't too primitive for you." I smirk at his suitcase as he puts his stuff down.

Nick looks around, a broad grin on his handsome face. "This'll do just fine."

In spite of my words, I think the cabin is pretty great. Bright cerulean curtains hang at the windows, and there's a dark indigo woven rug in the center, in front of a small gray sofa. A tiny kitchen is off to the right. A tall ladder leads up to the loft bedroom and — my favorite feature — an epic skylight. White clouds float by, skimming sky the same shade as the curtains.

"All that's missing is a fireplace," he says. "But I guess you don't want campers burning the place down by accident."

"Wouldn't be good for business," I agree. Which makes me remember again why he's here. There's an awkward silence.

"So." Nick looks at me. "I guess I'll see you at dinner?"

"Right," I say. "If you want to wash up, the showers and bathrooms are just behind Pegasus." Walking over to the sofa, I pull open the drawer underneath. "Here are some towels." I nod up at the loft, clearing my throat. "There's clean sheets on the bed."

He looks at me, and I swallow.

"Thanks, Julia." His voice matches his eyes. Warm. Like black coffee.

"You're welcome. I hope you'll be comfortable here," I say, tone polite, just in case Caleb's whole honey/fly theory has any merit.

"I'm sure I will," he says, and I leave him to further inspect his surroundings, feeling his eyes follow me. I'm pretty sure Caleb meant that I'm the honey and Nick's the fly. But as I close the door gently behind me and jog down the steps, I contemplate just who is what in the whole equation.

*

"Can you pass the peas, Jules?" Dan asks. He and Taylor sit side by side, both fresh-faced and glowing from their time in the sun.

"Sure." I hand them over, barely resisting the urge to dump them on his head. So far dinner's off to a slightly better start than yesterday's, but not by much.

"Don't forget to say peas and thank you," Taylor singsongs. Dan laughs as I try to hide an eye roll. Nick must catch it because he smiles down at his plate — not the typical expression Mom's burgers inspire. The adults are at one end of the picnic table and the five of us sit at the other, Caleb holding court at the head.

"So, Julia, happy to be done with school?" Mrs. Schaeffer calls from her end. I'm pretty sure everyone's making an extra effort to be nice, what with the humiliation of Dan bringing his girlfriend here. All it does is make me feel even more like a reject. It's like the elephant in the room (or, rather, backyard). An elephant with blond hair, a great bod and the face of a Disney princess.

"Yes." I become extremely interested in the salad on my plate.

"What are you going to be doing this fall?" she says, pouring vinegar on the wound.

I'm a little miffed with Mr. and Mrs. Schaeffer. One: they had to have known how awkward it would be for Dan to bring Taylor. Two: they were basically the ones to set this sale stuff in motion. (Though they probably thought they were helping us out.) And now, three: she calls attention to my total lack of plans, making me look like a big loser with nothing set for September except skulking around the campground.

"Julia was a bit preoccupied this year," Mom says to Mrs. Schaeffer. "So she'd planned on sticking around here to give me a hand." Meaning I was so focused on Caleb getting better I didn't get my applications into schools on time. Of course, Mom doesn't come out and say this, not wanting to add to Caleb's feelings of guilt, but Mrs. Schaeffer seems to get her meaning.

"Oh. How wonderful!" she exclaims, like Mom's just told her I'm going to Africa to save the endangered white rhino. "I'm sure your mom will appreciate the help."

"What about college?" Dan asks, not as intuitive. "I thought you really wanted to go." I shoot him a look and nod at Caleb, who is obliviously downing the soda Mom let him have as a special treat.

"Did Julia get you set up all right, Nick?" Mom interrupts.

"Yes, thank you, Mrs. Ducharme," Nick says. "That's some great work you guys have done there."

"Anna, remember?" Mom says. "And thank you. Did she mention she helped out with the cabins?"

"She did," Nick says. "Beautiful artisanship." He looks at me, eyes twinkling.

"She's also got her grandfather's knack for tinkering," Mom says, her words like helium to a leaking balloon. I do love building and playing with things, seeing how they work, putting them back together.

"Tinkering?" Taylor laughs her charming, how-quaint-and-by-quaint-I-really-mean-pathetic laugh.

I deflate a little.

"You know," Caleb says. "Like fixing things and building stuff."

"A girl after my own heart," Nick says. That makes me feel slightly better. Not that I care about his approval. Much.

Losing interest, Taylor turns to Dan. "Are you taking me to see the island tonight?" The adults have gone back to their own conversation, the tinkering comment having sparked a debate on whether colleges versus trade schools are better for getting jobs these days.

"Sure," Dan says. "Why don't we all go? Done your ATV-ing for the day, Jules?" He arches an eyebrow as if to imply he knows I was making excuses earlier.

"All?" Taylor does a little pout.

"I'd be up for it." Nick looks at me. "What do you say, Tinkerbell?"

My eyes narrow. What's with the cute nicknames? He *must* be reverse honey/fly-ing me so I'll think selling is a good thing. Caleb kicks me under the table. Ouch. Well, two can definitely play at this game.

"Sure." I sit up straighter, taking a note from Mrs. Schaeffer in the fake positivity department.

"Great." Dan grins. I don't know why he's so bent on having us all hang out together.

"Great," Taylor intones, like she's just made plans for a root canal.

"Great," Nick says, crossing his arms and staring at me.

"Great." What the heck have I just signed myself up for?

"Anyone want another veggie burger?" Mom calls down to our end of the table.

"No." We answer at the same time, still staring at one another like some kind of stand-off.

She looks a bit taken aback at our synchronized response. "Okay, I'll just go get dessert ready then."

"Great." Caleb burps.

*

I shove the canoe, and it scrapes the bottom of the sandy shore, pushing through the muck before gliding into the water. It's dusk and the mosquitoes are feasting.

Nick slaps the back of his neck. "Mother. Think that guy just made off with half a pint."

"Girl," I say. "Only the females bite."

"Typical. Leave it to the females to bleed you dry," Dan says, offering his hand to help Taylor into their canoe. He's already tossed in his backpack, which most likely contains marshmallows and beer.

"We're worth it," she says airily, taking her place on the seat like a queen. Dan hops in their canoe and hands her a paddle.

"Ready?" I ask Nick, stepping into the canoe. It teeters slightly as he joins me. "Careful."

"Don't worry." He smiles at me. "One unexpected dunk is enough for the day." Picking up our paddles, we stroke, trailing behind Dan and Taylor. The moon is rising, embracing the four of us in an ivory glow. Staring past Nick's shoulder at the boat in front, I sigh. This isn't exactly how I pictured my moonlit canoe ride with Dan.

"Penny for your thoughts?" Nick says.

"Gave them to you last night for a few M&M's," I say. Won't be making that mistake again.

"So, chocolate's your weakness?"

Dammit. I change the subject.

"What do you think?" I gesture around me. "So far." Out in the middle of the lake, away from the few lights of shore, the stars are ablaze, the inky velvet sky a treasure chest of dazzling sapphires and rubies, glittering diamonds and topaz. The shadowed trees of the shoreline stand tall, silent protectors over the creatures in their midst. If we sell the campground, who will protect them?

"It's amazing. You're lucky you got to grow up in a place like this." His voice sounds … wistful? My heart, unfurling at the wild beauty of the evening, opens cautiously against my will, like some night-blooming flower.

"Where did you grow up?" I ask, feeling exposed.

"All over," he responds. "Mostly New Jersey. Toronto."

"You guys moved a lot?"

"I lived in Jersey until I was twelve. Then I went to live with my grandparents in Toronto."

"Why did you move?"

"My mom died." He states it so matter-of-factly that I find myself nodding. Right. The last time he saw Dan.

"So you and your dad moved to be closer to your grandparents?"

"No." He clears his throat. "Just me."

Why wouldn't he stay with his dad after his mom died? Wouldn't he need to be with his father at a time like that? The one thing that got my family through Caleb's illness was one another. I keep my questions from bubbling over.

Nick smiles. "Since you spilled your guts last night, I guess it's only fair I return the favor." I look at him. "Besides, I can tell you're dying to ask."

"It's none of my business." I strive for blasé.

"He didn't want me then," he says. "Or maybe he couldn't take care of me. Whatever. The end result was the same."

I keep my voice as level as the canoe. "And now?"

Nick gazes out at the water. "Now, it's different."

I hesitate. "How did your mom die?"

"Cancer," he says. "One minute she's fine, complaining about a sore arm, the next she's in the hospital, tubes everywhere. Then she was gone. It was so fast."

My heart goes out to him. "I'm sorry." The sentiment is completely inadequate, but I don't quite know what else to say.

"Thanks." He digs his paddle hard into the water. "It was a long time ago."

Not that long ago. Besides, losing a parent sticks with you.

He continues, "When you were telling me about your brother last night, I wanted to say I know what it's like. Those long nights in the hospital. Scared to leave in case it's the last time you'll see them."

I'm silent as I paddle. The difference being that Caleb's very much alive and on his way to being healed. Despite the lame joke I told Nick last night, I lost count of the number of stars I wished on. My only wish was for Caleb to get better.

"When did your dad come back into the picture?" I say. I'm thinking of my own.

"When I graduated from high school. I saw him occasionally, of course, holidays, vacations and all that, but we didn't live together again until I was eighteen."

"He wanted you to follow in the family footsteps?"

"Something like that." His face is remote.

Up ahead, Taylor and Dan have reached the shore of the island. Dan hops into the water and pulls the canoe up, tying it to a stump. Feeling like it's an awkward place to leave the conversation but not really sure how to continue, I give one last hard paddle and the canoe scrapes bottom. Splashing out before I can, Nick pulls the canoe the rest of the way onto the shore. He offers me his hand and I take it, jumping onto the sand beside him. As our eyes meet, a loon cries in the distance; its mournful trill seems to say it understands. Something passes between us. Flustered, I let go of his hand and busy myself tying up the canoe.

"So what's so special about this place again?" Taylor asks, looking around.

"Are you serious?" Dan says. "It's awesome. Totally private, being at one with nature. Jules and I have some pretty great memories exploring this place."

"In the summers we were allowed to set foot on it," I say, giving him a testy look. Last summer had been one of them. "Every few years, biologists designate it as a nesting site for loons. Then it's closed and no one's allowed here."

"That didn't stop us a few years ago, did it, Jules?" Dan grins at me and a familiar yearning tugs at my chest. He turns and walks up a faint trail, holding Taylor's hand. Nick and I follow. What on earth has he told Taylor about me? His offhand comments seem to barely register with her. Then again, it's like Beach Bombshell Barbie feeling threatened by Clumsy Campground Skipper. Laughable. I'm still completely bewildered at how nothing's worked out like I thought it would.

"You guys crashed a loon sanctuary?" Nick says.

"We were really careful," I say, though it had been pretty stupid. I'll chalk it up to wanting to impress Dan and the thrill of doing something forbidden. For the most part, I'm pretty straitlaced, much to Paige's exasperation, but every once in a while the urge to do something I'm not supposed to overrides common sense. Like pushing boys into lakes. "Besides, they ended up mating successfully, and we had two little chicks that summer." I look at him. "I didn't realize you were so concerned about loons. Maybe you'll let them gamble in your resort?" Remembering what he just told me about his mom, I immediately feel like a jerk. Plus, that was a really bad joke.

But he laughs, ebony eyes twinkling in the moonlight. "Only if they have ID."

"You guys coming?" Dan turns and calls down the path. It rises up over a small hill, brush on each side, long grass swaying in the wind.

"Where are we going?" Nick asks.

"There's a little area on the other side of the beach where we can have a fire," I say.

"If I'd known, I would've brought marshmallows," he says.

"Got 'em," Dan calls over his shoulder, raising an arm.

"Did you know they're made out of animal bones?" I say.

"As a matter of fact, I did." Nick's grin is a flash in the dark. "Doesn't make them any less delicious."

"What's made out of animal bones?" Taylor asks as the trail starts to dip down.

"Gelatin," I say. "The stuff in gummy bears, Jell-O, marshmallows. It's made from boiling animal bones or hooves so long that the connective tissue oozes out."

"That's disgusting." She makes a face.

"Yup." Which is why I try not to think about it when I eat s'mores.

"If you eat meat, it's all the same," Dan points out.

"It's still gross," Taylor says.

The trail ends and we're on a small beach facing the other side of the lake and a thick wall of trees, the mountains rising up behind them.

"Why don't Julia and I collect some wood for the fire," Dan says, looking at Taylor and Nick. "You two can chill here."

"I can help," Nick offers quickly.

"We know where we're going. You guys don't." Dan shrugs off the backpack he's wearing. "Wouldn't want you to step on a loon's nest accidentally."

"So what should we do?" Taylor asks, lower lip slightly out. Sheesh. Even *I* think her pout is adorable.

"Find some big rocks to ring the campfire." Dan looks around. "There's usually some scattered around here."

"Rocks?" Taylor looks unimpressed.

"Here." I throw the aged Leatherman jackknife I always have on me to Nick. "Whittle some sticks for roasting marshmallows."

"Whittle?" Nick echoes Taylor. "And I thought you were grossed out by their ingredients."

I shoot him a brief smile and repeat his words. "Doesn't make them any less delicious."

He clutches his chest like he's just been shot. "Oh, God," he croaks, stumbling around. "She smiled." I turn before he sees a second one playing on my lips and walk off to get wood.

"Jules," Dan calls, hurrying to catch up. "Hold up a sec."

I'm not sure I'm ready to be alone with him, but curiosity wins out. I stop and turn, nerves dancing, and take a deep breath. This should be good.

Chapter Nine

"What is it?" I say. Then change my mind. I don't want to know. Under the pretense of looking for sticks to use as kindling, I turn back around.

He grabs my hand to stop me. "I want to talk. To explain."

My hands flutter him away. Striving for nonchalant, I say, "Don't worry about it. Obviously we weren't on the same page." Or chapter. Or genre.

His tone is beseeching. "Taylor and I hooked up just after Christmas. I wanted to tell you, but it didn't seem like a good time, with your brother and everything you guys were going through."

I blink at him. "Sorry, am I supposed to thank you for being considerate?"

He sighs. "I didn't plan for it to happen, it just did and we'd never really talked about — you know — us."

"I thought it was implied." I bend over to pick up some sticks. Apparently our make-out sessions only meant something to me. God, I'm so glad it didn't go any further.

Dan tries again. "I didn't realize what it would be like, with her here." Straightening up, I look at him. "This is our place. Being here reminds me of all the time we spent together."

I'm not sure how to respond or even what he's saying. It doesn't change the fact that he still brought her here. It hits me that I have no reason to feel badly toward Taylor. It's not her fault.

"What did you tell Taylor about me?" I ask. This time he's the one who walks to pick up a couple of broken branches.

"That we're old friends," he says, finally looking at me. A loon sounds again in the distance. "Aren't we?"

No, I want to say. *You put a dent in my heart like it's nothing.* But I stay silent. Five years we've known each other. Five years his family's been coming to our campground. He's everything I associate with summer, and now I've been cast into the role of "friend."

"What about your parents siccing your uncle on us? Why didn't you give me a heads-up?"

"My parents were trying to help your mom out. I thought you knew."

"Yeah, well, I didn't." My throat is tight. "There's been a few not-so-great surprises recently."

"I'm sorry. I know how much you love this place." He lets his collection of firewood fall to the ground and grabs my free hand. "I love it, too. I'm an idiot. Can you forgive me?"

"Sure," I manage, pulling my hand from his. "Friends." I start back to the fire, splinters in my hands and in my heart. Back at the clearing, I unceremoniously dump my stockpile next to Taylor's perfect stone circle.

"Nice job," I say.

"Thanks." She looks at me, big blue eyes wary. Guys don't give women's intuition enough credit. We pick up on things. Subtle currents, unspoken words, body language. Not to mention the totally obvious comments he's been making. She has to know there's more to his story than he's telling.

"Where's Nick?" I ask, looking around.

"He went for a swim."

"Seriously?" I peer out at the dark water.

"Seriously," he shouts, treading water. "Fire, please."

Crouching, I take the kindling and crisscross the smaller stuff, layering bigger pieces of wood on top of each other. Dan comes back and drops a huge pile of wood beside me.

"Here." He reaches into his backpack. "I've got some paper." He wads up the newspaper and sticks it under the twigs, lighting one corner, then another, and blows gently. The flame licks the paper and takes hold, burning bright, then dims as it goes about the more labor-intensive work of consuming the wood.

Nick makes his way out of the lake, pushing hair out of his eyes, water running down his chest.

"That was refreshing," he says.

"You didn't get enough of the lake this morning?" I ask.

He laughs and brushes the water from his toned body. How would it feel if I touched it? *Oh my god. Am I actually thinking that?* Averting my gaze, I stare at the fire. Taylor and Dan are cuddling a few feet back. Nick comes and sits beside me, still clad in boxers only.

"Aren't you going to put your clothes back on?" I ask.

"Might as well wait until the fire dries me off. No sense getting my clothes all wet. Again." He leans back against the log. We sit there in silence around the campfire. This is so freaking awkward.

"So, Taylor." I clear my throat. She looks up from where she's cooing at Dan. "What are you planning to study at college?"

"Math."

Of course. Not only blonde and beautiful but smart, too. I should've known.

"Yup," Dan says, giving her shoulders a proud squeeze. "Taylor's been offered a scholarship to Penn."

"Awesome," I say. The campfire crackles and crickets chirp, both literally and figuratively. Why on earth did I agree to this? Roasting marshmallows with my ex-summer fling, his stunning gifted girlfriend and handsome campground-robbing cousin? What the heck am I doing here?

"So, Cuz, what are your plans for this place?" Dan says to Nick, but with a pointed look at me.

Right. I sit up straighter. I'm supposed to be convincing Nick not to buy.

Nick clears his throat and picks up a stick. "It's still early days."

"Yeah, he's just assessing the property," I say.

"We both know how fast you and Uncle Tom move once you decide you like something. You're ruthless. I heard about that Miller deal." A muscle jumps in Nick's jaw as Dan looks at me again. "It really sucks that your mom's considering selling, Jules."

"Why is she?" Taylor asks, curious. Guess the boys haven't shared.

"My brother was sick this year," I say, grabbing at a stick close to me. "We have a lot of medical bills." It's been sharpened.

"Oh," she says as I shove the stick into the sand. "Sorry to hear that."

"Yeah," says Dan. "I knew a little bit from what you told me and from my parents but didn't realize how bad it was."

"Nice job," I say to Nick. "Where's my knife?"

"Here. So, hey, can you point out some constellations for us?"

"Sure." I shoot him a grateful look. "There's Cassiopeia."

Everyone looks where I point. "She was a vain queen in Greek mythology. And there's Scorpius."

"I can never find the Little Dipper," Nick muses. "I always think I've found it, but I don't think it ever is."

"See the last bottom and upper right stars in the bowl part of the dipper?" I say.

"Yeah." Nick cranes his head.

"From the last star go straight up to Polaris." I point at the bright star. "Also known as the North Star."

"Fiftieth brightest in the sky, right?" Nick says.

"Yes." So he'd been listening. "And the star that all other stars in the summer revolve around. Polaris is the last star in the handle of the Little Dipper."

"So are you into astronomy, or something?" Taylor asks.

"A bit," I say.

"You have a telescope," Nick points out. "And those." He nods at the binoculars around my neck.

"Yeah, well, it's just something to do to pass the time." And to distract me those nights during last fall and winter when no one was at home. It sure beat not sleeping.

"What's that over there?" Taylor points up at a section of the sky.

I squint up at where she's pointing. "Um, I don't think that's anything."

"Oh." She sounds disappointed. The moon goes behind a cloud and the sky darkens.

"Here." I take off the binoculars. "Try these." She holds them up to her eyes. "Other way."

Dan laughs and she turns them around.

"What am I looking at?" she says.

"Want to see what another galaxy looks like?" I ask.

She looks at me over the binoculars. "Really?"

"Go back to Cassiopeia," I instruct. "The W-shaped constellation. Now, see the deepest part of the second V?"

"Yeah."

"Follow that point; it aims directly at M31."

"M31?" She doesn't seem impressed.

"Also known as the Andromeda galaxy, if you prefer fancy names," I say.

"A star by any other name would shine as bright," Nick murmurs.

She follows the invisible line to a hazy object in the sky. "I think I see it!"

"Look to the side of it, instead of straight on," I say. "You can see distant objects better that way."

"So cool." She's sitting straight up. "There's a big bulge of light and, like, super faint spiral arms coming out from it."

The boys look in the direction she's looking.

"Let me see." Dan makes a grab for the binoculars.

"Wait your turn." She smacks his hand away.

"You both can probably see it if you look really hard, now that your vision has adjusted to the dark," I say to them, tracing my finger to where Taylor is looking. "The Andromeda galaxy is the farthest object that can be seen with our eyes. It's only two-point-five million light-years away."

"Only?" Nick echoes.

"It's beautiful," Taylor says in a dreamy voice.

"It's the closest galaxy to ours, with more than a trillion stars," I say. "And getting closer to us every day. About seventy miles per second, actually."

"Will it get bigger as it comes closer?" she asks.

"I'd imagine so," I say, folding my hands behind my head and leaning back against the log. "Seeing as how it's on a direct collision course with our Milky Way."

"What?" She puts the binoculars down, looking panicked.

"Don't worry, that won't happen for about another five billion years," I reassure her. She passes me back the binoculars.

"Well, that's just great." Dan gets up and grabs his backpack, rummaging through it.

I shrug. "By that time Earth will have other things to worry about. The sun will have swelled up into a red giant and consumed all nearby planets. Not to mention there's always the possibility of being wiped out by a random asteroid or a nearby massive star explosion."

Everyone looks at me, mouths hanging open. The moon comes out from behind the clouds, illuminating the alarm on their faces.

"Um, but no need to worry." I hasten to lighten the mood. "By that time we'll probably have offed ourselves due to some cataclysmic environmental catastrophe or nuclear war or something."

That didn't come out quite how I wanted it to.

"So, uh . . ." Dan breaks the millionth awkward silence of the evening. "Who wants a drink?" He holds up the beers from his backpack.

"No thanks." Beer ranks almost as low as Mom's kombucha, taste-wise.

"I got something special for the ladies." He holds up a liter water bottle, filled with what looks like orange juice.

"Screwdrivers." Taylor claps her hands, imminent demise of all life-forms forgotten. "Wanna drink, Julia?" It's the first time she's said my name, and it sounds weird.

"Sure," I hear myself say.

Dan passes me the bottle and our fingers touch briefly. I take a chug. It's strong. Wiping my mouth on my forearm, I pass the bottle to Taylor.

She takes a swig. The boys crack their beers and start talking about sports.

"So, math, hey?" I say.

"Yup." She hands it back to me.

"That's cool." I take another drink and try not to cough.

"Thanks." She takes the bottle from me. "Sucks you're not going away this year."

"I don't mind." Much. Of course I'll be sad when Paige leaves, but she's not going far. Just to college a few hours away. And my family needs me right now. "There'll be other chances."

Nick overhears me. "Most of my buddies ended up pissing away their first year, anyway." He gives me a brief smile. "They don't know what to do, so they just spend the year doing keg stands and becoming professional beer pong players."

"I'm awesome at beer pong," Taylor says.

"Never played," I say.

"I'd teach you, but we need cups," Dan says. "And a flat surface."

"Let's play another game," Taylor suggests. "How about 'Questions'?"

"How do you play that?" I ask.

"It's like truth or dare but without the dare," she says. "One person asks another a question. They have to answer, no hesitation or laughing, or they have to drink. The oldest person goes first."

"That's you, Grandpa." Dan nods at Nick.

"All right." Nick looks at me. "Julia, if you could have any kind of superpower, what would it be?"

I think for a second. Flying would be really cool. So would turning invisible. But I know what would be even better. "I think I'd like the power to heal instantly."

"Wolverine style." Dan nods.

"Okay, Julia, your turn," Taylor says. "But first you have to drink because you took too long to respond." She hands me the bottle.

"Okay." I take a swallow; it seems less strong now. Or maybe my taste buds have been anesthetized. "Um, Taylor."

She looks at me and I rack my brain for something to ask. "What's your most embarrassing moment?"

"When my parents caught me having sex," she says immediately.

Whoa.

Dan looks at her. "Your parents never caught us …" His expression darkens, and Taylor tosses her hair over her shoulder.

"It was before we were together." The challenge in her tone is unmistakable.

"Well, I'd hope so," Nick murmurs.

"No judgment around the campfire," I say. It's so nice to hear that Dan and Taylor are having sex. Gives me warm fuzzies. Also makes me feel like rolling around in the fire pit.

Suddenly, the annihilation of the solar system doesn't sound so bad.

"My turn," Taylor announces, not giving Dan any time to jump in. "Nick, do you like Julia?"

This game is the worst. The heat from the fire is nothing compared to that beaming out of my cheeks.

"Of course," Nick says.

"I mean, do you *like* her, like her?" she clarifies.

"He just met me," I say, staring resolutely at the flames.

"Doesn't matter," Taylor says. "When you know, you know."

"Yeah, I'd say there's an attraction there," Nick says. The heat in my face has spread down to my belly.

"Too bad you're here to buy her family's home," Dan says, having regained his composure.

Right.

I look up at him. He still looks grumpy at his girlfriend's revelation that his wasn't the only comet to enter her stratosphere.

"Dan, don't be so negative," Taylor chides him. "This is perfect!" She seems weirdly overjoyed by Nick's admission. "Let's give the love-birds a little time alone." She leans over and whispers, "Go for it. He's hot!" Before I can ask what exactly is the "it" I should go for, Taylor hops up and holds her hands out to Dan to grab. "Come on, baby, let's go for a swim."

"With or without our clothes?" Dan says, visibly perking up.

Taylor lifts her pink sweater over her head and throws it on the ground. "What do you think?" She giggles and runs off through the bushes. When Dan chases after her, Nick and I are alone by the campfire.

"Julia, you can look at me, you know," he says.

Our eyes meet. His face is mostly in shadows.

"You seem a little nervous."

"Do I?" My voice is a squeak.

He laughs and moves closer to me. "Why do you look so surprised? Don't tell me you didn't feel anything last night on the dock."

I'm also feeling something right now, but I'm not about to tell him that. "That was before I found out who you are and what you're planning on doing."

"What if I'm not exactly sure what I'm doing?"

"Come on." Everything about Nick screams that he knows exactly what he's doing.

"What if I want different things than my dad?"

"Like what?"

He sighs. The campfire crackles, and the crickets have settled into an easy rhythm. "It's complicated."

"You just said you want different things than your dad. So what are they?"

"A life." He bites the word off. "Don't get me wrong, my dad's extremely successful. I know this sounds arrogant, but let's just say we don't have to worry about money."

"Must be nice." My tone is acerbic.

"I'm sorry." He picks up a stick and pokes the fire, exposing crumbling ash on the other side of a large blackened log. "What I meant is, for him, work is everything. It's all he does, all he thinks about. Deals and how to make more money. That's his life."

"And you don't want that?"

"I know you guys are strapped for cash right now, but think of what you do have. You get to live here." He gestures around. "From what I've seen, your family seems pretty tight. What you have is better than money." He doesn't know the whole truth about my family, though. When he talked about his dad, I didn't mention mine.

"You're forgetting that without money, we won't have 'here' for too much longer." I imitate his gesture, throwing my arms wide. "Forgive me, but you seem a little, um, privileged. It's easy to talk about how money isn't everything when you have it."

"You're right." He gives me a long look. "I have thought about walking away from it all, you know."

Right. "How and why would you ever do that?"

He's silent. "I want to do music."

"The guitar. Are you any good?" I ask him. His playing last night had sounded amazing.

"I was in a band in Toronto. We were this close to making it." He holds up his finger and a thumb, a millimeter apart. "I could taste it." His voice is raw.

"What happened?"

"My dad came back last year. Said if I wanted my share of the family business, I'd have to work for it."

"He made you quit?"

"Yup." He laughs; its hollowness bothers me. "Pretty standard father-son stuff, actually."

"So if you don't follow in the family footsteps, you're cut off?"

"My dad's a pretty traditional guy. I'm his only son. Only child, actually. He thinks he's *saving* me from myself. From throwing my life away." Nick jams the stick in the fire; flames flare. "Maybe he's right."

I don't know what to say. Clearing my throat, I change the subject. "So what kind of music do you play?"

"Indie rock, mostly, but we infuse other sounds. Reggae, ska, some folk and blues. You kind of have to hear it." He grins. "We were really big in Japan." Ah, that explains the Osaka comment.

"So from rock star to real-estate developer, huh? Bet there were more girls in the first line of work."

He laughs and grabs the binoculars to look through, bringing them level with my face. "Actually, believe it or not, it's the real estate that's … brought into focus? … the most interesting girl I've met in a long time." His voice is mischievous.

Something in my chest actually *flutters*. All it takes is a few pretty words?

"Must be tough having beautiful girls throw themselves at you." My words come out sharper than I intend.

"No, it's actually pretty great." He puts down the nocs, his smile appropriately wolfish. "But those girls are different. They're not throwing themselves at you but their image of you. The rock star. Everyone wants to touch a little bit of fame …" I watch his hand come toward me and tilt my chin up so I'm staring right at him. "It's hard to find things and people that are real these days, Julia." His breath is warm on my cheek. "I knew you were going to push me off that dock. I can see every thought flash across your face. Your transparency is a rare quality."

"What about my temper?" I manage.

"Also something to behold. It means you're not afraid of showing passion." He lowers his mouth. "I like that," he whispers, just before his mouth comes down. His lips are warm, soft but firm, and they part mine slightly. My brain explodes like a supernova as something is unleashed deep within me. Something that Dan's kisses never came close to touching. It scares me.

I pull back, my breath coming hard and irregular.

"What are you doing?"

"Kissing you?" Despite the amusement in his voice, his breathing is also uneven.

"I mean, why?"

"I thought we've established that, despite your prickliness, I find you attractive."

"You're not just trying to seduce me into giving away my family's property?"

He sighs and pulls back, running a hand through his dark hair. "I thought *I* was jaded. Actually, I'm pretty sure I'm screwing myself and my dad, though I'm not really sure that I care. If your mom finds out I kissed you she might not be so keen on selling, desperate or not."

"We are not *desperate*." Something about the word nettles me, and I look up at the sky, not sure what exactly it is I'm looking for. There's a streak of light as a meteor enters Earth's atmosphere and is vaporized, burning up in a blaze of dust and gas. A quick intake of breath from Nick beside me tells me he's seen it, too.

"What if I help you?" he says, abruptly.

"Help me what?"

"Figure out a way not to sell, like I was trying to do last night."

"Why would you do that? Seriously … why?"

He ignores me. "You guys need money, right?" He rubs his chin, musing. "Maybe some kind of auction or something …"

I jump up, unfocused. "You think I'm just going to auction off my virginity to the highest bidder like some crazy girl on the internet?"

Nick looks at me and bursts out laughing. "Wow, that's quite the leap." I stand there, frozen, realizing the idiocy of my accusation; my only defense is that his kiss made me temporarily insane. "I was thinking more along the lines of helping you guys raise some money so you wouldn't have to sell. Don't you have some kind of local festival coming up?"

"Wakestock," I say, forcing my fists to unclench. "It's a local wakeboarding event, with competitors coming from all over the county. The campground's always full."

"I read about it during our prelim research," Nick says. "Sounds pretty cool. But what if we made it bigger?" He gets up and starts putting his clothes on.

"Bigger?" I say, distracted, watching him pull his shirt over his head.

"Attract corporate sponsors, some musical acts. Big names. Charge for tickets."

"That sounds like a lot of work. It's only a month away."

He shrugs. "I could call in a few favors. I can even get the band back together."

"Who *are* you?"

He looks at me. "You know who I am. In the past twenty-four hours I've told you more about myself than I've told anyone." He *has* been extremely open. Telling me about his mother and father leaves me feeling like he's almost a kindred spirit.

"It doesn't happen like that," I say, blood roaring in my ears. He takes another step toward me.

"Oh yeah? What if it does?"

Chapter Ten

Nick takes another step toward me. Then something cracks in the bushes and our heads swivel toward the sound.

"Hey, guys." A sopping wet and — thankfully — fully clothed Taylor steps out of the bushes. "I'm not interrupting anything, am I?" Her look is sly as she sidles on over to the fire. Rubbing her hands together, she holds them up to the warmth. Dan's right behind her, and he throws on another log. Properly raging now, the hungry flames are quick to lap at the untouched wood.

"I should be getting back," I say, grabbing my binoculars and putting them around my neck. I can't think. The alcohol might also have something to do with that.

"I'll come with you," Nick says.

"No, you stay here." Paddling with Nick on a moonlit night isn't going to clear my head any.

"I'm coming," he says firmly. "We can talk about my idea some more."

"Bye!" Taylor chirps and waggles her fingers in our direction.

"Later." I turn and start off back to where we tied the canoes.

"Julia, wait." Nick grabs my hand. "Why are you in such a hurry? Did I offend you in some way?" I look down at our hands. He pulls me toward him.

"I just don't believe that you …"

"That I what?"

That someone like you is interested in someone like me. Oh, man, that must be the vodka — fertilizer to the seeds of insecurity. *Pull it together, Julia.* "That you'd want to help us."

"Why not?"

"Won't that piss off your dad?"

He shrugs. "Nothing I haven't done before. Besides" — his voice is teasing — "you're much better-looking than my dad. Gorgeous, in fact."

I make a face.

"You are."

"I have freckles," I point out. "Since when are freckles gorgeous?"

His thumbs come to my nose and sweep up along my cheekbones to my temples. "Your freckles are adorable." He bends down and kisses my nose. I can't believe this is happening. "Since meeting you, I can't get you out of my head. I've even somehow managed to write an entire song last night. Something I haven't done in a long time."

"So you're saying I'm your muse?"

"I'm saying you inspire me. And how I feel about you in such a short time is … disconcerting. But right now, I'm not thinking about that."

"What are you thinking about?" My voice comes out as a whisper. Something in my core shifts. Maybe irrevocably.

"This." He bends his head and presses his lips to mine in a kiss that has me practically swooning as he savors my mouth. My hands go to his chest and I clutch a little at his shirt as my knees give way.

What is happening to me? The response that Nick's kiss elicits from me is overwhelming. And scary. I put my hands on his chest and take a few deep breaths. "I need to be getting back."

He looks as stunned as I feel. "Okay."

We get to the canoe and climb in; it wobbles unsteadily. Legs shaky, I barely manage to sit down without tipping us both in the water. I grab at the paddle at the bottom of the boat. We face forward, paddling in silence. The moon goes behind the clouds again.

"Look up," Nick says, voice hushed. I do, and though I've seen it thousands of times, it's still glorious. "I've never seen so many stars. It's even better than last night."

"Not as much light pollution in the middle of a lake." Dip. "Of course that will change if a casino goes up." But my voice sounds quietly resigned, even to my ears.

"Julia, I'm not going to let you lose your home." Nick's voice is firm.

"What?" I wonder if I've heard him correctly.

"I've decided I'm going to help you and your family."

"Won't you — and your dad — miss out on the opportunity to make a lot of money?" I stare at his beautifully curved back.

"It's just money. What you guys have here is special. Like you."

I don't know if I should trust him or not. "How are you going to do that?"

"Any way I can. I still think amping up Wakestock could be awesome and earn you guys some extra cash. Plus, once you get the public involved you'd be surprised how many people will help fight to save this place." He strokes, the dip-dip of the paddle luring me into hope. "You'd also be surprised how many people aren't too fond of mega resorts."

"You'd be surprised how talk of a few jobs on the table can change minds."

"Well, if you're open to them, other opportunities can be created."

His paddle hovers over the water. "I'd need to do a bit of research first." It dips in.

"Thank you," I say. My chest hurts, like maybe I pulled a muscle paddling. Rotating my shoulder back, I try to release the tension, rolling it a few times. The tightness remains. We're almost at the shore. "So what are you going to do with your time now that you don't have to officially assess the property?"

He smiles. "I thought you were going to give me a few astronomy lessons? Plus, don't we have a fort to fix up?"

"In case you haven't noticed, we're pretty busy around here," I say, but the tension is leaving, like after a yoga class.

"I can help."

"Really?" I say to his rippling trapezius muscles. "You want to spend your time helping me do campground maintenance?"

"Doesn't sound so bad to me."

"Okay." I'm the worst. Why can't I say something light and flirty? "Why don't we start with the boards on the dock?"

He laughs. "Deal." Jumping out of the canoe, he pushes it all the way up to shore. I hop out and help him, tying it up by the others. I have no idea how, but Caleb's honey/fly theory — against all odds — appears to have worked. Even though I've really been more vinegar than honey.

Maybe Nick likes vinegar?

He grabs my hand and I feel a jolt. The way I react to him makes me realize that my feelings for Dan were not as strong as I'd imagined. I'd liked him, but the goose bumps Nick gives me are at a whole other elevation.

"I'll walk you home," he says. "You can point out a few other constellations on the way."

*

With the clouds dissipating and the large trees blocking out most of the sky, I decide to forgo the stars, taking Nick off into the woods instead.

"Where are we going?" he asks as we traipse down a trail in the dark, stumbling over small rocks and pushing pointy branches out of our faces.

"Here," I say, stopping short as we emerge out on the bank of a tiny lake. The water is perfectly still. Just off center to the right is a large dome of sticks piled precisely and methodically.

"Another swim?" he says, coming right up behind me, warmth radiating from his body like a solar flare.

Something strange is happening to my skin. It feels like it's crawling with fire ants. "Do you want to get smacked?"

"What'd I say?" His laugh is throaty as he puts his hands lightly on my waist. My heart jumps, like a fish at dusk.

"Not by me." I nod at the center of the lake. "Watch." After a few seconds of silence, a large brown head appears, breaking the glassy tranquillity of the water.

"What is that?" His breath is soft on my neck. "Some kind of hairy fish?"

A breathy laugh escapes. I turn to look up at him. "It's a beaver."

"You brought me all the way out here to check out a beaver? How incredibly romantic." He grins down at me.

"That's their lodge over there." Suddenly shy, I turn back around and point to the middle of the lake. "The whole colony lives in it together." One big happy beaver family.

"Cozy," he murmurs, wrapping his arms around me.

"You want romantic? They are one of the few monogamous animals on Earth." Another thing I've always admired about them.

Nick laughs. "Tell me some more sexy facts about beavers, Julia. I love it when you get all ranger girl on me. It's hot."

And I love it when he says my name. "I bet," I croak. "So." Clearing my throat, I attempt to calm my heart rate. "More sexy facts, hey? All right. Besides being busy bundles of energy who take exceptional care of their home, which *I* happen to find *very* sexy" — I glance sidelong at him — "they also secrete a chemical from their glands that smells like vanilla."

"Just when I thought things couldn't get any more risqué," Nick says. "How and why do you know that?"

"It's used in natural flavoring. Generally, Mom doesn't like Caleb and me to have any artificial flavors or colors," I confide. "Red dye number seven, especially, makes him a little crazy."

"I've never met someone with such a passion for beavers before." The way he looks at me makes me nervous. But in a good way. Like a chaos-throughout-my-body way.

My throat is dry, my voice a whisper. "Did I mention they have transparent eyelids that act as goggles while they swim underwater?"

His voice lowers even more. "I don't believe you did," he says, mouth coming down to mine. I forget about the beavers.

*

I turn around on the porch step, feeling electrified, like a tree struck in a lightning storm. "It's okay, I'm home now."

"I'll just wait until the door is shut behind you."

Another laugh escapes. "You know, I have lived here seventeen years without being mauled by a wild animal."

"That streak is over," he quips, pulling me to him. His mouth comes down on mine and the voltage of it almost makes my hair rise. I don't think I'll ever get used to it. The porch light comes on and we jump apart.

"Julia?" I hear Mom call out.

"Yes?" My voice is squeaky and breathy.

"Just checking."

I can't stop a giggle from sneaking out. Then another. I put a hand to my mouth.

"Goodnight," Nick whispers, one hand coming to cup my cheek, brown eyes letting me know he doesn't want to say goodbye. Waving him off, I close the door behind me and climb the stairs in a dreamy fog, going straight to my room, not wanting Mom to see me.

And with good reason, I think, a few minutes later, staring at myself in the mirror. Green eyes overly bright, cheeks flushed, lips swollen, hair disheveled. I touch my face in wonder; it feels tender and raw from Nick's scruff.

"Julia?"

I startle and turn around. "Cale."

He inspects me. "Did it work?"

This time my laugh isn't breathy. It's loud and delighted; my first real laugh in a long time. "In a way." I'm sure Caleb didn't actually mean for me to fall for Nick, but that is exactly what is happening. Like a giant piece of rock entering the mesosphere, tail burning bright.

Caleb comes into the room, half jumping, half dancing, seemingly not bothered by his weak side. "I knew you could convince him." He looks at me, and now I feel as tall and strong as one of the giant redwoods out back. On an impulse I pick him up and twirl him around. He's so light, and his tiny ribs almost break my heart. But he's strong like me. He'll heal here, in the fresh air and under the stars, and he'll be back to himself by the end of the summer. I just know it.

*

After Caleb goes to bed, I flip open my laptop, too wired to sleep. I have to tell Paige. But first I go to Google and type in *Nick Constantine*.

There he is. And his band.

Wow.

Pages and pages of search results pop up. I click on a few articles. The group was an indie darling. I keep reading. By the look of it, Nick was being modest. They'd just begun to make it, no "almost" about it. What would that feel like, I wonder, to finally touch something you'd worked so hard for, then have it ripped away? I keep on reading. Fans loved them. Critics, too.

Nick is legitimately famous.

Of course, living in total Hicksville, it takes a little longer to hear about some of the newer acts. But if things had kept going for the band, there'd be no way I wouldn't know his name. I watch a few YouTube clips of them playing. Bright lights, music that infects you and makes you dance, even if you're not in the mood. Screaming fans. Lots of girls. Gorgeous girls. My spirits start to fizzle. Girls as pretty as Taylor. I wonder if she knows. Dan must have told her, right? Then again, he seems to be a little envious of his cousin. And no wonder. Rich. Good-looking. Semi rock star. He probably never said a word to her. That does seem to be his MO. Good thing, because I'd never stand a chance against someone like Taylor if she decided she wanted Nick. Actually, now that I think about it, I wouldn't stand a chance against any of these girls. My heart bottoms out. Compared to them, I look like I just tumbled off the back of an ATV.

I remember something else. What was that "Miller deal" Dan mentioned? I type in the phrase along with Nick and his dad's last name and an article appears, the details eerily familiar. Property adjacent to a new shopping mall. All the other neighbors had sold, but there was an elderly couple, the Millers, holding out because they didn't want the trees razed down for a parking lot. They were offered staggering amounts of money but wouldn't sell to any developers. Until Nick and his father came along. Somehow, they ended up getting the Millers to sell them the property, which they then flipped to the company who wanted it, for a crazy profit. The article lauded their efforts, calling them the "Constantine Closers," and showing before and after pictures of the lot. Where giant trees once stood, now there was nothing but gray concrete.

I feel my good spirits vanish in a puff of smoke, like the bad guys in one of Caleb's video games. I'm such an idiot. At best, I'm nothing but a trivial distraction to pass Nick's time while he's stuck in the middle of nowhere. At worst, he's totally playing me for the property.

I go to the bench under the bay window and sit with my arms crossed around my legs, chin resting on my knee. This is only going to end one way. With me getting hurt. Gazing up at the sky, I see another shooting star and, despite knowing the complete futility of it, wish that I'd never met Nick Constantine.

Chapter Eleven

I smash the hammer down, ruthless in my attack on the nail. Sweat drips down my face, and I stop to wipe it off with the back of my hand.

"Need any help with that?" Nick's silky smooth voice has every synapse in my body snapping to attention.

"All done, thanks." I stand and pick up the two old boards, destined for the fire pit.

"Can I get those for you?" I shrug and dump the boards into his outstretched arms, avoiding direct eye contact.

"Everything okay?"

How, after only two days, can he read me so well? He'd said I was an open book, but apparently I'm more of a flashing neon sign.

"Fine." I attempt a smile.

"I came by the house this morning, but your mom said you'd already left."

"I wanted to get this done before someone else tripped." I put the hammer into the loop on the tool belt Mom made for me last birthday.

"You ready to tackle the cabin?"

"I, um …" Shrieks of laughter from a family piling into their boat give me a second to think of an excuse. "I promised Red I'd help him with some stuff."

"Sweet. When do we start?" He looks at me, expectant.

I watch the family. Everyone's got a life preserver. Good. "Um, well. They're really more just one-person jobs actually."

A dark brow lifts. "Oh?"

"Yup." Hands go in my back pockets.

"Are you okay?' he asks, again.

"Fine. I'm fine. Everything's fine. Why do you ask?"

"You just seem a little … distant this morning," he says.

"Do I? That's weird. I'm totally fine." I bring myself to meet his eyes, which narrow in suspicion.

"You googled me. And the band." His tone is matter-of-fact.

"So?" I cross my arms.

"I told you, that's not me." He shifts the boards to one hand.

"Really? Because it looked a lot like you. Guess it was another Nick Constantine who opened for Discarded Unicorns, while thousands of fans chanted his name." I don't mention the other article.

"Fine, it was me, but …"

"Look, Mr. Rock Star, or Real Estate Wonder Boy, or whoever you are. I appreciate you trying to help, but we'll be okay." The words slip out. *No, no, no. Stop Julia. Stop it right now. You need him.* But my pride ignores my common sense, like a child whose parents warn her not to eat that third hot dog before riding the roller coaster.

"Fine." He doesn't object and I push down the disappointment that springs up.

"Well, if you'll excuse me, it's a super busy day." I push by him and he lets me go without protest.

*

I try to focus on whatever it is I'm doing, whether it's restocking toilet paper in the bathrooms, weed-whacking, pruning back some of the longer tree branches or sweeping the outdoor amphitheater where Sammy the Squirrel gives his weekend lectures on general camper safety and how not to start fires. But it's no use. I can't stop thinking about Nick. Or about our kisses last night. I sigh. Am I overreacting? Wouldn't be the first time. So he was semi-famous and good at his job. At least now my eyes are open and I won't be blindsided by unrealistic expectations. Besides, it's just a summer fling. I, of all people, know how temporary those are. As I finish repainting "The Sugar Shack" on the canteen, I decide to apologize. I've been keeping an eye out all day but haven't seen any sign of him. There's only one place I haven't looked. His cabin.

Unable to stop myself, I head for the A-frames. The sound of a guitar reaches my ears as I approach Nick's cabin. But it's not the melodic thrumming from the other night. It's harsh and jarring, with repeated stops and starts, almost painful, really. I walk up the steps of Aquarius.

"Good, good. You're getting it. Now the D chord looks like this ..." Nick's voice floats out the open window. There's a smooth strum, followed by a tentative one.

"Nice work."

"Really?" A small voice has me peering inside. Caleb sits across from Nick on the indigo rug in the center of the room. Both hold guitars. Nick's is shiny, freshly waxed but with the odd dent, the flaws adding to its character. Caleb's is even more banged up and seems big and awkward in his thin arms. Both cradle their instruments like they're the most precious things in the world. My mind flashes back to the way Nick held me in his arms last night. He's giving my brother guitar lessons?

As if feeling my gaze, the pirate looks up and smiles. My heart proceeds to dissolve into a sticky puddle of cardiac tissue and red blood cells. Crap.

"Hey," he mouths.

"Hey." I take a giant gulp of air and walk into the cabin. "Sorry to interrupt," I say.

"Nick's teaching me to play the guitar." Caleb beams like my Maglite 300.

"So I hear." His smile is contagious.

"Yup, the kid's got natural talent and some fancy finger work. A good combo."

"Must be from all the video games," I say. Turning to him, my smile falters. "About earlier ..."

"Don't worry about it, Tink." He grins, teeth even and white, incisors the teeniest bit pointed, adding to his dangerous air even as he sits cross-legged on a carpet teaching my little brother D chords. But the real danger is in how I respond to him. "All done your chores?"

"Yes, I ..."

"Sorry, Jules." Caleb looks guilty. "I should've been helping out."

"It's okay, Cale. How often do you get to take guitar lessons from a rock star?"

"Rock star?"

Nick rolls his eyes. "Wannabe rock star." He gives Caleb a little punch in the arm. I cringe, but Cale loves it, posturing with manly pride at the attention. "You ready to work on the fort now?" He changes the subject.

"Sweet!" Caleb jumps up, guitar clanging.

"Tink?"

"Let's do it." The man makes it way too easy to like him.

Nick puts his guitar back in his case, and Caleb leans his against the corner. "No case, bro?"

"Nah," Caleb says.

"Where'd you get the guitar from anyway?" I ask.

"Found it in Gramps's cabin."

"Really? Where?" A memory of my grandfather playing by a campfire wafts by, then drifts away like smoke.

"Wrapped in some old blankets under the hide-a-bed."

"A Gibson." Nick picks it up and examines it. He fingers a tune. "Still in great shape. With a little TLC, I bet this baby will have an incredible sound. Good vintage guitars always do."

"How come?" Caleb asks.

"See the top wood?" Nick raps lightly on the front of the guitar.

"Yeah?"

"Back in the day people had more skills in choosing the right kind of wood for instruments — wood that's harder to find now. Plus, older wood is drier and more stable. It gets stiffer and lighter as it ages, which translates into legendary sound." Nick gives it a light strum. "You're going to need a case to protect this baby."

Caleb looks at me, face shining. "Jules, can you tell Mom I want one for my birthday?"

"Sure." I hope cases aren't too expensive. Then again, I suppose he doesn't need the Louis Vuitton version.

"When's your birthday?" Nick asks.

"July twentieth."

"Cool. Well, you can borrow mine for now." Nick walks over and removes his guitar from the case, putting Caleb's in its place. That case probably costs more than our car. Nick turns and winks at me. "I've been meaning to get a new one anyway." He holds the door open. "Shall we?"

I follow him out into the sunlight, Caleb on my heels. It's another beautiful day. The sun is warm on our faces, reflection sparkling off the lake, and my little brother is oozing joy like tree sap. I breathe Nick in, along with air so fresh it turns my lungs inside out. One of Mom's random yoga phrases comes to me in spite of my racing heart. *Being fully present in each moment lies the way of happiness.*

I decide to listen for once. "Let's."

*

"Watch out for nails," I say. Some of the wood in the cabin is rotted and flaking, and I shake off the memory of a three-inch nail piercing Paige's flip-flop like it was warm butter.

"Here's one," Nick says, dropping it in the bucket beside me. "How far down to the studs do you want to take it?" He shields his eyes as the sun dips lower in the tree line. We've been working steadily for a couple of hours and have most of the big stuff cleared up. Debris lies in a pile off to the right of the cabin. I stand, tucking back wisps of hair that have escaped my bun. "Let's just make it safe," I say quietly.

Nick steps toward me. "You have a little dirt … just there." He brushes something off my forehead with the coarse work gloves we'd borrowed from Red.

"Thanks," I say, mouth dry. We hadn't brought enough water with us. I put my hands on my lower spine and bend backward, stiff from working all day.

"Massage?" Nick says, taking his gloves off and walking around behind me. I stand there and he rubs my shoulders, replacing the physical tension in my body with a different kind.

"Thanks." His hands feel so good. "Cale," I call. "Ready to pack it in for the day?" His head pops up at the window.

"Okay." He sounds reluctant, and I smile. These past few days are the most he's been outside in ages. He comes outside, and I tear myself away from Nick's magical fingers.

"Should we just leave the stuff here?" Nick picks up his gloves off the ground.

"Yeah, I'll just put it all in the cabin." Gathering up the tools, I go inside while Caleb and Nick discuss his next music lesson.

"Under the bed, hey?" I mutter under my breath, figuring that's as good a place as any to leave the tools. Not that we have to worry too much about someone finding the place. But still, there are some expensive pieces of equipment. Depositing the tools on the ground, I lift the creaky frame of the storage bed, moldy mattress heavy. Propping it up with the wooden post lying there and pushing aside one of the blankets that must have shrouded the guitar, I place the tools inside. When I remove the post, something at the far end catches my eye — a faded and worn leather journal, tucked behind one of the wooden slats.

I lean forward over the low ledge and reach for it, my legs coming up off the ground. If anyone were to walk in right now, it would look like the bed is eating me. Managing to snag a corner, I pull it out.

Escaping from under the bed, book in hand, I scrunch up my nose. Mildew. The brown book is stuffed with papers, worn and half-decayed, just like everything else in the cabin. Unwrapping the twine wound around the journal, I open it and see my grandfather's writing. Unexpected tears prick at my eyeballs. Blinking them back, I walk out into the fresh air.

"… probably a new bridge, a few replacement tuners, some decent strings and a good buff, but …" Nick catches sight of me. "You all right?"

"Fine." Nostalgia combines with dust motes, making my eyes watery. "Just found something of my grandfather's."

Caleb looks up. "What is it?"

I lift it up. "Think it's an old journal."

"Sick." Caleb bounces awkwardly from foot to foot. "Maybe it mentions the treasure."

"Treasure?" Nick looks at us, dark brows raised. Caleb catches my expression and freezes mid-hop for a second, then relaxes.

"It's okay, Jules, we can trust him."

Can we, though?

Look how well it worked out with the last guy I liked.

Look how well it worked out for my mom.

"It's nothing," I say, and really it isn't. Just a few threads of a story, woven more to get Caleb's mind off things than anything else. "Our grandfather thought there might be something valuable hidden on the land."

"Really?" Nick says. "That's cool. Any idea what he was talking about?"

"He died when I was little," Caleb informs him. "Jules remembers him better than I do."

I remember the smell of scotch mints, a cheerfully cantankerous man who swore too much and loved walking the woods with his dog, Hoss. I hadn't thought about the sweet black lab in years. Actually, now that I *am* thinking about him, I'm pretty sure he's buried somewhere around the cabin. Nick follows my gaze around the forest.

"What are you looking for?"

"A grave site," I say.

He startles. "Your grandfather's?"

Caleb lets out a high-pitched "Huh?"

"Not him." I laugh. "His dog, Hoss." Nick relaxes. "We put Gramps's ashes in the lake."

"Oh." That doesn't seem to make him feel any better.

Caleb's stomach lets out an insistent grumble. "Wonder what Mom's making for dinner," he muses, rubbing his stomach with the singular focus of a boy who has spent all day playing outside.

"Probably a few celery and carrot sticks with some hummus and pita," I say. "She teaches tonight and will be busy helping Red check people in."

"But I'm so huuungryyy," he moans.

"All this fresh air does work up an appetite," Nick agrees. "I could really go for something more substantial." The boys look at me.

"What? I don't cook, remember?"

"Aw, come on, Julia," Caleb says.

Nick digs a granola bar out of his pocket and throws it to Caleb. Does he always walk around with food in his pockets? "Well, I'd offer to make something, but you'd have to let me use your kitchen."

"Be my guest," I say. "I'm sure it will appreciate the attention."

Caleb walks ahead of us, humming the tune he and Nick were playing earlier. Or rather, the tune Nick was playing. Caleb was plucking it like a chicken, to a slow painful death.

"You're handy, you're a rock star and you cook? Is there anything you can't do?" I say.

"Make you trust me?" he says, voice quiet. The sunlight filters through the trees, and they take on an ethereal glow.

"Wait up, Cale!" I shout, pretending not to hear. I'm reluctant to tell Nick he might be on his way to checking that one off the list, too.

Chapter Twelve

"More chili flakes?" Nick asks.

"Mom's not a big spice fan," I say. She walks into the kitchen, overhearing.

"Beggars can't be choosers when someone else is cooking," she says.

Nick puts the container down. "We'll skip it." He continues sautéing the eggplant. "Just warning you, this is going to be a pretty weak moussaka." We didn't have time to pick up any groceries; he's just using what's on hand.

"Beggars can't be choosers." I groan. My back is really killing me.

"Long day, guys?" Mom asks. I know she worries about the amount of work we have to do around here. But honestly, it doesn't bother me. I love the campground. I feel more grounded here than anywhere else, my roots sinking as deep as one of the giant trees out back. The thought of not going away in the fall hadn't bothered me much when I thought I'd be here. Now, with that maybe uncertain, it feels like being told to jump out of a plane without a parachute. "Why don't you come to yoga tonight, Julia? It will be good for you."

Actually, a good stretch is just what I need. "Sure," I say, looking at Nick. "Wanna come?"

"Are you asking me out?" he says with a sideways look, putting the eggplant on top of the pasta in a casserole dish.

"In front of my mother? Please. I just want to see if there's anything you can't handle."

"And you're going with yoga?" he asks, tone implying this is a serious error. "Let me just say that my downward dog is unparalleled." He sprinkles some No-Moo mozzarella on top of the eggplant. "At least among the roadies."

"Not yoga. Hot yoga. Totally different." I pause for dramatic effect. "Where there's no dog to be found, downward or otherwise."

He sizes me up, hands now in oven mitts, yet still looking totally hot. "I can sweat with the best of them."

"Perfect!" Mom says brightly. She opens the oven door for Nick as he puts in the moussaka. "It's a date." My eyes go to hers in a flicker of panic. "Ah, I mean, not a date. I mean it's an outing." My eyes narrow. "I mean, um …" She holds up the plate of veggies. "More carrots, anyone?"

*

Mom begins: "If it's your first class, the goal is just to stay in the room. We start with a breathing exercise, Pranayama. It looks and sounds a little funny, so again, newcomers, just watch me first." I turn to Nick, standing beside me on his mat, and give him a this-means-you look. I join in the exercise, hands folded under my chin, elbows rising to the count of six, then down for the count of six as my head tilts back, a slight buzzing noise coming from my throat. Nick joins in the next set. He follows along the next few postures admirably, and I try to focus on Mom's instructions, trying not to think about the fact that we're sweating beside each other, half naked.

It's just like being in our bathing suits. Except there's something slightly more intimate about a candlelit yoga class.

"Next is standing bow pose," Mom intones. "Pick up your right foot with your right hand, hold from the inside at the ankle, all five fingers together. Kick back and up, slowly, smoothly. Bring your body down from the lower spine, stretch your right hand fingertips toward the front mirrors, try to touch exactly between your two eyebrows." I hear Nick panting beside me and feel a very non-yogic desire to rock this pose, showing off my dubious athleticism, flexibility and grace. I go further into the posture than I ever have before. I'm in the zone. It's forty degrees Celsius with forty percent humidity, and sweat runs in rivulets down my entire body, making me look like I've just come out of the lake. Eyes zero in on my reflection in the mirror. There's a small movement beside me, and they go to Nick, who sits back on his heels, sitting the difficult posture out, eyes on me. I lose my balance and stumble forward, falling out of the posture, catching myself just before I sprawl across the wooden floor.

Scowling and embarrassed, I get back on my mat. "Quit looking at me," I mouth to him. His gaze is unnerving.

"I'm trying," he mouths back. Ignoring him, I get right back into the posture.

"Psst," he whispers. "I feel like I'm going to vomit. Or pass out."

"Totally normal," I whisper back. Mom shoots us a disapproving look. No talking in the yoga room. "Just lie back in Savasana."

He obeys, going into corpse pose and lying flat on his back. The rest of us join him a second later after the posture is over. My chest rises and falls with exertion, feet spread open as the heels touch, arms palm-up along the length of my body. I focus on slowing my breathing. Calm breath calms the body, calms the mind. Candlelight flickers and soft music plays in the background. There's a brief, fluttering feeling in my stomach as Nick's hand rests tentatively on top of mine and squeezes.

"Arms above your head, cross only your thumbs, and sit up, double exhale," Mom commands, and we obey. The rest of the class passes dreamily as the repetitive postures lull me into a mild meditative state, though not as deep as usual, most likely because of Nick's presence.

"We're going to finish with a breathing exercise, good for abdominal muscles and internal organs, helping to rid our body of all the toxins we've just released. Sit Japanese-style, Buddha-belly, hands on your lap. Focus only on the exhale, the inhale happens automatically. And begin." She claps out the breaths in a solid rhythm to the count of sixty. "Good job, let's do it one more time, only faster, like you're blowing out a candle." We puff out any residual negative energies, and Mom thanks everyone for coming, bowing to us. "Namaste."

"Namaste," we chant back. Some people get up to leave right away; others take their time on the mat, breathing slowly as they lie in Savasana, usually my favorite part of class. Every so often, the extreme physical exertion gives way to mental exertion and an odd feeling of peace will float over me, as my body settles onto its bones. If that makes sense. Tonight, though, I'm left feeling keyed up and unsettled. Then Nick's hand closes over mine again and my breathing slows. We're the last ones left in the room.

"Not bad for your first time," I murmur, taking a sip from my water bottle.

"You were amazing," he says, voice low. "I knew you were a warrior, but ..."

"But what?"

He shakes his head and takes a chug of his water. "I'll tell you later."

I get to my feet, hang my damp towel around my neck and lift my yoga mat up off the floor. Nick does the same and we walk out of the darkened studio into the light.

"Do you want to shower?" I can't help but look at his flawless body, still glistening. He looks at me, a smile playing around his lips.

"Is that an invitation?" His tone is teasing.

"No, I mean, I just thought, since you, um, sweat a lot and … but that's totally normal, I sweat a lot. Not all the time, just in class. I mean, we're hot, right? Temperature-wise. That is …" Fanning myself, I finally manage to stop my mouth. "Anyway, the showers are over there." I point.

"Great job." Mom comes up behind us. "How'd you like the class?"

"Honestly? I never thought the most intense workout I'd ever do would involve yoga," Nick says, taking another long drink of his water. That he doesn't try to hide it makes me like him even more. Dammit.

"The heat combined with the style of yoga makes it very challenging, cardiovascular-wise," Mom agrees.

"You're telling me." Nick wipes his face with the towel. "Is it the same every class?"

"The postures are. This allows you to see your progress and frees your mind to meditate instead of wondering about what's coming next. It can be very therapeutic." Mom looks at me and smiles. "You'd be surprised what hot yoga a few times a week can do for your mind as well as your body."

"Okay, enough with the spiel, Mom."

She laughs. "Sorry, I can get a little evangelical, but only because I see the difference it makes in people's lives. I myself would never survive without it." She notices another student hovering close by, eager to talk to her. "Excuse me. See you at home, Julia." She looks at Nick. "Don't forget to drink lots of water tonight and tomorrow. Stay hydrated." Turning, she walks over to the student.

"So …" I clear my throat. "Um, are you going to have a shower …?"

"I was thinking a swim in the lake would feel amazing right now. Your mom did say to stay hydrated."

"What's with you and lakes? And she meant internally."

"My grandparents had a cabin on a lake a few hours out of Toronto. Used to spend every summer up there. This place reminds me of it." We pack up our things and leave the studio. I give Mom a wave goodbye, and she raises a questioning eyebrow at Nick, which I ignore. A cool breeze ruffles the trees, feeling incredibly refreshing after the humidity of the yoga room.

"I still can't get over how hot it was in there." Nick looks up at the sky. The moon is getting fuller, waxing, not waning.

"You get used to it," I say.

"Come on. I was like a fish flopping around on dry land, gasping for its last breath."

I laugh. "You weren't that bad."

We approach his cabin. The crickets are chirruping, and water laps gently against the shore. He shakes his head. "All I wanted to do was run out of that room. Then I look at you and you're as tranquil as a" — he looks around at the moonlight on the water — "as this." He gestures. "You were glowing."

"Glowing?"

"Incandescent." He seems at a momentary loss, then smiles as something flits past. "Like that firefly."

I try to brush off his remark, but I feel the glow he's referring to, and I'm pretty sure he's the reason it's there.

"That's it," he says in a satisfied tone. "I really nailed it with the Tinkerbell nickname."

"Pretty sure she's a fairy, not a lightning bug."

He shrugs. "Close enough."

I look up at him. "They are not even remotely the same thing ..."

He walks up the steps, dropping his bag on the deck, and motions for me to follow him up the stairs. "I believe you owe me an astronomy lesson."

I really shouldn't. I should be going home. I need to stop this. Whatever it is. But his gaze has a gravitational effect, like the moon on the waves, pulling me toward him.

"I thought you wanted to go for a swim." My voice comes out as a whisper.

"I do," he says, reaching for and pulling me up against his chest, lifting up my chin with a finger. "But first I want to do something else."

"What's that?" I hear myself ask. Only it doesn't sound like me. The voice is low and throaty and, dare I say it, seductive?

"This." His lips settle on mine. Sensations overwhelm me, all of them highly pleasurable, but there's anxiety underneath.

He's playing you. He's good-looking. He's rich. He can have anyone he wants. You're so naive. Why would he want a freckly little redhead with bruised shins and tree sap in her hair? Because he wants something from you.

But I don't care anymore.

Needing to get away from the voice in my head, I pull away. "Last one in's a rotten egg." Running down to the water, I strip off my T-shirt; anything to shut the voice up. Diving into the cool lake, still in my sports bra and short shorts, I kick hard, swimming under the water until my lungs burn. Surfacing, I scan for Nick. He's there, outline visible on the beach, illuminated in the moonlight. He grabs the waist of his shorts, and I inhale; he's not seriously thinking of …? He pulls them down and I let my breath out. Boxers. Whew. Wading in, he dives under. Wow, he can hold his breath for a long time; where is he? I peer down into the dark lake, not wanting to fall for the same trick he pulled after I pushed him off the dock. But he surfaces just in front of me and flashes me that grin.

"Guess that makes me a rotten egg?" He lifts his arm and sniffs at an armpit. "Not surprised after that yoga class. Oh, and by the way, you're twelve."

I splash water at him and swim away. He grabs my foot and I shriek irrationally.

"Not so fast, Firefly," he growls, pulling me back through the water. "Always flitting away."

I laugh and splash at him, kicking out of his grasp. "Make up your mind. Am I a fairy or a bug?"

Nick treads water, eyeing me. "Take your pick. Either way, you're luminous."

My cheeks redden. Sheesh, all it takes is one of Mom's yoga classes and he's describing my aura. But still. No one's ever called me luminous before.

"Maybe the lake's radioactive," I say, looking down. "Think your dad will fall for that one?"

"Until he gets the water tested."

The playfulness in my voice turns slightly desperate. "We could fake the results?"

He pulls me close to him in the water, our legs kicking languorously under the surface. "Let's not talk about my dad right now. Astronomy lesson. Go."

"Where do you want me to start?"

"How'd you get interested in it?"

"It started with a book actually."

"Star Wars?"

I laugh. "*Cosmos* by Carl Sagan. Someone left an old copy of it behind."

"I've heard of that."

My eyes narrow. "I thought you knew nothing about astronomy."

He holds up his hands in a defensive gesture, droplets of water flying. "There's a reboot on Netflix."

"Oh." I lean back in the water, face tilted toward the sky. "Anyway, it got me interested a few years ago. I'm a bit of a worrier, and what he had to say, I don't know, kind of comforted me somehow." I look back at him. "Then when Caleb got sick and Mom was at the hospital a lot I began to come out and look at the stars. You know how when something sucks really bad, and you get all caught up and consumed by it?"

"Yeah," he says, voice quiet. I wonder if he's thinking of his mom. "I do."

"I was angry and anxious all the time and didn't want to bring that energy around Caleb." I'm glad it's dark so he can't see me blush. "Sorry, blame Yoga Mom for that." Nick laughs as I grab my wet hair and sweep it to one shoulder. "It also gave me something to think about. Humans are just an insignificant blip in time and space. We've only been around for about point-zero-zero-four percent of Earth's lifespan. When I look up at the stars it gives me perspective. Reminds me to be thankful for each moment I'm here. And for each moment my brother is, too." Feeling chilled, I start to kick toward shore.

"People should definitely make the most of each moment," Nick says. "But I don't think our lives are necessarily insignificant." He swims alongside me. "In fact, I think that's the point. Life is about making your time here matter."

"How do you do that? Even if you do something great, only a few people are remembered after they're dead. For most of us, after a hundred years or so, it's like we were never here." Our feet touch the sandy bottom. The night air is cooler than the water and I sink back down up to my chin.

Nick does the same, angular jaw grazing the water. "Maybe it's not about being remembered but making a difference to someone or something else. Leaving things a bit better than how you found them."

"Like replacing a run-down family campground with a shiny new resort?" I can't resist.

He ignores the jab. "It sounds like you're having a bit of an existential crisis." We float in silence for a few minutes looking up at the stars. There are quadrillions out there.

"Do you know that there's ten thousand stars for every grain of sand on Earth?" I say.

"Seriously?"

"Yup. It's mind-blowing how big the universe is."

"Do you believe in heaven?" Nick asks abruptly.

"What?" My teeth are starting to chatter. That's a random question.

"Heaven. Do you think it exists?" He must be thinking of his mother again.

I take a minute to think of how to word my response, not sure of his beliefs. "I used to. Now I'm not sure anymore. Or if I do, it's in a different way."

"How's that?" His voice is curious, not offended.

"See, that's how the stars make me feel better. Because I don't know for sure if there's a heaven like in the Bible, or whatever. But there are *heavens* above us in the literal sense. We're essentially made out of stardust." I think of Grandpa's ashes. "Our bodies are composed of all the same elements — nitrogen, carbon and oxygen — that we go back to when we die. In a way, I guess it's kinda like going home."

"Deep thoughts, Tink."

Embarrassed, I look down into the water. Talk about rambling.

"Another one of the things I like about you." He rubs his hands down my arms in a brisk warming motion and takes my hands. "Come on, you're shivering."

Leading me to the beach, he grabs his shorts. "Last one in the cabin's a rotten egg."

I laugh, exhilarated and freezing my ass off, chasing him up the sand to his cabin and up the stairs.

He turns, smiling. "I win."

"What do you want?" I look at him from under lowered lashes. Paige would be impressed with my newfound guile.

"To warm you up. Your lips are blue." He opens his door and motions for me to go inside. I hesitate, not sure I trust myself to be alone with Nick Constantine. But then again, not sure I care anymore.

Chapter Thirteen

The night air is fragrant with the smells of the earth, and an owl hoots somewhere off to our left. I really want to go in. Not to mention both of us are dripping wet, and a fluffy towel would feel so nice right now. I picture them, folded neatly in the closet, scented with lavender. I take a step toward the threshold, mouth dry. "Nick …"

"Julia?" a small voice pipes up.

Nick and I startle. "Caleb?"

He steps into the light cast by the lone bulb above the door, which is currently being swarmed by moths.

"What are you doing here?" I ask.

"I wanted to talk to you about something." His chin angles up, and I suppress a sigh. Then feel bad for feeling frustrated. Didn't I promise myself a few nights ago that I was going to pay more attention to my little brother?

"What's up?" I say, steam rising off my body.

"I, um, found something."

Nick holds the door open wider, a resigned smile on his face. "Why don't you both come inside? I can make some hot chocolate."

"Really? Sweet." Caleb runs up the stairs, past me and into the cabin.

"You have hot chocolate?" I murmur, following Caleb in. He immediately makes himself at home, plopping himself on the couch, kicking sandals off haphazardly along the way. Nick closes the door behind us.

"Stole a few instant packs from my aunt and uncle." He opens the cupboard beside the sink and pulls out the little red kettle that comes in every unit. "Thinking if I had any guests over I should have something to serve them."

"Plan on having lots of guests?" I'm in the closet helping myself to the towels. Wrapping my hair in one, turban-style, I flip the tail back and tuck it under, not wanting to drip all over floors I just mopped the other day. I wrap another one around me and throw one to Nick, who catches it easily.

"Just one." His smile is languid, like his movements, as he wraps it around his waist. I'm reminded of pirates again. Minus the gold fillings.

I clear my throat, nod at his clinging boxers and then back at Caleb, who's caressing Nick's guitar.

"Right. Keep an ear out for the kettle." He goes to the stairs toward the loft.

I sit on the rug, towel wrapped around me, and ask my brother, "So, what did you find?"

Caleb leans forward, face animated. "A map. In Gramps's journal."

"What kind of map?"

"Of the property. It looks like it goes back into the mountains."

"Cool. Probably from when Gramps first surveyed the place. Did you ask Mom about it?"

"Not yet. She won't think much of it, though."

"And you do?" Clearly. He's practically levitating off the sofa.

"What if it leads to the treasure Gramps used to talk about? I think there may be some kind of clue on it or something, there are these lines on it that are kinda weird." I'm not sure how to proceed. Cale's just so into this, and I don't feel like being the one to dash his treasure dreams.

"Don't you think someone would've found it by now?" I ask, tentative.

"Found what?" Nick comes down the stairs in a damp T-shirt, his short, dark hair curling up at the nape of his neck. There's a green shirt in his hand, which he throws to me. "Put that on." I pull it over my head. It's baggy, falls mid-thigh and smells like him. I bring my knees up and under the shirt, resting my chin on top.

"Treasure," Caleb announces, triumphant. I wait for Nick to laugh.

"Where?" He's serious.

"Well, I haven't found it yet," Caleb amends. "But if we read my grandpa's journal to see if there's any clues — and follow the map — I bet we could."

"That's pretty cool," Nick says, sitting beside Caleb on the couch. "Is there anyone you can talk to that maybe knows a bit more about it? What about your mom?"

"Yeah, maybe," Caleb says, thinking. "Or Red!"

"Great idea." Nick ruffles his hair. Caleb looks up at him, all devoted puppy eyes and wagging tail. My heart isn't the only one that's going to have a few cracks when Nick leaves. I swallow. Nick's leaving. Right. When?

"How long are you staying for?" I ask.

"I talked to my dad today," he says. "Told him I need a few more days to finish the assessment. And then asked for a week's vacation."

Surprised, I look at him. "Really?"

"Awesome!" Caleb says.

"It's been a while, so I figured I deserved some time off." He grins. "This cabin available?"

"I'll have to check registration." I try not to let him see my delight. "Why would you want to spend your vacation here? Wouldn't you rather be on, like, a yacht in the south of France?"

"Been there, done that." His tone is teasing. I roll my eyes. "Besides, this is shaping up to be a pretty awesome vacation. Beach, lake, building forts." He nudges Caleb. "Hunting for treasure."

Caleb jumps up from the couch. "When can we start looking?" he asks.

"Why don't you go through the journal some more and see if there's anything else useful. Then we can talk to Red," I say, standing up.

"I left it at home, though. I'll go get it and bring it back."

I cut in. "It's getting pretty late, Cale. I'm sure Mom will want us home soon."

"How about I walk you back," Nick says, getting up. This time we don't refuse his offer.

*

"Well," I say, turning to Nick. "Thanks." Caleb's already raced up the driveway and into the house, intent on poring over every page of that book. Nick looks at me. His expressions range from mysteriously smoldering to lighthearted and sweet. Currently, his gaze is at a mild simmer.

"You know what the best thing about this place is?"

"The Sugar Shack?" Nerves equals lame joke. I make a lot of them.

"You." He pulls me closer to him, wrapping his arms around my waist. "Are you happy I'm staying?"

"Sure. I mean, it gives us more time to figure out how we're going to keep from selling the campground."

"And?" he presses.

"And …" I lean back, looking up at him. "It gives me more time with you." More time to keep on falling. Just what I need.

"I hope you think that's a good thing?"

"You are a nice distraction from cleaning toilet stalls and stacking firewood."

"So I smell better than human excrement and give fewer splinters? I think that's the nicest thing you've ever said to me."

"Don't let it go to your head."

"Too late." He lowers his lips to mine and this time I kiss him back greedily.

The porch light comes on and we pull apart. "Julia?" Mom calls.

"Coming," I say.

Nick releases me and lets out a sigh. "This feels familiar."

"I think mothers have a sixth sense when their kids are up to no good."

"Who says I'm no good?" Nick says.

"Oh, no, you're good." Too good. "But try not to let that go to your head, either."

He smiles and holds up his hand. "Promise. Hey, where can I get decent cell service around here? I need to make a few calls."

"If you walk up to the main road by the entrance you should be able to get a few bars. We were set to put Wi-Fi through the campground last year, but then, you know …" I shrug. Money had to go to other things.

"Thanks." He runs a finger down my arm. "See you tomorrow?"

"I'll be here all week," I crack. *Stop it, Julia.*

"Night, Tink."

"Night," I say and walk toward the front door. I can make Mom's shape out in the front window.

"Good day?" Mom says, looking at me.

"Yes, why?"

"You look a little starry-eyed."

"From looking at the constellations." I give her a grin. It must be goofy, because she half rolls her eyes. "Julia, you look positively dopey right now. And I'm pretty sure you're not still on a yoga high." More like a Nick high. "You like him." Her tone is matter-of-fact.

"He's a nice guy." I hope.

"Yes, he is. But he's older ..."

"Only a few years. Girls are more mature than guys anyway ..."

"He's also a lot more experienced. And have you forgotten why he's here?" That knocks me off my cloud a bit.

"He says he's going to try to help us find a solution, where we don't have to sell."

Mom sighs. "Don't you think Red and I have also been trying to do that? We don't want to sell."

"Don't you?" I challenge. Mom's usually pretty chill, and it takes a lot to get her angry, but when she is, watch out. Typical Taurus.

"You don't think we've exhausted every possible avenue?"

"What about the treasure?" Caleb pops around the corner.

Mom throws up her hands. "What on earth are you talking about?"

"I found a map," he says, "and one of Gramps's old journals."

"Your son seems to think your father has buried treasure somewhere on the property," I inform her.

"Maybe not buried," Caleb says, thoughtfully. "It could be hidden in a tree or something."

Mom takes a deep breath. "Can someone explain this treasure nonsense?"

Caleb looks at me for help. I sigh. "I remember Gramps used to tell me stories about something valuable hidden on the land."

"This place was his whole life," Mom says. "Of course it was valuable to him. Those were just stories, Julia. He loved entertaining you with his tall tales." I'd figured as much. The only reason I'd said something to Caleb was to get his mind off his illness. It kind of snowballed …

"But what if they weren't just stories?" Caleb persists. "What if he was telling the truth?" Mom gives me a look. She can see Caleb's enthralled by the idea, and I know now she's thinking the same thing I did. Whether or not there's anything of any worth hidden here, it's a harmless distraction. And she doesn't want to drag him back to reality any more than I do. Nine-year-olds *should* be having these kinds of adventures. Especially nine-year-olds who've been laid up in a hospital for half a year.

"Well." Mom sighs. "I guess it's worth looking into. I do remember Dad going on about the 'riches of the land' and all that."

"I knew it!" Caleb yells.

"And I think we might have an old metal detector lying around here somewhere. Maybe in the barn? Oh, that reminds me," Mom says to me. "The McGregors want to book the barn for their vow renewal next weekend."

"Next weekend?" I say. "Why such short notice?"

"Their original location was at Pedro's, but they just had a bad kitchen fire."

"How are we supposed to get it ready in a week?" I ask.

"They're handling everything. Bringing in decorators and caterers and whatnot." Mom sighs again. "He's Dad's old pal, I couldn't say no. Besides, it's their sixtieth. That's pretty special." I wonder if she's thinking about my dad. I wish she could find a nice guy. But she's so busy running this place I don't even know when she'd find the time for a relationship.

"I guess we can give it a good sweeping and air it out," I say.

"Ahem." Caleb clears his throat. "What about the metal detector?"

"We can look for it tomorrow. Go get ready for bed and I'll come and tuck you in."

"Okay," he says, practically skipping off to his room.

"Your brother seems a lot happier," Mom says quietly. She puts her arm around me and we walk to my room.

"Yeah, he does." I look at her, waiting for what she has to say.

"You've been great with him. He seems to really like hanging out with you and Nick." Ah, there it is.

"Yes, he does seem to be around an awful lot." I squint my eyes at her. "You wouldn't have anything to do with that, would you?"

"I don't know what you're talking about," Mom says. She's a terrible liar.

"Have you been getting him to spy on me?" I say, indignant.

"Shhh. Not spy, just keeping an eye out." That explains his uncanny timing this evening.

"So, basically, spying."

"It makes him feel important. Besides, what am I supposed to do when there's a handsome young man hanging around who obviously finds my daughter attractive?"

"You think he thinks I'm attractive?" He'd said so, but hearing someone else say it is different. Even if it is my mother.

"You are attractive, my love, but that's not what's important ..."

"I know, I know. It's more important to be kind and smart and blah, blah, blah." I recite back the words she's been saying to me my whole life. "But seriously, what makes you say that?"

She sighs. "When you two are together, the energy flowing between you, it hums."

"Really?" Humming is a good sign. "You're sure it's not just flowing one way?"

"I could see it in class tonight." We reach my doorway. "Look, sweetie, Nick seems like a great guy. But older guys have certain ... expectations."

"So do younger ones, Mom." I don't mention the pressure Dan put on me the past couple summers to go for it. Not like *pressure* pressure. But basically he's done everything in his power to convince me that sex-on-the-beach isn't just a fancy cocktail. I'm glad it didn't end up happening. Probably the reason why he brought a girlfriend this summer. But all that's a dull ache at best now.

She turns to me at the doorway to my room. "I'm sorry you're not going away to school in the fall."

"What?" Her comment comes out of nowhere.

She tucks a piece of hair behind her ear. "We were so busy; I didn't have time to help you." Her eyes are watery. "And I know you were worried about the money." She takes a deep breath. "I'm so sorry, sweetheart."

"It's okay, Mom." I give her a hug and she holds me tight. "There's always next year."

She stifles a half sob into my hair, not my intended effect, and pats my back. "I love you so much."

"I know." Awkwardly, I pat her back. "I love you, too."

She sniffs. "I just want to do the right thing. For you and Caleb."

"What do *you* want?" I ask, half fearing the answer.

"Only for my kids to be healthy and happy." She looks at me. "I don't want to sell, Julia; this is our home. And besides, these past few days Caleb seems much more like his old self, and I think this place is helping him get there."

I smile. "He wants a guitar case for his birthday."

She looks at me blankly. "Wouldn't he rather have a guitar?"

"He found Gramps's old one. Nick says it's in pretty good shape. He's giving him lessons."

"Nick plays guitar?"

"He's in a band."

She rolls her eyes. "Of course he is."

"You don't have to worry about me, Mom."

She sighs. "That's like telling the sun not to shine."

Her words trigger a memory. "Gramps called me that. Sunshine."

"He did." She smiles. "He used to sing you that old song. He loved you and Caleb so much."

"I miss him."

"Me, too."

"Do you think there really is a treasure?" I look at her.

"I think we would've found something by now if there was."

I feel silly for being disappointed; I'm not a nine-year-old boy. Still. The thought of finding something hidden in the woods had a certain appeal. "But what if he was going to tell us and never got the chance?" My grandfather dropped dead from a heart attack; just how he said he always wanted to go. No fuss, no prolonged suffering. Just, BANG and gone. The downside being it's quite traumatic for those left behind.

She gives me another hug. "There's always a possibility." I feel her smile into my hair and know she's humoring me the way we humored Caleb. "No harm in looking. That reminds me," she says. "Don't let me forget to ask Red to dig out that old detector."

We say goodnight. Alone in my room, I check my phone to see if a text from Nick managed to make its way through the spotty airwaves. Or whatever it is texts float on.

Sweet dreams, Tink.

There's a peculiar fullness in my chest as I get under the covers, leaving the phone by my bed. I'm slowly lulled to sleep, the soothing melody of "You Are My Sunshine" playing in my head.

Chapter Fourteen

"I know I saw the darn thing somewhere in here." Red roots around in the little room at the back of the barn. Caleb stands back, wringing his hands in excitement. My eyes water from all the dust in the air, and I sneeze. "A-ha! Here it is." He's got his arm under a bunch of boards and pulls out a dull metal bar with a long cord wrapped around it. It's about the length of Caleb and looks like something out of an old movie about ghostbusting.

"Now to see if this old feller still works." Red flicks a switch and we hold our breath. Nothing. Caleb's face falls. "Ah, well, kind of expected that. I'll have a look and try to get it up and running."

"Hey," says a voice from behind, and our heads swivel. "Nice space you got here." Nick's looking up at the rafters, dusty shafts of light shining down on him from the high windows. He's bathed in sunlight and for a ridiculous second he could be a Greek god come down to earth.

"Thanks," Red says, breaking my trance. "We use it for storage mostly, and the odd shindig. I helped Julia and Caleb's grandfather build it." His voice is nostalgic.

"Hey, Nick, check it out," Caleb says, proudly showing off the metal detector.

"Sweet," says Nick, walking over. Just then something swoops down from the rafters and Nick ducks. "What the ...?" An owl settles on one of the high beams, ruffling its golden feathers. Its white heart-shaped face cocks to one side as it takes in our guest.

"That's Henry," I say. "Henry, Nick. You're up late, buddy. Busy night last night?"

He gives his customary screech in response, and nestles his head into his feathers, apparently saying goodnight.

"You have an owl?"

"Well, he's not ours; he just likes to chill in the barn."

"He pays his rent by keeping the mice away," Red says. "I hear you'll be staying with us awhile longer."

"Yes, thank you. I'm happy the cabin was available."

"Can we go work on it now?" Caleb says, eyeing his new toy.

"Right, well. See you two later." Red waves and picks up the unwieldy detector, Caleb trailing behind. Nick and I are alone in the barn. I try to tamp down my feelings, but they keep fizzing up and over, like when you crack the tab on a can of shaken soda.

"So," Nick says, dark eyes penetrating mine, "I have something to tell you."

My stomach does a roundoff back handspring. "What's up?"

"Remember how I was talking about amping up your Wakestock event?"

"Yeah," I say.

"I have some good news."

"What is it?"

"I contacted a few buddies of mine and they agreed to come and play."

“Play where?”

“Here.” Nick gestures around him at the barn. “This place is perfect. We just slide the doors all the way open, set up a stage. Hang a few fairy lights or whatever. It’s a pretty sick venue.”

“Pardon?” I’d heard him but don’t really understand what he’s saying. “You invited some bands to come play at Wakestock?”

“Yeah.” He looks uncertain. “Is that okay? I mean we’d talked about a way to raise money. I hope you don’t think I’m overstepping or anything. I just thought …” I fling myself at him and he catches me, laughing. “So you’re not angry?”

“Thank you,” I say, arms wrapped around his neck and looking up. He’s really trying to help. He actually cares.

“You’re welcome.” He kisses the tip of my nose. “Wait till I tell you who’s playing.”

“Who?”

“Well, yours truly for one. This is all just a big ploy to get the band back together, you know.” He winks.

“If it saves the campground, I’m all for it.” There’s a tingling in my spine at the realization that I’ll get to see Nick perform live. Wait, does that make me a groupie?

“Then another of my good buddies who happens to be in that band you mentioned the other night also said they’d play a few songs.”

I stare at him, stupefied. “Discarded Unicorns. Is coming. Here?”

“Well, I already told them to save the date for my twenty-first. It’s my champagne birthday. I didn’t want to steal Caleb’s thunder when he mentioned it the other day, but it just so happens it’s the same weekend.”

“Your birthday? You’re a Cancer?” I wince after the word comes out, but it doesn’t faze him.

“Cancer-Leo cusp,” he clarifies.

“Hmm. Had you pegged as a Scorpio for sure.”

"I don't know enough about astrology to be offended or not."

"I can't believe Discarded Unicorns is coming," I shriek. "Every single one of their shows has been sold out for the last year. Wait till I tell Paige; she's going to die. I'm going to die." Maybe I have died; maybe this is all a dream. Discarded Unicorns, saving the campground, keeping our home. Caleb getting better. Nick.

"Please don't," Nick says, eyes crinkling. "I really want you to see my show."

"Do you think it's going to be enough? Raise enough money, I mean?"

"Depends on what your tipping point is. Do you know the minimum you need to stay afloat?"

"No," I say, some of the despair starting to settle back in. "I can ask my mom. What if it's too much?"

"We can probably get away with charging a hundred bucks a ticket."

"A hundred dollars?" That seems crazy to me.

"Like you said, sold-out shows. Besides, factor in the cool location, and maybe we can do an auction or something, where a date with a few of the guys goes to the highest bidder. Throw in a few corporate sponsors who can plaster their signs everywhere and *voila*!" He shrugs. "We should be able to rake in some pretty good cash."

"No offense, but this kind of seems like a huge undertaking." I massage my temples. Also, I'm not sure how Mom and Red are going to feel about throwing what is essentially a massive party at the campground.

"Well, you're lucky you know people. Or rather, one person."

"What about all the other details, like, like ... security? Or, or parking?"

"Let me handle those," he says, taking my hands in his and lowering them down. "My mom was an event planner. A very good one. I kind of inherited her knack for details."

I sigh. "Is there anything you don't do?" One of these days I will find it.

"Dance."

"Dance?"

"Yup. Can't dance. Just kind of nod my head to the beat." He demonstrates. "Maybe throw in an arm here and there if I'm feeling really crazy. Been told I resemble a T. rex bobblehead." I snicker. "Actually, Alex told me that."

"Alex from *Unicorns* Alex?"

"I mentioned we were friends, right? You're not going to get all gooey around him and forget about me, are you?" His voice is husky as he pulls me close.

"I don't get gooey," I inform him, despite the fact that it's happening this very moment. If you pulled my ankles in one direction and arms in the other, I'd stretch and stretch, like a piece of soft taffy.

"Not even a little bit?"

"Nope." My voice comes out as a whisper as knees melt into shinbones. Nick picks me up, wrapping my very malleable legs around him, and walks to the back of the barn where it's darker.

"What about if I do this?" He kisses my neck, feather-light, down to my collarbone. The polar opposite sensations of soft lips and coarse facial hair have my head falling back and he kisses lower still. "Or this ..." He backs me up against the wall, hands coming up, and I gasp at the sensations overtaking my body.

There's a loud "Screeeeech!" the equivalent of "Get a room!" as Henry lets us know he's less than impressed about being woken up. Nick's head lifts as if expecting talons to come raking down the back of his neck. I take a steadying breath.

"I'm sorry," he says, setting my feet on the ground. "I know it's ridiculous, but something about you overrides my common sense. You make me feel like a, a ..." He grasps at words. "Like I have no self-control." He shoves a hand through his hair and backs away from me. "Your mother … I like her and she would kill me if she even guessed I was this close to … to … mauling her daughter."

"Mauling?" I raise an eyebrow. "You make yourself sound like Old Claw." It's nice to see him equally affected by the undeniable chemistry between us. It makes me feel strong. Like he's not the only one with power. "Don't you think you're maybe being a bit melodramatic?"

"Yes. I mean, no." His eyes are like the sun and I'm wearing all black. "I've never felt that way about anyone before, and I've met a lot of girls."

He must see something in my expression because he's quick to amend. "I mean, like met met, not *met* met." A frustrated sound rips through him. "Come here," he says and yanks me toward him. I know what his body will feel like pressed against me, and shiver, wishing I could feel it without anything between us. *Skin, there's not enough skin.*

"Julia?" a voice calls. Dear God, you'd think you could find a few moments alone in a freaking campground.

"Yes?" My voice is hoarse. Dimly, I recognize the voice as belonging to Dan.

"There's a situation out here."

"What?" Unless someone is in the midst of drowning I really don't want to hear about it.

"One of the toilets is plugged and flooding the men's bathroom."

Are you freaking kidding me? The fever in my body evaporates in an instant and I want to cry. I'm furious. At Dan for making me feel like the hired help. At Mom for not having enough money to hire proper staff. At Nick for making me feel embarrassed, because if he wasn't here I wouldn't give a rat's tail about having to fix a plugged toilet. I mean, I would because it's gross and a pain in the ass, but I wouldn't be feeling so humiliated about it.

"Coming," Nick hollers over his shoulder. He looks at me and tucks a piece of hair behind my ear. "I'll take care of it."

I stare up at him, at a loss. "You don't know where the plunger is."

"I'll find it." He leaves me there, gooier than I thought possible, and goes to deal, literally, with the shit going down (or rather not going down) in the bathroom.

*

"That's disgusting." Leaning over Nick's shoulder, I pull my shirt over my nose, while he works the plunger. Someone had decided to use an entire roll of toilet paper on their presumably now very clean bum.

"I've seen worse," he grunts, giving a final yank. The mess comes loose with a loud plop. "Some of the more seedy places we played got pretty nasty by the end of the night."

"Having enough bathrooms." I count off on my finger, referring to Wakestock. "Another thing to think about."

"Just rent some porta-potties."

"Let me guess. You know a guy?"

"This ain't my first rodeo, sweetheart," he drawls with a thick accent.

"What is that? Australian?"

He looks up, surprised. "No, Texan. It's not good?"

"I'll take it from here," a gruff voice says. I look over my shoulder to see Red standing there with a mop and bucket, yellow Caution Wet Floor sign splayed open.

"Thanks, Red," I say, relieved to escape the funk of the men's bathroom.

Nick straightens, holding the plunger away from his body. "What should I do with this?"

"Leave it outside. I'll take care of it," Red says.

I walk over to the sink to wash my hands. "Did you manage to get Caleb's metal detector working?"

"'Course I did. Coulda taught you something, as well." He gives me an inquiring look.

I avoid eye contact. "I've just been showing Nick around."

He makes an *mmm-hrphm* noise deep in his throat. Nick washes his hands, and we leave Red to finish up, feeling only slightly guilty.

"Thank you," I say.

"At your service, Tink."

Dan's with Taylor on a towel at the beach. He sees us and lifts his hand in a beckoning wave. "Guys." We walk over.

"What's up?" Nick asks.

"Taylor and I are going into town tonight, want to come? It could be fun. Like a double date."

"How are you getting there?" I doubt Mr. and Mrs. Schaeffer are letting him take the giant motorhome into those tiny streets.

"We were wondering if you'd mind driving?" He flashes a smile, which I'm sure he thinks masks his ulterior motives.

"Um ..." I don't know what to say. Nick jumps in.

"We already have plans."

"Really?" Dan arches a brow. "You two seem to have really hit it off."

"My father's coming in tonight," he says.

"He is?" Dan and I say together.

"I'm having dinner with him. Would you like to join us?" Nick looks at me. He wants to introduce me to his father? Well, not introduce exactly, seeing as we've already met, not to mention I assaulted his son in front of him, but still, dinner seems a bit ... official. Nick's studying me, and I realize he's waiting for me to respond.

I swallow. "Um, sure."

"That's cool. Say hi to him for me." Dan and Taylor walk off, holding hands.

Nick looks at me. "You don't have to, you know." Wait, so now he doesn't want me to come? "I just thought maybe we could talk to him."

"About not selling?" I say, hope glimmering.

"Yeah. He's not a terrible person. He might understand."

"Might?" Something about Nick's expression has the hope evaporating like mist on the moon.

He shrugs. "It's worth a shot."

"Anything is worth a shot."

"Including helping your little brother look for treasure?" He raises an eyebrow and it's my turn to shrug.

"These last few days it's like a new Caleb, or more like the old Caleb. He's outside, being a kid, excited and thinking about things other than being sick." I look up at him. "And a lot of it is because of you. Maybe you think it's not cool to send him on a wild-goose chase, but I haven't seen him like this in a really long time and it feels good to have my little brother back."

"Happy I could help."

"So you really want me to come for dinner?" A thought hits me. "Where should we go?"

"You're asking me? I thought you'd have a few recommendations."

"Um, Indelicato's is always good. Their pizza is incredible."

"It's a date." He smiles.

"With your dad."

The smile fades a bit. "With my dad."

Chapter Fifteen

The red stain grows bigger, and I dab at it desperately, cursing myself for wearing white.

"So, Julia." Nick's father's low baritone has me looking up from my lap, napkin hovering over my water glass.

"Yes?"

"How are things at the campground?" He helps himself to another slice of pepperoni. "Any more dock mishaps?"

"We got the boards all fixed up," I say, dipping the napkin in my ice water and blotting subtly at the tomato sauce. Frigid water drips onto my leg.

"Nick tells me you're extremely … competent in that area."

"Yes." I'm not really sure if he expects me to elaborate. "My grandfather taught me."

"I've heard a lot about him. Sounds like he was quite the character."

I look up at him. "How did you hear about my grandfather?"

"Dan's parents told me a bit about him." He nods at his nephew, who's sitting with Taylor on the other side of the room, looking all schmoopy over breadsticks. Should've figured he would take her to this place. It's his favorite. We used to come here all the time. I wonder how they got here? Shifting in my seat, I look back at Nick, who has yet to broach the subject of not selling. The heat of the pizza ovens is suffocating. And now I wonder if the cold water I keep applying is actually setting the tomato sauce.

"Will you excuse me for a second?" Holding the handbag I borrowed from Mom in front of the stain, I get up from the table. Nick gives me a reassuring smile and I totter toward the bathroom in the one pair of wedges I own. Dinner so far has been awkward at best. Sighing, I push on the door. It swings back hard as whoever's coming out pulls at the same time. Half stumbling into the ladies' room, I murmur a "Sorry."

"Julia?" I look up at the familiar voice. It's Paige's older sister, Hannah.

"Hey, Hannah. How are you?" I exclaim. Seeing my best friend's face — more or less — and familiar shade of dark hair has me desperately missing Paige. "I didn't know you were home for the summer." Last I heard from Paige, Hannah was living with her boyfriend in the city. She still isn't talking to their dad. Their parents' divorce was pretty messy. But at least their dad still wanted a relationship with his kids.

"Wasn't planning on it, but my advisor had other ideas." She rolls her eyes. Hannah is doing a master's in something or other to do with birds and conservation. "He wanted help on a project that, according to him, was a 'perfect fit' for me."

"Have you heard from Paige lately?" I ask.

"She's only been gone a few days." She laughs. Nick looks over, catching my eye, and winks.

"Was that for me or for you?" Hannah murmurs, turning her perfect face so he can't see her.

"Me, I think." Though seeing him in a setting like this makes me less sure. Pretty Hannah is more his type.

"Ah. I thought so." She gives me an approving look. "Go, Julia."

"Thanks." My face is warm. "Say hi to your mom for me."

"Will do." I watch her stroll away, an ingrained swing in her hips that has most of the male eyes following her, but not Nick's. I hold a paper towel under hot water then pat at my dress. The orangey-red color fades, but the surrounding ring of water expands. Sighing, I stand under the hand dryer and push the knob, holding the fabric up under the warm air, feeling dumb for even wearing a dress. This is so weird. I just want to be back at the campground. When I give up and return to the Constantines, they are very involved in their conversation. Mr. Constantine looks up, sees me and smiles in a way I'm sure is meant to be friendly but has something in the way of a fox about it. I sit down.

"So, Julia, Nick tells me you feel strongly about not selling." Relief sweeps through me. At last.

"It's my home."

"I understand." He clears his throat and looks somewhat sympathetic. "But have you thought about what will happen if your mother doesn't sell?" I look back and forth between the men. Nick's expression is somber as his father lowers his voice. "I've reviewed her finances. The situation isn't good." He pauses. "I'm not sure how much she's told you. She may be angry with me for sharing this information, but I think you need to know so you can appreciate the extent of the problem." Nick reaches for my hand as his father lowers his voice even more. "She's in the hole for a quarter of a mil and on the verge of declaring bankruptcy. It will destroy her credit for the next decade. Minimum. She won't be eligible for things like credit cards, a mortgage or maybe even a job for a while. It's like scrawling a black *X* over all of your financial futures." He drops this little grenade in my lap, blasting away any further worries about the stain on my dress. This is a stain on our lives. On my future, too, if I need loans to go to school. I swallow, feeling the blood drain from my face. "And if it's not us who buy the property, it will be someone else." The "us" rankles. I wait, but Nick is conspicuously silent. I need to get out of there before I do something humiliating like throw a breadstick or faint. I pull my hand from his and stand up.

"We'll figure something out." I turn to Nick. "At least I thought that's what we were doing." Without waiting for a response I stride out the door, bell jangling overhead.

"Julia, wait." Nick follows me out. "Where are you going?" He catches my hand again and gently tugs me to a stop.

"Home." Tears spring to my eyes as I gulp in air. "I thought you were going to try to convince your dad." I feel like such an idiot.

"He was just trying to level with you."

He'd leveled me all right. "You were pretty quiet in there."

"I was just letting him say his piece. You didn't even give me a chance." He sighs. "I know how my dad works. If he thinks he's being pushed into something, his guard goes up. We want to make him think it's his idea. That he doesn't want the property."

A tidal wave of fear washes over me. "But what if he's right? About all that bankruptcy stuff? Two-hundred-and-fifty thousand is so much money." I feel my face crumple and Nick pulls me to his chest. He puts a hand on the back of my head.

"Sssshhh," he says, stroking my hair. "It's going to be okay."

I know that it's not, but it doesn't stop me from wanting to believe him.

*

"So your dad seems to think our situation is pretty hopeless," I say as we walk down the flower-lined main street of town. Feeling bad for leaving the table, we'd gone back, but Nick's father had been on the phone. He waved us off. We were free.

"Don't pay too much attention to him," he says. "He's just a bit jaded."

Aren't we all. "What do you mean?"

"After my mom died, he kind of went off the rails a bit. Despite all his money, none of it could save her in the end. I think he feels like he failed her." Nick's arm is warm and solid around my shoulders. "So now all he cares about is making more of it. That's my theory, anyway. We don't actually talk about it."

"That's sad."

He shrugs. "It's what I'm used to."

"So what *do* you talk to him about?"

"Sports. The business. How being a musician will ruin my life. Pretty girls pushing me off docks."

"So not *all* superficial talk."

"We've been making some progress. Actually, this deal and the one before that we were getting along pretty good." He must mean the Miller deal. I don't think he realizes the note of wistfulness that's entered his voice.

"And now you might potentially be damaging your relationship because of me." I know what it's like to want to be close to your father.

"It's not your fault. It was already damaged."

"But you were repairing it."

He sighs, and I'm silent.

He nudges me. "So how does it feel to leave a multimillionaire cooling his heels at a restaurant?"

I stop in my tracks. "You think we should go back?"

"Nah, he's a big boy. He'll take the rental back to the airport." Mr. Constantine had picked us up after chatting briefly with Mom. He'd had some more questions for her about the property — and apparently her finances — and zipped in for the day.

"That was a quick visit."

"He'll get the full report after my vacation."

"So you're on your own time now?"

"Yup. And you're sure my cabin's available?"

"It is. You can come to pay for it up at the registration house tomorrow."

"You know you guys seriously undercharge for those, right?"

"You think so?"

"Know so."

I glance down the main road. It's still a ways to the campground. "Maybe we should call a cab?" Just as the words are out of my mouth, Taylor and Dan pull up beside us in Red's truck. My jaw drops.

"Hey, guys, need a ride?" Dan asks. Then sees my expression. "He offered, Jules. Overheard me talking to my parents." I don't even know what to say. The. Freaking. Nerve.

Nick puts a hand on my rigid back. "Thanks," he says. Then leans forward to whisper in my ear, "Do that breathing exercise from yoga, okay?"

Inhaling deeply, I walk around to wrench open the back door on the passenger side. It is a long walk back to the campground.

"How was your dinner?" Taylor chirps. "Ours was pretty good, but now I reek of garlic." She waves a hand in front of her face.

"Fine, thanks," I say, despite only managing a few bites of my pizza before everything went wrong. Having a short fuse is really not conducive to enjoying a meal. Maybe it's all part of a vicious cycle: I'm hungry, so I do or say something stupid. My temper might be a lot more manageable if I carried around a couple of granola bars at all times. Like Nick.

"What do you feel like listening to?" Dan fiddles with the radio dials. I'm tempted to say, "Whatever the eff I want," but I manage to refrain. Barely.

A catchy song comes on, and Nick starts singing along, voice matching the tone of the singer exactly. Then I realize: it's one of his. Dan realizes it, too, and I look up in the rearview to see him grimace. Taylor does a double take.

"Are you kidding me right now? You're *the* Con Man?" she screeches so loudly Dan almost drives off the road. I grab on to the front seat. "Oh, my God. I thought you seemed familiar, but figured it's just because you're Dan's cousin." She smacks Dan's arm. "Why didn't you tell me?"

"Surprise." His tone is bitter. "My cousin's a famous rock star, in addition to being heir to a real-estate tycoon."

"The Con Man?" I look at Nick. He looks amused.

"Just a little nickname." I think of the "Constantine Closers." How many does he have?

"It's because he's got such a smooth voice." She looks over her shoulder. "He can talk you into anything."

My face freezes. Is that what is happening here?

"It's obviously a play on my last name. My buddies started it." Nick looks over and reaches for my hand across the seat. "I know what you're thinking," he says, voice quiet. "It's not like that."

I look out the window at the passing trees. Taylor continues to chatter, peppering Nick with questions about the band and what it's like being a rock star. Nick downplays it in that humble way of his that makes you think he doesn't buy into it. Taylor's perked up considerably, flirt-o-meter revving with a famous musician only a foot away. I pretend I'm not listening, but really my ears swallow every word.

"Lemme get this straight. The band. Is coming here?" Taylor's voice rises a few octaves.

"Yeah, thought it would be cool to get the guys together and help out with Julia's situation." My situation? He makes it sound like something of my own doing. Taylor continues to freak out as we turn into the campground.

She interrupts herself. "But don't you want to buy this place? Why are you trying to help her?"

"Because he knows they're going to get it anyway, and he's trying to make himself look like a hero so he can get in her pants." Dan, who's been silent during Taylor's squealing, finally speaks.

"What the hell did you just say, man?" Nick's voice is incredulous. His demeanor clouds over in an instant, like a tornado materializing out of nowhere. "I don't care if you're my cousin." His voice is low and menacing. "You got a problem, let's deal with it."

"Relax, bro. I'm just kidding." Dan contorts his face into a smile that comes off as more of a sneer.

"Yeah, well, I don't find you very fucking funny."

"Chill, guys. Dan's just feeling a little jealous," Taylor says. Which only makes the tension in the car more oppressive. Dan slows over a speed bump, and I take off my seat belt, open the door and jump out.

"Julia." I hear Nick call my name as he follows. Dan keeps driving, presumably to drop the truck off to Red, who will be getting an earful later. I walk in the direction of the lake. Nick calls my name again. "Stop." Something about his tone stops me. "He's full of shit. You know that, right?" I don't say anything. The tornado is still spinning, and I'm directly in its path. "You're so willing to believe the worst about me. Don't you have any faith in people?"

"Look at Dan." The words burst from my mouth. "I thought he was … I don't know … anyway, it was all a freaking lie."

"Dan's an asshole."

I want to tell him about my father. But I can't. "Your dad wants my family's property."

"It's not personal. Do you have any idea how rare this place is? Anyone with a shred of business sense would want it. We just happen to be the first because of the family connection."

"And you're in a band."

"Was." His tone is bitter. "Not anymore. So?"

"You could still have any girl you wanted."

"Apparently not." He looks at me. "Look. I have a few weeks here. I'm not making any promises. But I really, really like you. And I think you feel the same. Not sure why you're refusing to acknowledge that or why you're giving me such a hard time. Despite the fact that I play a musical instrument and my father's in real estate, I'm essentially a good human being. But I'm not going to force you into anything. You know where I am." This time he's the one who turns and starts walking to the lake.

I watch, but I don't follow.

Chapter Sixteen

Feeling drained, I lie down on our trampoline in the backyard, staring up at the clouds. A monarch butterfly flits by, most likely on its way south. It floats lazily on the breeze, its delicate orange wings lined with bold black veins dotted with snow-white spots. The vibrant colors seem pretty to us, but are actually a warning to predators of its toxicity. Too bad people don't come with similar warnings.

I sigh. Is Nick right? Have I been judging him unfairly? If he knew the real reason, maybe he'd understand. *Then why don't you tell him?* I push the voice out of my head. Some of what he says makes sense. And didn't I already decide this is just a summer fling? It's not like I'm going to marry him or anything. Paige would say I should just have fun and not worry about tomorrow. Tomorrow it could all go to shit anyway. Look at my dad and Mom. Look at Caleb. I mean, things could be very different right now. He was lucky. We're all lucky to be here, random couplings of eggs and sperm. I watch the butterfly circle off. Even she is lucky to be here, her species currently being decimated due to pesticides on the plants she feeds on. As I'm reminding myself to plant some more milkweed for the monarchs, my body launches a foot into the air and I yelp.

"Jules." Caleb bounces toward the center of the trampoline where I lie.

"What's up?" I prop myself up.

"Guess what I found?"

"A treasure chest full of gold, jewels and a mummified hand."

He sits back on his heels, looking at me like I've lost it. "What's with the hand?"

I shrug. "I dunno. Maybe it was put there to guard the treasure, kind of like an ancient curse."

"Oh. That makes sense. But no, you're wrong."

"Darn." I lie back down and look up, one arm going across my face to shield it from the final rays of the sun. The sky is gradient shades of fuchsia, the clouds fluffy pink marshmallows. Caleb begins to jump.

"So Gramps's journal talked a lot about the land's bounty." He uses air quotes around the word "bounty."

"Yeah, there's fish in the lake, deer in the forest, etcetera, etcetera," I say.

"I think he was talking about something else." He bounces higher.

"Like what?"

"Did you know there's an abandoned mine?"

I sit up. Caleb's bounces each lift me a few millimeters off the taut black fabric. "What?" But there's a tingling of recognition. Wait. Did I know that?

"Yeah," Caleb says emphatically.

"Where?"

"Not sure exactly, but it's on the map."

"What map?"

"Gramps's map. Remember?"

"Right. Where is it?"

"I don't know. A couple miles into the forest, maybe? Looks like it's at the base of the mountains."

"Not the mine, the map." I stand up and begin to bounce alongside him.

"Oh. Upstairs in my room." He turns as he jumps, facing the house.

"Did you show it to Mom or Red?"

He does a flip. "I thought it could be something just you and I look into." My heart breaks a little at his sweetness. "And Nick," he adds.

"You really like him, don't you?" I say, bouncing higher now.

"I could say the same thing about you." He fixes me with a cagey eye. "He's a cool guy."

"I had dinner with him and his dad."

"Yeah, Mom mentioned it. How was it?"

My words are timed with my jumps. "I got up. And left. Halfway through. Our meal."

"I'm surprised you made it past the appetizers." His grin is cheeky and infectious.

"I do love their calamari." I execute a flip of my own and land on my face. It's been a while.

Caleb laughs. "At least you didn't throw anything."

I get up to my knees, difficult while Caleb's launching hard off the tramp. "I showed incredible restraint."

Caleb giggles again. "That word doesn't really describe you."

I continue bouncing with my brother, already feeling lighter.

*

I stand outside Nick's door, listening to the guitar, hesitant to knock. The air is thick and humid, like it is right before a summer storm. There's a lull in the music and, before overthinking it, I lift my hand

and rap softly, insides churning, nerves going berserk. Part of me hopes he doesn't hear, while other parts ache with anticipation. I hear the guitar clank down and footsteps cross the room. A drop of water lands on my forehead.

The door opens.

"Hey." Nick's hair is tousled, getting too long. It frames wary dark eyes and a face full of scruff.

"Hey." I take a deep breath as more drops fall. "Can I come in?"

He opens the door wide. "Sure." The moisture in the air carries the woodsy smell of cedar to my nose, and I breathe in again, walking into the cozy cabin.

"I'm sorry." I turn to face him. "For acting like such a —"

"You don't need to apologize." He stands there, hands in shorts pockets.

"But I do. I haven't been very nice to you."

"I don't completely agree." His look is amused and suggestive all at the same time. I blush. "Besides, who says you have to be nice to me, anyway?"

"My mom and Red," I say, automatically. "And it's just basic manners."

"Well, I'd say you have every right to be a bit … conflicted." He walks up to me; his closeness takes my breath away. "I wouldn't blame a lioness for defending her territory any more than I'd blame you for trying to protect yours."

"So now I'm a giant cat?" My voice sounds weird, throaty, almost purring.

He tucks a strand of hair behind my ear, like he had in the barn. "It suits you, with your beautiful mane." His voice is husky. "Copper, strawberry, cinnamon."

My knees are once again refusing to stay locked. "Don't just the boy lions have manes?"

"Technicalities." He lowers his mouth to mine, then stops right before our lips touch. "Did you come here just to apologize?"

"No. I came. To see you." My voice is tremulous above the raindrops that have started to patter at the roof and windows.

"Why?"

"Because I want to tell you you're right about my misjudging you. And I want to tell you something. About my father." He pulls up short, face serious but open, waiting for me to gather the words. Taking a deep breath, I begin. "He left after Caleb was born. I was eight. My last memory of him is his coming into my room to kiss me goodbye. He said he loved me and that he'd be back. I don't know where he was going or what he was doing. It was only later that I figured out he was leaving us. Maybe it was the stress of two little kids and the around-the-clock work around here. And maybe it just would've been for a little while. Maybe he just needed a break and would've come back." My voice falters on "back." Nick stays silent but takes my hands in his. "Anyway, he didn't." My throat is tight. "He met someone else. Eventually they had a baby. He has a whole other family somewhere. Toledo, last time I cared to search for him online. We weren't enough. And though I've mostly worked through all this, I guess a part of me still thinks when people leave they might not come back. That they'll find something better out there."

Nick wraps his arms around me, hugging me tight to his chest. "I'm so sorry, Julia." And I know he means it. He, of all people, knows what it's like to lose a parent. But his didn't choose to leave. Mine did. "I can't even imagine what that was like."

I take another shaky breath and my eyes lock with his. "And I came here to tell you that I trust you." There's a flash at the skylight. The rain gets harder, and a low crack of thunder sounds from somewhere far off.

"I'm glad," he says, "because I would never want to hurt you."

"I believe you." Taking his hand in mine, I turn to the stairs leading up to the loft. He follows me, silent, as I climb the rungs, light-headed. I lie back on the double mattress, on the soft blue blanket as another flash of lightning illuminates Nick's face through the skylight. I'm so used to seeing a twinkle, or the tug of a grin, that his expression now stops the hands that are reaching for him. He grabs one and kisses it, more tenderly than I'd ever expect, before coming to lie beside me.

I exhale. "Kiss me."

"I can do that." He lowers his head, bringing his mouth to mine. He's giving off so much heat, it feels like I'm about to be incinerated. And I'm enjoying every second of it.

He pulls away, his breathing ragged. I'm glad to see I'm not the only one. "Since that night on the dock I haven't been able to stop thinking about you," he says. "I was managing just fine. With accepting my life. My dad. Then you come along and ..."

"Fall on my face." A smile curves at my lips.

"Fall on your face." He gives a low chuckle. "And you get up. And it seems like every time you're hit with something — finding out about the campground, Dan and Taylor, me being on the other team, so to speak — you get right on back up. You fight. You're brave, you know."

His words are a balm to the ache in my heart. "Braver than me." I look up at him, and the moon comes out from behind clouds. "Brave and beautiful." And though I hadn't thought I need the flattery, it, too, is sweetly soothing.

He bends down, lips brushing mine, and my body arches toward him, as if an invisible string is attached to my navel and being pulled upward. The kiss reverberates through my body, like all his kisses do, sounding off some sort of internal gong, like in one of Mom's classes. She says gongs affect us on a cellular level, vibrating even the smallest particles of our bodies.

Kissing Nick definitely messes with my molecules.

The rain has stopped and the moon is out in full. "You still never got your astronomy lesson," I whisper.

"You dazzle me more than any stars." He trails a finger from my shoulder, down across my body, ending at a hip, across to the other hip and back up to my collarbone. "Besides" — he rolls on top of me, kissing my forehead — "that was just a ruse to get you to spend more time with me."

"So you're not really that interested in whether you're looking at Ursa Major or Ursa Minor?" My hands trail down the middle of his back, the valley between two hard and smooth curved ridges.

His laugh is soft in my ear. "Either way, it's a spoon right?" I'm about to correct him but as his kisses trail down my neck and lower still, words flee.

*

I lie beside Nick, head on his solid chest, one hand threading through the soft dark hair there, both of us looking out the skylight. My body feels weightless, untethered to the earth, like gravity has somehow been temporarily suspended. Being with him feels so perfect and right. My mouth curls up in a slow smile that I imagine must look pretty feline, were anyone to witness it. A giddy feeling runs through me, and I feel powerful, liberated and a little overwhelmed all at the same time. Paige is going to freak the eff out. It's midnight and the sky has cleared. I'll have to leave soon or Mom will be worried. But I push the thought out of my mind as I give Nick his lesson.

"The Big Dipper isn't actually a constellation, you know," I say.

His hand comes up to cover mine, fingers entwining. "Could this night be any more earth-shattering?" he murmurs in my ear.

I laugh. "It's an asterism. A familiar pattern of stars in the sky."

"Isn't that what a constellation is?"

"Sort of. It's a recognizable pattern that's usually part of a larger constellation. The Big Dipper is a part of Ursa Major, the Great Bear."

"One of Old Claw's relatives, hey?"

I smile.

"What about the Little Dipper? Not a constellation either?"

"'Fraid not. Part of Ursa Minor."

"Little Bear?"

I nod and raise our hands upward and trace a pattern. "You can make your own asterism. Just find a pattern in the sky of something that looks familiar."

He sits up. "Come on."

I stare at him. He's so beautiful. "Where are we going?"

"We need more sky to work with." He starts down the ladder and I follow him, feeling exhilarated, free and intoxicatingly happy. We run outside into the night, laughing. Nick grabs my hand and we race down to the beach. The short rainfall has refreshed the night air, the fragrant smells of damp earth and dripping leaves and plants give off a heady, sweet scent. The moon is filling out. Its light shimmers off the water in a river of milky white.

Nick pulls down his boxers and runs into the water, diving under. I watch from the shore as he comes up, pushing the hair out of his face, body looking like it's carved from marble in the moonlight. "It feels amazing. Come in."

I know the water will seem warm, the rain making the air cooler. I lift the dress over my head, emboldened by the moon and the night, and slowly wade into the water, goose bumps erupting from my skin. I'm not sure if it's from the shock of the water or the look in Nick's eyes as he stands there, watching me, taking me in.

I take a deep breath and plunge; the temperature of the lake feels divine. I surface next to Nick; he grabs me and pulls me into his arms, his body infusing heat into mine. I cast my eyes heavenward.

"How's this for more sky?" The stars are as bright as I've ever seen. So many billions, so far away. I can't believe they're there every night, and some people rarely get the chance to see them, blocked by light pollution or general busyness.

"You got a nice view here, Tink," Nick says, looking up, arms still wrapped solidly around me. It's not deep and I sit on his legs.

"I know. Can you see why a casino would ruin it?" It makes me sad to think of mindless zombies, pulling away at slot machines, while all this is just wasted upon them.

"I can. But what if it wasn't a casino?" Nick spins me in a slow circle, so I'm facing the shore. I study him.

"What do you mean?"

"What if we did something else with the property?" The light of the moon reflects in his irises.

"Like what?"

"My father and I are developers. We don't work for the casino. We broker the deal."

"What does that mean?" My brain feels fuzzy.

"It means we have a bit of say in who we sell to once we acquire the property."

"Wouldn't you just sell it to the highest bidder?"

"That's usually the way it works."

"And the people that want the casino are probably the ones who have the most money."

"They're also the only ones who know about this place at the moment. We've been looking for a spot for them for a while now and told them about it when we realized it might be an option."

"So what are you saying? If other parties are interested they might have some competition?"

"You just seem really bothered by the casino part. If you could convince your mom to put a clause in the contract where we had to sell it to someone she deemed acceptable, maybe we could find a more suitable fit."

I look down at him, my legs still entwined around his waist, just under the surface. "I think a family campground is the best fit."

"I agree," he says. "I'm just trying to come up with some creative alternatives in case that doesn't happen." His words make me sad, and I lower my legs, feet touching the sandy bottom. I know that what's happening isn't his fault and he's trying. But the thought of losing my home depresses me. Where would we go? What would I do? A big fat tear falls into the water, creating small concentric ripples. "Tink, don't be sad. We can still stick to Plan A where we don't sell at all."

"Remind me how that happens?" I start wading toward shore. Nick follows beside me, one hand on my lower back. Having serious conversations in the nude is a bit disconcerting. I grab my clothes and the moon disappears behind some clouds, along with my earlier euphoric state.

"Epic Wakestock weekend, remember?" Nick tugs on his shorts and smiles as I try not to stare. "Throw in some savvy social media marketing and we might make enough money to hold off the creditors for a while."

I nod my head, cheeks flushed. "Let's do it."

"On it," he vows. "Get ready for the craziest Wakestock this campground's ever seen." We'll have to tell Mom and Red — I hope they'll go for it. But if she's cool with renting out areas of the campgrounds for weddings and vow renewals, what's a little benefit concert?

"And what's Plan B again?" Making a beeline for the warmth of his cabin, I toss the words over my shoulder. I hear his feet on the crunching sand behind me.

"Your brother finds his buried treasure?"

"Right." I let out a long, slow breath. "Plan A, it is."

Chapter Seventeen

Over the next few days I become aware that some sort of thermonuclear reaction is taking place inside me. Like a new star forming, it happens quietly, atoms binding together as time passes in a blur of electrifying kisses and stolen moments. We work on Caleb's clubhouse, and even the more mundane tasks of daily maintenance take on a rosy glow, because we're together. Crazy text conversations fly back-and-forth between band members during the week, adding to the thrill, even if I'm just a peripheral part of them. Nick's social media marketing strategy is brilliant; by the time Friday rolls around, the event page already shows over a thousand people coming. I feel a little dizzy when I see that number.

"Do you really think we can fit in that many people?" I ask, as I look over his shoulder at the screen in his hands.

"Are you kidding me? There's as much space here as one of those big music festivals. Check out this video Unicorns just did to promote Wakestock. Once it goes live, the numbers will triple." Nick's gone into full-on event-marketer mode. Mom and Red could learn a thing or two about all this social media stuff, I think. Our campground doesn't even have a decent website.

Mom seems cautiously optimistic, though slightly worried about hosting such a big event, but I explain to her and Red that it will be just like the vow renewal we're doing tomorrow for the McGregors. On a much larger scale, of course. Not sure they realize exactly how much larger, but I'm trying not to think about that. Instead, I'm focusing on helping them get ready for the McGregors' sixtieth this weekend, kind of like a warm-up for the main event.

Nick plays the video. I can't believe these guys are talking about *my* family's campground. They're promoting it as a pop-up concert and benefit. I wonder how Nick's dad will feel if he sees his son actively campaigning to save something he's trying to acquire.

"Join us and special guests The Con Man, who are reuniting just for this event. It's going to be epic. What could be better than dancing barefoot on the beach to sweet sounds as the sun goes down?" The video flashes to an image of Nick and his band rocking out at a previous show. The video production is slick and professional, and I'm amazed at how fast it was put together. When I say so, Nick shrugs.

"My buddy Peter did it. He filmed most of our videos. The man is a genius."

"You know so many interesting people," I say.

He holds my gaze. "I do. The most interesting one happens to be this girl with green eyes the color of polished sea glass and hair like the flames of the sun." I blush and he laughs, knowing full well how awkward his ridiculous compliments make me feel. He loves to tease me. And despite the intensity of the chemistry between us, he brings a levity to things, a lightness that helps ease my anxiety. Caleb must sense it, too. He's been hanging around, either with his nose in Gramps's journal or strumming semi-recognizable tunes on the guitar. He's had a few more lessons, and Nick's proclaimed him the next Hendrix. Caleb googled him, and it seems the guy was a big deal back in the day, so he's been pretty pumped.

"Are you ready to go?" I ask Nick. We're heading to the clubhouse to put the finishing touches on it, like in one of those home reno shows. We're kicking Caleb out so it'll at least be somewhat of a surprise when he sees it.

"Yeah, just let me grab something from the cabin." He holds out a hand. "Come with me?"

I grab his outstretched palm and it covers my much smaller one. We reach the cabin and Nick says, "Wait here." I obey, looking around at the lake, heat rising in my cheeks as I remember the night of our moonlit swim. The screen door of the cabin bangs shut.

"What is that?" I say as he comes out, though I know what it is, as well as who it's probably for. It's a guitar case. Covered in stickers and autographs, it's pretty much the epitome of rock 'n' roll.

"I got my buddy to send my old case." He frowns at it. "Do you think he'd rather keep the Vuitton?"

"I told my mom he wanted a case." It's sweet that Nick got him one, but I think she already has it covered. Though this one, I'm sure, is much, much cooler.

"I just thought that ..."

That we can't even afford to buy my brother a birthday present? The rogue thought flits through my brain, but I keep my voice even. A few days ago I would've let go of the reins, but now I pull them back. "That's incredibly thoughtful of you. He'll love it."

"Really? I feel bad for stealing your mom's gift idea. Maybe I'll buy the other one from her. Or we could do a swap, and she can say it's from you guys."

"What about the Vuitton?"

"I thought we could auction it off at Wakestock?" He grins. "Could fetch a pretty penny."

I laugh. "Who says that?"

"What?" Nick looks baffled.

"Do you know the night we first met you reminded me of a pirate."

Nick grins. "I can live with that. As long as you realize I'm a pirate with good intentions."

"That's what they all say," I tease. Nick grabs the guitar case and swings it over his shoulder.

"Can I drive the ATV today?"

"Race you for it," I say, and take off running at full speed. Nick lets out a shout and chases after me, still holding the guitar case. I'm such a kid.

"This seems a bit unfair," he half yells, half pants, case banging off his back.

"That's life," I call over my shoulder. Though I feel that life has been reasonably fair with planting him in my path. Reaching the quad, I laugh, breathless with exhilaration.

He drops the case and sweeps me up in his arms. "You cheated," he complains, bringing me down and kissing me full on the lips.

"All's fair in love and quadding," I tease. Then realize what I've said. "I mean, like and quadding," I stammer. "I mean, I like you. Not the other thing." Being with him right now is one thing, but I would not love Nick. I know this is only temporary.

Nick laughs. "I like you, too." His whisper is soft in my ear. "As a matter of fact, I'm crazy about you." He kisses the tip of my nose, enveloping me in happiness; but underneath, now, is something else. Not wanting to examine it too closely, I hold up the keys.

"All right," I say, "you can drive."

*

I add the final coat of paint to the trim of the windowsill. "I hope he likes it."

"He's going to lose his mind," Nick says, installing a new doorknob. He squeezes the drill and it spins round and round with a high-pitched hum.

"You think so?" I put down the brush and walk over to the entrance, my glance sweeping the interior. The cabin's had quite the facelift. It may still be pretty run-down, but at least it's safe and clean now.

"This place is a kid's paradise. Outdoors, adventure, privacy. I would've loved to have had a place like this when I was his age. Still would, actually."

"Oh, really?" I lift an eyebrow. "You'd give it all up for a little cabin in the woods?"

He shrugs and looks around. "It's peaceful out here." He reaches for me. "It would be especially great with someone to keep you company. And by someone, I mean you."

"What would we eat?" I say from under lowered lashes.

"We could forage for berries and things. I don't like hunting, so we'd have to go vegetarian."

"My mother would be overjoyed. You don't think we'd get bored?"

"I'm sure we could think of ways to occupy ourselves." He bends his head down and our lips meet. And I picture it. Him, me. Our cozy little home in the forest. The vision is only a second long but real enough to jolt me into realizing I can see the rest of my life with him.

It scares me. And I recognize that as the sensation beneath my happiness a moment ago. Because odds are that the vision is not the reality that is going to come true. Pulling back from the kiss, I open my eyes and look at him. He gazes back.

"What's wrong?"

Tears fill my eyes. "I'm trying to live in the moment. But all I can think of is how I'm going to feel when you leave."

You'd think I'd be used to it, living in a place like this, where people come and go every year. But maybe that's why it bothers me so much. Because I know. I know that despite the "stay-in-touches" and the promise of "see you soon," or whatever, it always fades into nothing. People leave and that's it. Sometimes they come back. Most times they don't. And sometimes they come back and it's not the same. They might even have a gorgeous blonde girlfriend in tow. I'm just a summer fling for Nick. And while that had been good enough for Dan and me and what we had, I know it's not enough for what I have with Nick. I thought it would be, but it's not. I need to stop this. Now.

I take a step back and a big breath along with it, before the words rush out. "Maybe we should just be friends." The forest is silent, the birds have ceased calling; not even a leaf rustles. Hazarding a glance up, I see his pained expression as he shakes his head.

"You still don't trust me."

Maybe. But I think it's more that I don't trust myself not to be shattered when he leaves.

"I'm sorry." My voice trembles. "Please don't be mad at me."

He sighs and runs a frustrated hand through his hair. "I'm not mad. Just crushed, actually." We stand there. A second ago we'd been so close, but now we're light years apart.

I bite my lip. "I'll understand if you want to leave."

"I don't run out on my commitments, Julia." His tone is cool. "I promised you and Caleb I'd help, and that's what I'm going to do." Guilt must show in my face because he sighs again. "Come here." He pulls me close and I don't resist. "Fine. Friends it is." He kisses the top of my head. "Though it's going to be hard to keep my hands off you." Then he lets me go, abruptly. The space around me feels empty without him in it. "Are you sure that's really what you want?"

No, I want to shout. *It's not what I want. It's the only way I can keep myself from feeling excruciating pain when you leave.*

But I nod.

His face is tense and he turns. "Come on. Let's go get Caleb."

I follow him, mind racing. Am I doing the right thing? The sounds of the forest have started up again, and branches crackle under our feet as we make our way back to the quad. He tosses me the keys.

"You're in the driver's seat, Tink."

*

We look everywhere for Caleb, my excitement for the big reveal tempered by the hollow feeling of having done something very wrong. We drive down to the lake where he's been the last few days, wrangling his metal detector, but he's not there. Mom and Red, getting the barn ready for the party tomorrow, say they haven't seen him in a few hours, either. We decide to go the house, hoping to catch him on the trampoline or find the other quad gone. But the tramp is empty and the ATV is parked. I sigh and turn to Nick. "He's probably in the basement."

"The kid can't be outside all day," Nick reasons. He's been quiet since the woods.

"He used to be," I grumble, but it's good-natured. I can deal with a little gaming now that he's getting outside again.

We head downstairs, but the basement is dark and empty.

"Where is he?" I say out loud.

"Did you check his room?"

We go upstairs, and I poke my head in the doorway. A little form is huddled under a few blankets, eyes closed. I struggle with the urge to wake him, to make sure he's okay. Poor kid's probably just exhausted from all the activity these past few days. Then he rolls over, and I see his hair is damp with sweat, his face paler than usual.

"Cale?" I say, walking into the room and putting my hand to his forehead. He's hot. "Cale?" I say, louder this time. Nick follows me into the room.

"Hey." He opens a sleepy eye.

"Are you okay?" The fear that was a constant companion when he was in the hospital is back, creeping along my skin.

"Yeah." Caleb's voice is quiet. "Just tired."

"Do you want me to get Mom?"

"Nah, she's busy."

"But you're sick." My voice sounds panicked, and Nick puts a hand on my shoulder.

"Think it's just the flu." I'm skeptical. "It's not like before, Jules. That was different."

"You're warm." Going to the bathroom, I bring back some Advil and a glass of water. "Drink."

"It's just hot from this stinkin' blanket," he says, throwing off the covers.

"What did you have?" Nick's voice is soft, curious. "When you were sick?"

"Guillain-Barré syndrome." He pronounces it carefully, complete with French accent.

Nick whistles. "Sounds fancy." He sits down on Caleb's desk chair. I take a seat on his bed.

"Real fancy." Caleb offers a tired grin.

"What was it like?" I look at Nick, unsure if it's a good idea for Caleb to relive his illness, but my little brother inches himself up on his pillow, leaning back against the headboard, seemingly wanting to talk.

"Painful. Weird. Like being pricked by a billion needles, all over my body, under my skin."

Nick winces. "Fun times."

"It's an autoimmune thing where your body attacks your nerves.

Eating away at the myelin sheath so they're exposed," I say. "It causes muscle weakness and paralysis." And sometimes death. Though most people do eventually recover from it.

"How did you get it?" Nick asks.

"Nobody really knows how you contract it." Caleb shrugs. "The doctors figure it was maybe from slicing my foot on a broken beer bottle someone left on the beach or something."

"Ouch."

"Yeah. I felt really weak and couldn't move; then my skin felt like it was on pins and needles. It spread all over my body, and I couldn't breathe."

An involuntary shudder runs through me, recalling those long weeks when he was intubated.

Caleb looks at me and grins. "Jules thought I was faking because I didn't want to go to school." I still feel guilty about that. Giving him a hard time when he said he wasn't feeling well. When he fell over after trying to stand up, I knew it was serious. What if it's serious now? What if it isn't just the flu, and he's having some kind of relapse? There is no cure for GB; it either goes away, sometimes leaving traces behind, or it doesn't.

"Maybe we should go to the hospital just to get you checked out?" I say.

"I don't want to go." Caleb's voice is stubborn. "I spent enough time there. It's probably just a bug." I know it was hard for him. Being paralyzed and relying on everyone else to do everything for him. We used to have to move his arms and legs so he wouldn't develop blood clots or get bedsores from being immobilized so long, hooked up to a hundred machines that kept him breathing, kept his heart going. Feeling nauseated, I walk over to his window. A breeze floats on in and I breathe deeply.

"She's a bit of a worrier," Caleb tells Nick, and I whirl around.

"Can you blame me? This crazy disease strikes you at random.

Anyone can get sick and die at any moment. Or drop dead of a heart attack or, or …" Hot tears form at my eyes and I leave the room, with a choked, "Excuse me."

Rushing down the hallway, I fling myself on my bed with such force it shifts over a few inches. I blink hard and try to swallow the hard lump in my throat that's swelled to the size of a grapefruit, breathing in the fresh laundry scent of the pillow. Caleb's illness had taken a toll. On all of us. And now, with the worst of it behind, I begin to see just how much it affected me. I take a steadying breath. We made it through. He's getting stronger every day.

"So this is your room, hey?" Nick stands at the doorway.

"You can come in," I say, sitting up, pushing the hair off my face. "Sorry about that."

"What?" He walks into my room, dominating the space with his large frame.

"Being such a wuss."

He laughs. "You're one of the least wussy people I've ever met. Do you mind if I sit?" I shake my head, and the bed creaks under his weight. "You've been through a lot this year. It's understandable that you worry about your brother. When my mom got sick I was a mess. Cried like a baby." It's difficult to picture him crying, but I guess he wasn't so … strapping back then.

"I know. I just want to be strong, you know? For Mom and Caleb. They've had enough to worry about. They didn't need to worry about me falling apart."

"That's what a family does. They support each other. And from where I'm sitting, you look very much together." He shifts on the bed, facing me. His body is the positive charge, pulling my negative ions closer. I want nothing more than to lean my head against his broad chest and have his arms come up to encircle me.

But. We're just friends. My decision. The push and pull of electric currents pulse in the magnetic field around us.

"Jules?" Caleb stands in the doorway. "I'm feeling better now; can we go check out the cabin?" The Advil must have kicked in.

"Are you sure?" I tear my gaze away from Nick's, trying to gain a sense of equilibrium. "What about dinner? Are you hungry?"

"Oh, yeah. Mom's helping out at the rehearsal. She said we could come by and grab some lasagna if we wanted." He looks at Nick and shrugs. "Crashing other people's family functions is a thing around here."

"It's actually how we get most of our food," I agree, feeling slightly better. Caleb wants to eat. That's a good sign. "We're not unlike feral children."

"Great name for a band." Nick smiles, getting up from my bed and offering me his hand. There's a palpable fizz of energies as currents meet. I pull my hand back.

"Hmm," Caleb muses, oblivious. "Feral Children?" His nose wrinkles.

"Might be too metal-sounding for us." Nick scratches his chin. I look back and forth between them.

"You guys are starting a band?"

"Just working on a number for Wakestock," Caleb says, nonchalant. I put my hand on his forehead. It's definitely not as warm. Just a bug, then.

"Shoot, that reminds me. I have a few calls to make about the event," Nick says. "Do you guys mind if I meet you at dinner?"

"Sure," I say, following them both out of the room. "We'll be the ones huddled around the garlic bread."

"Save some for me."

"Not making any promises," I say, turning to close the door behind me. My eyes fall on some papers peeking out from under the shifted bed. Forgotten college applications. There had been a few conservation programs I'd been looking into. I think of Paige's sister, Hannah. Maybe I could ask her a few questions about the process. I follow the boys down the stairs. Caleb walks down, hands animated, not bothering to use the railing. He *is* getting stronger. When someone in your family is sick, everything else is pushed to the side as you focus on getting through one day at a time. But now, despite living in the present being the way to happiness, maybe it's time to start thinking about the future again.

Chapter Eighteen

"Are you sure you're feeling better?"

Caleb sounds slightly exasperated. "It could've been something I ate."

We walk along the path to the cabin. Despite the lingering worry, I'm excited for him to see it. "Now, it's not that drastic," I say. "Just more of a general sprucing up than a whole makeover. Nick did a lot of work."

"He's a pretty cool guy, hey?"

"Yeah, he's pretty great." I wonder what he's getting at.

"So, like, are you guys dating or something?"

"No. I mean he's only here for a short time."

"But you like him, right? Like, *like* him like him?"

I'm unsure if this is an appropriate conversation to be having with my little brother.

"I just think that if you like him, then you should go for it." Since when does Caleb play Cupid?

"Mm-hmm?" A noncommittal sound emerges from my throat.

"Life's too short to not go for things that make you happy." It's like he's been reading my mind.

"But what if the things that make you happy are the things that make you sad in the end?"

"I think worrying about stuff like that is pointless," Caleb says, all matter-of-fact. "Because what if it does work out? Then all the time and energy you spent stressing was for nothing. Better to put that energy toward something positive."

"Even if it'll leave scars?"

"Scars show you survived." He holds out his arm where, at one point, an IV had kept him alive. I know he's right. So why is it so hard to let go of the fear of getting scars in the first place? We reach the clearing and Caleb stops in his tracks. The cabin has been freshly stained and green gingham curtains hang at the windows.

"Happy early birthday. What do you think?" The question comes out high-pitched, nervous. He doesn't say anything, instead walking slowly up to the entrance. Fresh flowers hang at the windowsills, and there's the new brass knob, which he turns slowly, the door creaking open in welcome invitation. Battered and lined with deep grooves, the floor gleams underneath minimal furniture, the stuff we could salvage. A few repainted wicker chairs, a hexagonal coffee table. We'd been able to save the couch thanks to an old sheet that had been draped over it. I'd beaten out the cushions and covered the whole thing with matching plaid blankets found in the shed — they are clean and soft, if only slightly hideous. I can see the appeal of the place, why Gramps had chosen to live out here before marrying Grandma. It's kind of the ultimate off-the-grid bachelor pad.

The bookshelves are tidy; naked hardcovers line them in mute tones of blue-gray to beige, most parted from their jackets long ago. The covers that did survive are torn and moth-eaten, but still proudly protecting their occupants. "A book always has value, even when it is old and worn," I hear Gramps's baritone in the space. "Especially when it is old and worn. Then you know it's a good one." It is easy to picture him here, to feel him. I realize how much I miss him.

"I love it." Caleb's voice is muffled, and I pull myself back to the present. "This place is awesome!" The delight I'd been hoping to see is there in his face, and it spreads to me. He'd been there for most of the work, even contributed to it himself, but as Nick says, it's amazing what a little staging can do.

"Good," I say, feeling warm and content. "I'm glad." His eyes roam the rest of the cabin. Cupboard doors have been painted white to match the wicker chairs, and a maroon rug with a crisscross pattern covers the worst scuffs on the floor.

"This place makes me feel closer to Gramps. I wish I'd known him a bit better," Caleb says, walking over to the bookshelves.

"He was really wonderful," I say. "I remember him bouncing you on his knee, you giggling your head off, while he'd sing songs and tell us his silly stories. He always used to sing that one, "You Are My Sunshine."

"How does it go?" Caleb asks. Clearing my throat, I warble the first verse for him.

"I remember that," Caleb says softly.

"I think he'd be happy you did." We're quiet as the sunlight streams through the windows, which still have unbudgeable grime lining their edges, despite all the washing. "How's the treasure hunt going?"

His shoulders slump. "Not so good. I found an old watch and a few coins, a couple of bottle caps."

"But that's just on the beach, right? Don't you think that if anything were hidden it would be in a less obvious place?" I gesture around us. "Maybe out here. What about that abandoned mine you mentioned? Were there any more clues?" Guilt shoots through me.

We were supposed to look together but just haven't had the chance yet.

"There were a couple of notes, but it was closed because they never found much."

"What kind of mine was it anyway?"

"Gold."

There was an abandoned gold mine on our property? "But it was a bust?"

"Sounds like it." Probably not a good prospect for treasure then.

"What else did the journal say?"

"Remember that sentence I told you about? I'm not sure what got into Gramps but it was kinda weird; like, poetic, or whatever."

"What is it?"

Caleb makes a face but recites, *"The moon is a wide band of gold on warm silver waters. Overhead, an infinity of diamonds sparkles just beyond fingertips."*

I giggle. I can't help it. He looks so pained with the flowery words coming from his mouth. "Go, Shakespeare."

He fakes a right cross to my shoulder. "Stuff it." He'd just started to do that before he got sick. It's the first time he's done it since.

"Kidding." I hold my hands up. "Why don't I have a look at the book just in case there's anything you missed?"

"Sure." His stomach growls and I giggle again.

"Hungry?"

"Starving."

So was I, but not for food. I was craving the presence of a certain pirate. A "friend."

"How about we get some dinner?"

*

The rehearsal dinner for the McGregors' vow renewal is crazy. Multiple generations all converge down at the lake. Little kids run around, playing, darting between legs and screeching, while adults serve up BBQ chicken and potato salad alongside the lasagna and garlic bread. Nobody notices us, probably thinking we're just more grandkids.

The couple of the hour, and the ones responsible for the giant clan, sit on a pair of lawn chairs, chatting with family members and generally being celebrated. The matriarch is tiny, a little bird with silver hair and a smile that never leaves her face. She's vaguely familiar, and I hear someone call her Edith. She watches her husband with adoring brown eyes. He, too, is familiar, but his silver hair is thick and full with a slight wave to it. His eyes are bright and twinkly, and his wife isn't the only one who seems to adore him. Kids jump in his lap, flinging their arms around him, demanding songs and stories. He reminds me of my own grandfather, though slightly jollier, and the two were apparently good friends, along with Red, who's probably around here somewhere. I look up to see Nick striding toward me, effectively cutting off any rational thought.

"Hey," he mouths, eyes locked on mine as he gets closer, stepping around screeching toddlers and exasperated parents.

"How's the garlic bread?" he asks as he reaches me.

"I'm thinking I might go for the chicken instead."

"Really? You seemed so pumped for the bread."

"I don't want to reek of garlic," I say, mimicking Taylor.

"Why's that? Planning to kiss someone later?" Still teasing. Walking over to the long table holding the food, Nick helps himself to a giant piece of lasagna and two garlic breads. He offers me a slice. "Did you know that if both people eat garlic you can't smell it on the other person?" I take it from his hand and he grabs the other slice. "Cheers," he says, tapping his toast against mine.

"Cheers," I echo, trying not to read too much into his remark. After all, we're just friends, I remind myself. Again.

"Hey, Nick." Caleb bounces over to us, paper plate in hand. "Are we practicing after dinner?" Nick looks from Caleb to me. I take a bite of my toast.

"Sure," he says. "Let me take down some food first, and we can jam at my place."

"How's dinner?" Mom walks over, and I see Red chatting with Mr. McGregor. She looks at the toast in my hand. "Go help yourself, Julia, there's plenty to go around."

"She can have some of mine; there's no way I'm going to finish all this." Nick sits on the grass and gestures for me to do the same. We pass the plate back and forth, eating the gooey, cheesy pasta one bite at a time. There's something oddly intimate about sharing food from the same plate. But friends do that, too, I reason. Caleb wanders off to grab some chicken, and Mom watches him go.

"How's he feeling?"

"You knew he was sick?"

"He said his stomach was bothering him but nothing too serious. I took his temperature and it was fine." She smiles at me. "Let me guess; you were worried?"

"I found him with a fever and gave him some Advil. Besides, can you blame me?"

"Not at all, sweetie. But he seems to be fine."

"There's always a chance of relapse."

Mom sighs and sits beside us on the grass. "There is, but try not to think about all the bad things that can happen. You'll drive yourself crazy." Nick passes me the plate. "I hear you're teaching him to play guitar," Mom says to him.

"I am. He's a quick learner; his hands can really fly."

"He had all that practice playing video games," I say.

Mom laughs. "I guess that's something. He seems to have really taken to you."

"He's a great kid."

"So, how much longer are you here for?" she asks. I cringe, hoping Nick doesn't pick up the implicit "And what are your intentions toward my daughter?" tone.

"A few more days." Nick smiles reassuringly. "Then I have some things to do in the city before our big event next weekend."

"Yes, the big event. It's all under control?" Her brow furrows slightly.

"You won't have to worry about a thing, Anna. I have my best guys on it."

"It's really quite charitable of you to be so, uh, involved with helping the campground."

"It's a beautiful spot you guys have here."

"Yes, I'm sure that's why your father wants to buy it." Her tone is frank.

"I take it you're also not that excited to see a mega resort and casino go up?" His tone matches hers.

She sighs. "It would just destroy so much of the natural ecology of the area. The land has so much potential, but it would be nice to create something that contributes to the natural environment, not something that damages it."

"Any suggestions?" Nick asks. Mom looks taken aback.

"What do you mean?"

"What would *you* like to see on the property?"

"Well, obviously my first choice would be to leave everything as it is."

"Of course. But you said maximizing it to its full potential, which makes me think you have other ideas." My head swivels back and forth between the two, like I'm watching a tennis match. Mom's talking to Nick like he's an adult. Which I guess he is.

"I don't know, maybe some kind of eco-spa or something?" she says with a thoughtful look. "There's actually hot springs on the property somewhere. We could use the therapeutic waters in treatments, build a yoga and meditation retreat around that. A place where people can come to relax and rejuvenate. Like one of those digital detox places that are springing up everywhere. Get people to reconnect with themselves and nature."

I can see it, as she's talking. It's perfect. I had no idea this thought had ever crossed her mind.

"Mom, that's an amazing idea."

She gives a self-conscious wave of her hand. "I just like to daydream. Something like that would cost a lot of money. It would be a huge investment."

"What if you found the right investors?" Nick's gaze is level.

"Let me guess, you know some people?"

Nick lets that go, so she continues. "It seems like you're pretty invested in this place yourself. And in our family." I turn beet red.

"It seems like I am." His smile is directed at her, but his eyes shift to me, and it feels like I'm back on the trampoline, stomach executing a perfect quadruple somersault.

"And your father is fine with your … conflicting interests?"

"He's aware of them, yes." Aware. But not fine?

"Is everything ready for the McGregors' ceremony tomorrow?" I nod at the hordes, wanting to change the subject, though Nick seems perfectly cool in the hot seat.

"It's looking good. The barn's all clean and decorated and the men are assembling the chairs down at the beach tomorrow. Looks like the weather will be gorgeous, which is always a bonus." Mom stands up and brushes her bum off. She reaches her hands out and pulls me up. "I don't want Caleb's birthday to get lost in all the commotion of Wakestock next weekend, so we're having an early birthday breakfast this Sunday."

"Waffle bar?" We haven't had one in ages. Mom's banana quinoa waffles are solid but the best part is the toppings she lets us pile on.

From yummy fruit compotes and maple syrup to melted Mars bars, complete with Sour Keys and Jujubes raided from the canteen, birthdays are the one time when Mom turns a blind eye to her healthy ideals. That and when she delivers life-altering news, I guess.

"Yes." She sighs, shuddering. "I've also invited some of Caleb's friends from his old class."

"Really?" A few of his friends had come to see him at the hospital, but when he was completely paralyzed it was a bit rough for everyone involved, parents included. People with kids don't like to be reminded that tragedy can strike anytime, anywhere. The visits eventually slowed, stopping altogether as it became harder for Caleb to communicate. "Does he know?"

"It's a surprise, so don't say anything." She looks at Nick. "Would you like to come?"

"Waffle bar? Sounds awesome."

"Julia, can you grab a few things from the Shack tomorrow?" She looks at me. "I noticed you weren't there today?"

"Shoot! Sorry." I was so excited about the cabin reveal that I'd totally forgotten. "Did anyone complain?"

"Actually, Dan and Taylor ended up running it this afternoon." She sighs. "We need to hire someone else, with Paige not here. Luckily Dan's done it often enough with you over the years that he didn't have any problems."

"Not exactly rocket science," I mutter under my breath, but grateful just the same that he'd saved my butt. I've been avoiding him and Taylor as much as possible, but maybe it was time to let it go. If he'd come without her, I never would've fallen for Nick. Nick puts a warm hand on my back, and it feels like it's been there all my life. "Do you need help cleaning up?"

"It's okay. There's enough aunts, wives and sisters-in-law to have this place pristine in no time." She looks at me and Nick. "See you at home in a bit?" Flushing, I wonder how much she knows. She nods at Nick. "Say hi to your father for me."

Then she's gone, picking up a half-empty bowl of potato salad and scraping Dijon mustard–coated fingerlings into another half-empty orange bowl.

"Kinda felt a bit like I was getting the third degree and all that. You should tell her we're just friends." Nick looks at me and clears his throat. "Unless you've changed your mind?"

"You done eating yet?" Caleb and his new friend, one of the McGregor grandchildren, race over.

"You bet," says Nick. "Who's your pal?"

"This is James. He wants to come hang out."

"Sure. The more, the merrier the music."

"Neenerneenerneenerneeee!" James's epic air guitar has all of us looking at him. He puffs too-long bangs away from his face. "Dope."

"See you later? Friend?" Nick's smile shows that he senses my conflict.

Turning away, I manage a calm, "Sure thing."

Chapter Nineteen

I get home before Mom and go upstairs, turning on my computer. Automatically, my email pops up, and there's one from Paige. I click on it. My eyebrows lift. She's coming home a little earlier than planned. Apparently, she and her dad's latest do not get along, and she wants to avoid being alone with them in romantic Kyoto. She's already been, anyway. Pushing my foot against the desk to spin my chair around, I contemplate what to tell her. Knowing Paige, it will just make her crazy not being able to deconstruct every gory detail in person; I might as well wait until she's home.

As I'm spinning around absentmindedly, my eyes fall on the pieces of paper sticking out from under my bed. Without thinking, I snatch them up, thumbing through the applications. All of them are partially filled out. It looks like Caleb had gotten sick right around the Special Interests and Extracurricular Activities sections. They were blank. What would I even put down? Astronomy? Carpentry? Conservation? Nick Constantine?

What am I going to do when he leaves? Will I even have a home at that point? Mom's idea of an eco retreat had been so good. Maybe we could convince the buyers to do something like that. Though losing the campground would be completely traumatic, I could *maybe* handle it if I knew the area was going to be preserved in some way. A part of me is scared that the less people experience nature, the less they connect to it and care about it. And the less they care about it, the less likely they are to try and save it.

Sighing, I put the papers on the desk and go to Caleb's room. He's still not home. Noticing Gramps's journal lying on the bed, I pick it up and thumb through some of the pages, seeing Caleb's chicken scratch scrawled all over the place. We're both lefties, so writing in bound objects never works out great for us. A giant asterisk in fresh black pencil catches my eye. It's the poem Caleb recited earlier.

The moon is a wide band of gold on warm silver waters.
Overhead, an infinity of diamonds sparkles just beyond fingertips.

"*Warm silver waters*" triggers a sound bite from earlier today. Something Mom was saying about hot springs on the property? I wonder where they are. Could be cool to check out. Maybe with a certain friend.

I hear Mom come home. She's talking to someone. Red. Low murmurs signal that they're discussing something important. Of course I tiptoe to the door and lean out into the hallway.

"Not sure I want to sell but don't know that I have a choice." Mom's voice is soft. My heart, used to fluttering around in my rib cage these past few days, plummets to my toes. It's just like Mr. Constantine said. Things are bad. But then, I already know that.

Red answers, and Mom says something, then … "Talk about this in a minute, just going to check on the kids."

"Julia? Caleb?" she calls upstairs.

"Here," I call back, tossing the journal back on the bed and heading for the landing. "Caleb's not home yet." I jog down the steps.

"Hey, sweetie." Mom smiles, looking tired. "Nice to see you here. It feels like it's been a few days since you've been home."

"You're the one who wanted me to play tour guide to Nick," I point out, but my tone is gentle.

"Right." She sighs. "Well, of course you're home, and now Caleb's out till all hours."

"It's only nine, Mom. He's probably still jamming with Nick. Do you want me to go bust up the party?" Serves Caleb right. He's only been doing that to me ALL week.

She folds her arms. "Why do I get the feeling Caleb would then come home without you?" The screen door bangs, saving us from having to test her theory. Mom turns as Caleb walks into the living room. "How are you feeling, sweetheart?"

"Fine," he chirps, eyes bright with excitement, not fever. "Might have been something I ate. Speaking of eating, do we have anything? Playing really works up an appetite."

Mom smiles, fatigue melting away. "There's some vegan brownies in the fridge. One of my students brought them to class."

"Agatha?" I say hopefully. One of Mom's most dedicated students, she supplements her yoga fees with baking. It works out for all parties involved.

"Yes."

"And you're only mentioning this now?"

She rolls her eyes. "I literally just walked in the door, Julia." The three of us head for the kitchen. Caleb and I jostle through the hallway for first place, Mom following behind. Red's in there, tall glass of milk in one hand, plate of brownies in the other, guilt all over his face.

"Busted," I say, crossing my arms.

"You weren't planning on eating all of them, were you?" Caleb's voice is accusing.

"Uh …" He recovers quickly. "'Course not. Knew you raccoons would be down here sniffing things out. I was preparing a snack in advance of the onslaught."

Caleb and I look at each other, then at Mom. "Right," we all say at the same time.

"What? Can't an old man help himself to some dessert?" Red grumbles good-naturedly as he passes the plate around. "Caleb, how's the metal detector running?"

"Pretty good," he enthuses and starts telling him about some of his modest finds. I grab two brownies and murmur my goodnights, running back up the stairs with the chocolate in hand, now feeling adequately fortified to have another look at those college applications. There's always winter semester.

*

The morning of the McGregors' ceremony is beautiful, with clear blue skies that seem to stretch forever. Nick's final text last night sent me off to bed with dreams as sweet as the brownies in my belly.

You burn brighter than any star.

The last shred of resolve I'm hanging on to melts away. Enough with this "friend" nonsense. Who am I kidding, anyway? I'm going to feel what I feel now, and going to feel what I feel when he leaves, no matter what label I slap on our relationship. The dreams solidified my plan to enjoy these last few days with him. To the fullest. No more hesitation. Like jumping off the end of a dock into cold water. No sense agonizing about it, sticking a toe in here or wading in a painful inch at a time. None of that ultimately makes it any easier. You just have to jump.

And so I do. Out of bed and into the shower. Then back out again. "Mom! There's no hot water!"

No response.

"Mom?" I call again. The house is silent. She must be out prepping for the vow renewal. Bracing myself, I jump back into the shower with a quick lather to the places that need it most, then out again, shivering and trying not to think about why there's no hot water. Sunlight streams through my bedroom as I get dressed — my usual paint-splattered denim cut-offs and tank. The quiet of the place has me checking in on Caleb. My intuition is correct. His bed is empty.

Outside the air is warm. I hope Mrs. McGregor's dress isn't satin. Today is busy. Driving around in the golf cart, I rake the campsites of people who left this morning, picking up garbage and cleaning off their picnic tables. Whistling and looking around at my handiwork, I marvel at how many different shades of green surround me. From pistachio, chartreuse, avocado and lime to dark olive, mint, pine and hunter green, the foliage is a verdant rainbow of greens. People love the lushness of Charming Pines and the privacy between sites. Walking to the back of the site, I take a seat on one of the fallen logs, facing the forest. Moss-covered bark and small ferns and branches grow out of it and other nearby stumps. Trails thread off into the bush, whacked by overzealous kids exploring the woods. Other long-fallen logs support their own ecosystem with intricate tangles of roots at one end.

"Hey," Nick says, and I whirl around, heart speeding up. He's sweating, breathing hard, one headphone in one ear, the other in hand. "Fancy meeting you here."

"Nice day for a run."

"Beauty." He grins at me. Sweat stains the front of his shirt, but instead of being nasty, it's sexy. I try not to stare.

"So about this whole 'friend' thing …" I begin.

He takes a step toward me, stooping and kissing me full on the mouth. The work gloves fall soundlessly to the freshly raked gravel as coherent thoughts flee my brain. It becomes as calm as the Japanese Zen garden I'd tried to emulate, with the concentric circles expanding outward from the fire pit. At the center is heat. Nick and me, and a lot of smoldering embers.

"Knew you'd come around," he says, smiling at me, "and I wasn't referring to my run just now." Vaguely, some part of my brain recalls his "beauty" comment. His words breathe oxygen into the coals, emotions flare bright. "See you later."

It's a promise, not a question.

Holding up my hand in a dazed sort of wave, I watch him jog off, in the direction of the lake.

*

"Have you seen the flowers?" a harried-looking brunette asks, gurgling cherub on her hip as a mini-me version of herself peeks out from behind her skirts.

"Over there." I point at the guy unloading flowers from a delivery truck.

"Oh, thank God. Here." She hands me the baby. "Would you mind watching him while I run the bouquets and corsages to the wedding party? Or is that anniversary party?" she mumbles to herself as she takes off clutching the hand of the little girl. The baby and I inspect each other warily.

"Looks good on you." Nick walks up, showered and handsome in a white collared shirt that contrasts nicely with his tanned skin and dark hair. The baby shifts uneasily and emits a fussy squeak, lower lip starting to tremble.

"Tell him that," I say, starting to *sshh* and bounce him awkwardly up and down while scanning for his mother; but she's disappeared with the flowers.

"Here." Nick leans over and takes the baby from me. "Hey, little guy. Let's go see if we can find some fish." Child in one arm, he strolls down to the shore, past men setting up chairs in front of a large green trellis with yellow flowers woven throughout. Watching him talking softly to the baby at the water's edge, I sigh. If I wasn't a goner before … There's something about a guy who's good with kids. I think children, like dogs, can sense a person's true nature. I'm not sure what that says about me, seeing as how the baby was starting to fuss in my arms, but I decide not to dwell on that.

"Have you seen Caleb?" Red asks, coming up behind me.

"No. I thought he'd be down here with his metal detector."

"Ah. He might be at the cabin." He shakes his head. "I still can't believe you all fixed it up. I'll have to get over there and take a gander before …" He stops.

"Before we sell?" I say, still watching Nick and the baby, who's cooing away at something in the lake. Red follows my gaze.

"He seems like a nice fellow," Red says and looks like he wants to add something more.

"He is." The mother of the baby is walking toward Nick. Without children clinging to her she seems younger. She holds out her hand to the baby, smiling, and he dives forward. She looks up at Nick, shielding her eyes from the sun, and I see her smile. He says something and she laughs, seeming younger still. "When does the ceremony start?"

Red knows I'm changing the subject but lets it go. "In about half an hour."

"It's crazy that they've been together sixty years."

"Some people are lucky," he says.

"Were my mom and dad ever happy?" I ask, not sure what makes me ask that.

He hesitates. "They were."

"Do you know why he left?"

He clears his throat. "Maybe this is something you should talk to your mother about?"

"What's that?" Mom joins us, pretty in a turquoise dress that matches her eyes. I can't spoil the mood of the day, so I lie.

"I was asking Red how come he doesn't have a girlfriend."

She looks amused as Red sputters and coughs but doesn't give me away.

"Uh, I, ah ..." He stammers, and I feel guilty, but Mom gives him an out. "Do you mind showing the DJ where he can set up his equipment?"

With an exasperated look at me, he escapes, grateful to be off the hook.

"What's gotten into you, Julia? The poor man looked like he was about to pass out on the spot."

"Well, it's true. And the same goes for you? How come you don't date?"

"You, Caleb and the campground are all the company I need."

"You're still young, you know." I turn my scrutinizing gaze on her.

"Why don't we talk about this later?" she asks. "Right now I have a million things to make sure get done."

Later, always later. I can understand her reluctance to talk. I wonder if Dad leaving the way he had was one of the reasons she buried herself in work.

"I'm going to hold you to that," I say.

"Make sure you do, sweetie." Someone calls her name, and she gives me a little hug before hurrying off, nodding at Mrs. McGregor, who walks by in a pretty pink dress. Seeing me, she stops and smiles.

"You look very much like your grandmother," she says to me.

"Thank you," I say. I know from old pictures that I do resemble her somewhat. Her eyes follow mine, which are still on Nick. He's waving goodbye to the baby.

"Is that your young man there?" she asks.

It's my turn to be caught off guard, and I stammer out a response. "Um, well ... yes. I mean, no. We're just ... I don't know."

She looks at me, eyes twinkling. "Do you know how I knew that my husband was the one?"

"How?" I ask, surprised at her openness.

"I just knew."

"That's it?" I'm a little crestfallen.

She smiles, a secret smile that all women who're happily in love must share. "I know it's not very concrete, but it's the truth. When you know, you know. And if you don't know, or have doubts, then that person is probably not *the* one." I must look perplexed because she pats my arm. "Don't worry, dear. You're young." She pauses, thoughtful. "Though I met Johnny at fifteen."

"Edith, can we get you over here?" a man who must be the officiant calls over. "Just want to run through the positioning."

"Yes, of course," she answers and turns to join the group of people waiting for her. Before leaving, she touches my arm again, her voice sweet but firm. "Just remember, dear, when you know, you know." I smile at her and she walks away. Funny, Taylor had said the same thing around the campfire.

Nick stares out at the lake, hand in his pockets, breeze ruffling the dark hair at the nape of his neck.

This is what I'm afraid of.

Chapter Twenty

"And the next thing you know, I'm two hours late for my own wedding!" Mr. McGregor shouts triumphantly over the roars of laughter, holding his glass aloft. He looks down at his wife, expression tender. "But she waited for me. And I haven't kept her waiting since."

Mrs. McGregor's eyes twinkle as she sniffs. "Not unless you count getting into the bathroom most mornings." The crowd roars as Mr. McGregor says, "Touché, my dear. *Slàinte!*"

"Slàinte!" everyone shouts. Nick and I stand at the back, watching the happy couple share a kiss.

"They seem fun," he says.

"Totally," I say, suddenly wistful for my own grandparents. Didn't he live with his, once? "Do you get to see your grandparents often?"

"Not as much as I'd like," he says. "They're pretty great. I'd love for you to meet them one day."

Whoa. Surprised, I look at him just as Mr. McGregor says, "And now, a special gift for my dear wife." He peers out into the audience. "Where's my backup?"

"I'll be right back," Nick murmurs in my ear.

"Where are you going?"

"Onstage."

Caleb saunters by, carrying his guitar. Nick grins and follows him up to the raised wooden platform where people have been making speeches, as the DJ passes Nick his guitar. I notice the extra amps as the boys plug their equipment in and strum a couple of warm-up bars. Nick adjusts the microphone, lowering it so Caleb can reach.

"Hey, everyone. My partner and I wanted to play a little tune in honor of this special occasion. It's his first time performing, so let's all give him a round of applause."

"Ready?" I see him ask Caleb. My brother nods, looking nervous but resolute. "One, two, three, four." The boys start playing. The tune is familiar and sweet. Then they begin to sing "You Are My Sunshine," my brother's higher voice harmonizing with Nick's deep one. Mr. McGregor looks at his wife, singing only to her, no microphone needed to amplify the emotion in his voice.

Caleb picks a few tentative notes in a short solo and I hear Mom and Red cheer and whistle. Nick sings the bittersweet second verse alone, his eyes seeking mine out, voice as soft as the moss on fallen logs.

Mr. McGregor waves his arms like a conductor and everyone joins in for the chorus. Nick's fingers fly around the guitar, bringing the song to a close. There's a few tears in the room, including some of my own, watching Cale onstage, looking so proud, hair slicked to the side, purple-collared shirt straining at the buttons. That shirt was big on him at Christmas. My brother is growing.

Everyone claps and whistles as Mr. McGregor bends again to kiss his wife then leads her to a small dance floor at the front of the stage.

Cale and Nick walk off the makeshift wooden stage and head in my direction as the DJ, a short burly man with thick black frames and an even thicker beard, puts on a song where a man with a gravelly voice croons "*It had to be you.*"

"Nice job," I say as the boys reach me at the back of the barn. "You were awesome, Cale."

"Thanks," he says, cheeks flushed. "I messed up one little part but don't think anyone noticed."

"Nah. You nailed it, bro." Nick fist bumps Caleb.

He shrugs, looking down at the floor. "It's an easy song, only a few chords."

"Considering you've only been playing about a week, I'd say that's pretty great," I say. "How did Mr. McGregor even know you guys played?"

"One of the older grandkids recognized me at the rehearsal dinner yesterday and told him I was a musician. He approached me yesterday and asked if I could do something small for his wife. The song was Caleb's idea. I asked him to accompany me when we were rehearsing last night.

I turn to Caleb, seriously impressed. "You learned that song in twenty-four hours?"

"I had a good teacher." He looks at Nick. "Are you coming for waffles tomorrow?"

"That was supposed to be a surprise!" I say. "How did you find out?"

"Mom invited James, and he accidentally let it slip. Don't worry, I'll act surprised," he says.

"Dude, that was epic!" Big Mouth himself comes up to Caleb and slaps him on the back. Ah, well, it's nice to see my brother with a real friend his age, not one he just chats with online.

"Thanks, man," Caleb says, then looks back at Nick, who hasn't responded.

"I'm there, bud," Nick says.

"Cool." He turns to James. "Wanna go get more dessert?"

James pushes his hair out of his eyes, and the two race over to the sweets table, leaving Nick and me standing there. The DJ announces that the guests of honor would like everyone to join them on the dance floor as he switches up the song to "Marry You" by Bruno Mars. I gather my courage and turn to Nick.

"Want to dance?"

"You're forgetting that's the one thing I can't do," he says.

"Oh, right." I stare down at the floor.

He takes my hand and tugs me toward the dance floor. "But for you I'll make an exception."

People are getting up from the chairs as we walk to the already crowded space. A few people lean over to compliment Nick on his song, and he smiles his thanks. Nobody looks at us like we're crashing their family get-together, which we kind of are. They seem like the large family I've always wished I had; loud and crazy, but completely welcoming and really close to one another. Nick's dancing is as bad as he said, and I hold back a giggle at his one-arm T. rex move. But he's not afraid to make a fool of himself so I can have my dance. He crooks a finger at me and mouths, "*I think I wanna marry you.*" I play along, half turning around like I'm not interested, but my heart's pounding. A slow song comes on next and his arms come around me.

"This is more my speed." Dark eyes glint as he looks down at me. His hands slide down to my lower back as mine rest lightly on his shoulders. We sway back and forth.

"Watch those hands, Mister," Mom calls, wagging a finger as she dances by with Red. I overhear her muttering to him, "When did I turn into my mother?" Guess their official duties for the evening are over.

"They're above regulation," I call back, not caring that they're witnessing me dance with a boy. My first time dancing with a boy, actually.

Nick smiles and bows his forehead to touch mine. "Want to get some air?"

"Sure." He takes my hand again and leads me off the floor. A welcome draft reaches us as we approach the wide-open doors. I've left my hair down for once, and I lift it up off my neck, fanning myself.

"Your hair looks pretty tonight."

"Thanks." I drop it and it falls around my shoulders, grazing the top of the silvery dress that had been Paige's, with a little more cleavage than I'm comfortable with.

"Wanna take a walk down to the beach?" He nudges me. "Look at some stars? I've been studying, you know."

"Sure." Feeling bold, I slip my hand in his and we leave the party. "Your song was really good. I still can't believe you taught my brother to play guitar."

"Just a few chords," he echoes Caleb's words. "He's like a sponge, soaks everything up. How did he like the cabin?"

"He loved it. Thanks for all your help."

"My pleasure. Wish I could've been there to see his face."

I feel a little guilty at stealing all the thunder. "You had some calls to make, right? How did they go?" We reach the park halfway down the beach, and I sit on one of the swings. He stands in front of me, one hand on the chain links.

"Most went very well. I think Wakestock is going to be huge."

I look up at him, feet trailing in the sand. "Do you think it will raise enough money?"

He's silent.

"Nick? You said 'most' of your calls went well."

"I told my father I don't think we should do the deal."

"Really?" I want to throw my arms around him, but his face has taken on a stony quality, an expression I've seen before when he mentions his dad. I feel another prick of guilt that the campground's come between them. "What did he say?"

He sighs and walks around behind me. "You don't want to know." His hands press on my back, giving me a small push. I look up at the dark sky.

"So impress me."

"Huh?" he says over my shoulder.

I nod toward the heavens. "You said you've been studying?"

"Ah. Well. Did you know that all twenty of Uranus's moons are named after Shakespeare or Alexander Pope characters?"

"I did not know that." I tilt my head back farther to look at him, so he's almost upside down.

"You could fit one-point-three million Earths inside the sun." He walks around to face me.

"Didn't know that either." I sit up, slightly dizzy.

"And one thousand, three hundred and twenty-one inside Jupiter." Putting his hands out, he grabs the chains and pulls, halting their momentum.

"How many could you fit in Uranus?" I pronounce it the naughty way, unable to resist.

"Ha-ha." He smirks but takes my hand and leads me down to the beach. "How come I had a feeling you were going to ask that? If you must know, a modest sixty-three. Point one."

"You *have* been studying." I sit down on the soft sand and pat a spot beside me. "Tell me more."

He sits, picking up a pile of sand, letting it fall between his fingers. "Remember when you told me there were ten thousand stars to every grain of sand on Earth?"

"Mmm-hmm."

"That makes things like alternative realities, alien life forms and time travel seem completely plausible. We're seeing light that's millions of years old because it takes that long to reach us. If someone had a telescope and was looking back at us across the Milky Way, they'd see a bunch of Neanderthals running around."

"So you believe in time travel now?"

"Considering that our own galaxy, which has roughly four hundred billion stars, is one of quadrillions of galaxies, it's possible." He takes my hand in his lap. "I wish I could do a little of it myself."

"What do you mean?"

"Go back to the night we met. So I could be honest with you about who I was." He sighs. "It might have made things a lot easier between us."

"Maybe." Or maybe I would've had my guard up from the beginning and never have let myself fall for him.

"At the very least it could have saved me some laundry," he quips.

"I think you were being honest."

He waits for me to elaborate.

"So maybe you didn't tell me exactly what you were doing here, but you were honest about who you were, just by being you: kind, sweet, someone who listens. Even then you tried to help me figure out a way to solve my … problems." I squeeze his hand. "Though the man-eating bear suggestion probably wasn't your finest."

"You really think that?" His voice is low.

Do I?

"I think that despite the reason you're here, you're a good person. Your mom would be proud of you." The moment the words leave my mouth I regret them. Who am I to presume how his mother would feel? I pull my hand from his lap and look down at the sand, running my fingers through it, feeling awkward.

"She's the reason …" He stops. "I have something to tell you." His voice is terse. "While we're on the subject of being honest."

My body tenses.

"A few months ago I was involved in a deal" — he takes a breath — "similar to this one. Lots of property. Nice old couple. Kinda like the McGregors there." He nods in the direction of the party, still going strong. "I made promises, based on information I thought was true. But it doesn't matter. In the end, they got screwed, and it was partly my fault." I see the regret on his face and despite what he's saying — the implications — my heart hurts for him. "They took me at my word, and I let them down. I promised myself it wouldn't happen again. Business is business, but that doesn't mean I can't be the kind of person my mother would've wanted me to be." He lets out a deep exhale. "Anyway, I just thought you should know." He looks at me, face expectant. Waiting for me to condemn or pardon his sins. I look up at the sky, then at him.

"I knew about the Miller deal."

"What?" he says.

"Dan mentioned it, remember? I found an article online."

"Why didn't you say anything?"

"I don't know. Maybe I didn't want to hear about it." But I'm glad he told me. "Anyway, it sounds like maybe it was a good learning experience. Like you said, it taught you about who you want to be." I keep my voice light. "And that person seems pretty perfect most of the time."

"Hardly." But relief flashes across his features. "I wanted to tell you but didn't want you to think that my feelings for you came from a place of guilt." He picks up my hand again and turns it over, tracing the lines of my palm. "Because nothing could be further from the truth."

"Okay," I say, squeezing his palm back, letting him know he has my trust.

"Thank you." His voice is thick, like maple syrup. Not the liquid sugar stuff, but the real stuff, like we'd have for breakfast tomorrow with our waffles.

"Shoot!" My hands fly to my mouth and I inhale sand particles, immediately starting to cough like a smoker who's been hacking butts for forty years.

"Julia?" Nick's alarmed. "What's wrong? Are you okay?"

"Fine," I croak, waving my hand. "Just totally forgot to get the candy from the Sugar Shack for Caleb's waffle bar tomorrow." I cough again, eyes watering, mouth gritty. "That, and I just ate a pile of sand." *Smooth, Julia.*

Nick helps me to my feet. "Why don't I go grab you a drink from the party and meet you there?"

"Sure." I cough. I make sure he's far enough away before I start spitting and wiping my tongue. Ugh. When I reach the Shack, I pull the key from my pocket and unlock the padlock. I grab a can of Coke and take a big gulp, swishing the fizzy bubbles around my mouth to rinse the sand out. My conversation with Nick replays in my mind while I hunt for Caleb's favorites: Sour Keys, Big Foot, Jujubes, Fuzzy Peaches, Swedish Berries, Sour Grapes, Cola Bottles and Twizzlers. Placing the boxes on the steps, I lock up and pocket the key. Then I start back toward the party.

The barn is a live organism pulsating with music, twinkling fairy lights and laughter. Fresh Stargazer lilies perfume the night air. I see Mr. McGregor outside, mopping his brow with a red hankie, taking a break from dancing. He's talking to Nick, who's holding two drinks in his hands. What had Mrs. McGregor said earlier? When you know, you know?

I start toward them when a shadow crosses my path.

"Julia." The voice is quiet, soft.

Dan.

Chapter Twenty-One

"Hey." I peer over a stack of candy boxes. "What's up?"

"Looks like you need a hand."

"Thanks." I look around. "Where's Taylor?"

"She left." His blue eyes are unusually serious.

"What? Why?"

"It's complicated." One hand pushes the surfer blond hair back from azure eyes. "But mostly because of you."

"Me?" I'm mystified. "What did I do?"

"Sorry, that's not fair." He takes a step closer, the light from the party behind him casting him in a golden glow. "It's actually because of me. And how I feel about you."

"What?" I repeat again.

"I told her I still have feelings for you."

The candy almost falls from my hands. "And what kind of feelings would those be?"

"The kind that never go away and come back every summer. Like I do."

Talk about alternative realities.

"You come back because our parents are friends and they love the campground," I point out, only half processing what he's saying.

"You think I'd be here if I didn't want to?"

"I'm pretty sure you wouldn't have brought your girlfriend unless you wanted to, either."

"I know. That was stupid. She kind of invited herself, and I couldn't say no."

"I'm pretty sure you could've." I look over his shoulder. Nick's still talking to Mr. McGregor, but he's spotted me. His dark eyes watch, but he makes no move to come over. "Besides, why wouldn't you bring your girlfriend to a place where you knew another girl was waiting for you like an idiot? Makes perfect sense."

He winces. "I'm the idiot." I don't argue. Putting the candy on a picnic table, he takes a deep breath. "Seeing you with my cousin has made me realize how strongly I feel about you. I think I'm in love with you."

"What?" My voice begins to tremble. Not with eager anticipation. With fury. "How dare you!"

"How dare I what? Have the courage to admit how I feel and try to make it right?" His voice is calm, but there's a challenge in it. "You know we have a connection. We've had one for five years."

"A connection that obviously couldn't compete with Miss Teen USA." I go to get my candy and leave. If it wasn't for Caleb's birthday, I'd call it a loss and walk away.

"You have every right to be angry. All I'm asking is if you can somehow look past that anger to see if there's anything still there."

"Why would I do that?" I snap.

"Because I genuinely care about you. Yeah, I messed up, but at least I'm not trying to charm you into selling your campground."

My back stiffens. "Excuse me?"

"Come on, Jules, don't be naive. Don't you think it's convenient how the son of the man who stands to make a small fortune brokering this deal is coincidentally attracted to you?"

I hate myself for it, but his comment pricks awake a little voice at the back of my brain that screams, *I told you! I told you!*

"What do you mean 'small fortune'?"

"Not only does he get his commission, the corporation behind the casino is giving them a huge bonus for convincing your mom to sell, not to mention a huge cut of the profits once the casino and mega resort are up and running.

"You're lying."

He shakes his head. "I'm not saying he's not attracted to you. Look at you. You're gorgeous. But do you think you guys would be together if you'd met in other circumstances?"

He has a valid point, the voice says. I mentally tell it to take a long walk off a short pier. Something I also feel like telling Dan to do.

Starting to walk away, I call over my shoulder, "I think you watch too many conspiracy movies."

"Maybe," he calls after me. "Did he tell you my uncle's here?"

I stop. Chin on top of Fuzzy Peaches. Again? I seriously hope that man offsets his carbon footprint. "So?"

"He's presenting your mom with a contract tomorrow. So all Nick's Wakestock bullshit means nothing. Just something to distract you, something you could pin false hopes on. Like him."

A cloud crosses the moon, darkening the night further. Dan comes up behind me, his breath tickling the back of my neck. "I'm the only one who has the balls to tell you the truth. The campground's as good as sold, Jules." I stare straight ahead as a big fat tear rolls down my cheek. And there he is. Mr. Constantine, smiling, just as handsome as his son, while Nick introduces him to Mr. McGregor. One thing about having your party on a beach is that anybody can crash it. Mr. McGregor shakes Mr. Constantine's hand and says something that makes him laugh and pats Nick on the back. Nick looks startled but pleased.

Dan's arms wrap around me and the tower of candy. "I'm so sorry, Jules."

I shake him off. "Nothing's been signed yet." At least I hope not. I have to find Mom.

"Maybe this is what's best for your family. You guys work your asses off. After the year you've have had, wouldn't it be nice to ease the financial pressure? Cut you all a little slack? Maybe take a vacation somewhere warm?"

"It's warm here."

"I meant like year-round."

I whirl around. "First you tell me you love me, then you want me to go away, 'somewhere warm'? Which is it?"

"I want what's best for you." He stands tall, truth in his eyes, but truth realized too late. He nods at Nick. "Not just what happens to be convenient and best for the ol' trust fund."

I just don't know what to believe. Had I been right about Nick and wrong about Dan? Which would now make me wrong about Nick, and originally right about Dan? Shaking my head, I decide, for once, to wait before jumping to conclusions.

"Goodnight, Dan." Turning, I walk away.

Chapter Twenty-Two

"Tink." The gravel crunches as Nick hurries to catch up to me.

"Hey." My voice is flat. Just because I'm trying not to jump to conclusions doesn't mean that Dan's words didn't affect me.

"What's wrong?"

"Nothing."

"I saw you talking to Dan. It doesn't take a genius to see he said something to upset you."

"Congratulations, you're not a genius."

"Can I help you with those?"

"No!" I clutch the candy boxes to my chest and continue to march along.

"Okay. Do you want to talk about it?"

"Not really." My pace doesn't slow. "Let's talk about you. I didn't know your dad was coming in tonight."

"Neither did I."

"Really?" Out of the corner of my eye I see him flinch at the edge in my voice.

"You can ask him yourself." He gestures, holding a glass in his hand. My water, I presume.

"And why would I believe anything he has to say?"

I feel him struggle to keep his patience. "He's not a bad person. Things aren't always black and white, Tink. He sees it as helping your family out."

"Helping himself out is more like it."

"It's not a bad deal for him either," he concedes.

"Or for you. Let's not forget, you guys work together. You're a team. He benefits, you benefit."

"I told you, this isn't about the money for me."

"Really? You're willing to leave millions of dollars on the table because of some girl you just met?"

"She's quite a girl." His voice is quiet. "And it's just money."

Tears spring to my eyes. I wish I knew what to believe. I also could really use a swig of that water. Some stupid stubborn impulse prevents me from asking for a drink. "So is that why you were telling me that stuff about that other deal? Are you trying to prepare me?"

He sighs. "Tink, did you see me talking to Mr. McGregor?"

"Yes." I focus ahead, on the lights of home.

"Do you want to know what we were talking about?"

"Him joining the band?"

He ignores my sarcasm. "He told me to lock you down."

"What?"

"Well, he didn't use that expression exactly. But he said he's been watching us the last couple days and thinks we might have something special. He also said that he and Mrs. McGregor were almost our age when they got together and here they are sixty years later."

Funny, she'd pretty much said the exact same thing to me. "Did you tell him things are different nowadays?"

"No. I agreed with him."

"Did you happen to mention our ... conflict of interests?"

"I did. He was sad to hear about the campground. Apparently he and your grandfather were pretty tight." He pauses. "Not trying to sell myself or anything, but he thought your granddad would like me."

We reach my driveway.

"You're a very easy person to like," I say. Maybe too much so. But the brisk walking has cooled me down.

"Thank you. Does this mean that you're not mad at me?" Am I mad at him? I thought I'd made up my mind to trust him. It would be pretty crappy of me to stop the minute someone tries to test that.

"I'm not mad at you," I say. Maybe I'm the world's biggest fool, but I think I'd rather be that than the world's most jaded cynic. Maybe. I remember something else.

"Dan said your father has a contract."

"He does."

"When did you find out?"

"Last night."

"Let me guess, that was the not-so-great call?" I take a steadying breath. "Why didn't you tell me?"

"I was going to on the beach. Then I ended up blurting out all that stuff about my mom and you inhaled a mouthful of sand," he says, holding the glass he's carried all this way. "I was coming back with water and another confession. I'm sorry you had to find out from Dan. Can you forgive me?"

Just then a loud belch followed by giggles erupts from the direction of the trampoline.

Leaving his question unanswered, I walk around to the side of the house, dropping the boxes of candy on the doorstep. "Cale?"

More giggles. The light of the house shines, registering a new presence.

"Julia?" My brother looks at me, hair mussed, cheeks flushed from jumping. There's a slightly glazed expression in his eyes, which I recognize. His new BFF, James, lies on his back, burping the alphabet. Charming.

"What are you two up to?" I notice the candy wrappers littering the trampoline. Both seem to be peaking on a sugar high.

"James wanted to take the quads out."

"Probably not the best idea, in the dark," I say.

"I know." He looks down his nose at me. "That's why I suggested we come here instead."

Smart kid. "Has James even ridden an ATV before?"

"First time for everything!" James burps out in a hideous voice.

"Ugh. What have you been eating?" I wave my hand.

"Everything." He grins at me. "Nobody would let me have a beer, though."

Nick comes up beside me. "You do know that twelve is the legal drinking age only in Antigua, Barbuda and the Central African Republic?"

"Sweeeet. I'm thirteen. Let's move there," James says, standing up and bouncing, doing a few dizzying flips.

"How do you know that?" I ask Nick.

Nick grins, hands going behind his head to cradle it, elbows out. "I may or may not have done some research when my dad caught me drinking. I was trying to come up with a good defense."

James stops jumping. "I don't think I should have had that third piece of cake." He leans over the trampoline and vomits.

"Okay, kid, let's get you back to your parents." Nick goes to help James off the trampoline, careful to avoid the mess on the ground.

"Sorry," he mumbles. "I'll clean it up tomorrow. Hey, is that your cat? I always wanted a cat. Mom's allergic." He lurches off into the dark toward a small black object. "Here, kitty kitty." Too late, I see the white stripe as the tail goes up in strike position.

"James, stop!" I yell, backing up.

He lunges and the skunk sprays, letting loose a torrent of horrifying stench that has us stumbling backward. Hands come to my face in a feeble attempt to protect myself as Nick jumps in front of Caleb and me. The overpowering stink of sulfur sears my nostrils. James howls, having been thoroughly coated in the noxious reek.

"The lake!" I yell as we run, run, run. The only thing my brain can think is to get as far away from the toxic odor as fast as possible. We race for the water's edge, garnering startled looks from the late-night revelers. Running in fully clothed, we all dive under.

I come up from the cool water, wiping my eyes. The smell is still there. Irrationally, I dive back under despite knowing that simple water isn't going to cut through it.

A small crowd of onlookers has formed. I see Mom and Red gaping in our direction, and Mr. McGregor and another man walk closer to the water, then stop.

"James!" thunders the man with Mr. McGregor.

"Yes," James responds meekly. The shock of the skunk attack and unexpected submerging in the lake seem to have sobered him somewhat.

The man waves a hand in front of his face. "Dear God, what is that?"

"Either someone's smoking some wacky tabacky that's gone off or that's skunk." Mrs. McGregor walks up behind Mr. McGregor, who pulls his hankie from his pocket and offers it to his wife.

My mouth hangs open. Is she referring to what I think she's referring to?

"Only one way to get rid of that," she says, eyes merry over the red kerchief. "Good ol' baking soda, some hydrogen peroxide and dish soap. Works like a charm."

I would do anything to get rid of this smell. Mr. Constantine has made his way down to the water's edge, standing tall and pristine as we wade out of the water. "It seems every time you're around, my son ends up fully clothed in a lake," he murmurs as I walk past. I bite back the urge to tell him about the one time he wasn't clothed and head toward Mom.

"So, uh, I guess you want Caleb and me to help clean up the barn?"

"Um. No thanks, sweetie." Mom waves her hand in front of her nose as it wrinkles. "Why don't you head on home while Red and I and a few others take care of the worst of it. You can help us with the rest tomorrow."

"Dude, you're fast!" I overhear James say to Caleb. The boys are all still in the water. Mom and I look at each other wide-eyed. Tears form in her eyes, and slowly I turn. James is right. Caleb *is* fast. He'd kept up with us all the way to the lake.

Looking winded and pale but exhilarated from the exertion, he laughs. "The only thing you need to be when running away from an animal is faster than the other guy. Or girl," he amends, looking at me.

"Okay there, Flash, it was a skunk, not a grizzly bear," I call, but I can't suppress my own matching grin.

He shrugs. "This time." Nick laughs and pushes him back down into the water.

*

I head down to the lake carrying Mrs. McGregor's prescribed ingredients separately in a cloth bag. Apparently, they're unstable when mixed together and must be used ASAP. Mom's letting me bring the concoction to Nick, who is forbidden to go into his cabin until properly de-skunked. Caleb and I were hosed off and scrubbed down outside the house, eau de skunk still heavy in the air. I carry our clothes in another bag.

A small group hangs around the barn, laughing and chatting,

people in their twenties and thirties, probably McGregor cousins. I lift a hand in greeting, and they raise their bottles in return. Even though technically it's past eleven and quiet hours are in effect, I don't confront them — I don't want to interrupt their good time tonight. Nick sits off in the distance, down by the water, blue towel draped around his shoulders. My nose wrinkles as I get closer. "Hey, Stinky."

He looks over his shoulder and smiles. "Right back at you."

I sniff myself. "I'm not as bad anymore. Too bad it's not like garlic where you cancel each other out."

He stands up, clad only in boxers. "So where's this magic elixir?"

"It actually works well." I get out the three ingredients, mixing bowl and rag. "Red says it's the chemical reaction, but it doesn't last long so you have to mix it right before using it." Pouring the hydrogen peroxide in the bowl, I add the baking soda and dish soap. It starts to foam.

"So do I just slop it on?" He gives the concoction a dubious look.

"Yup." He grabs the rag and starts vigorously rubbing the solution all over his body.

"Maybe don't leave it on too long?" I say, looking at all his dark hair.

"Why? The smell is foul."

"True, but unless you want bleached body hair, I'd be careful."

"Don't blonds have more fun?" He grins, but heads toward the lake to rinse off.

I watch him dive under and come up, muscular back rippling, moonlight reflecting on the water in a narrow column. The man jumped in front of a skunk for my brother and me. The realization that I might be in love with Nick Constantine, regardless of what he's doing here and how long he plans to stick around, hits me with the force of an asteroid colliding. I sigh. That's unfortunate.

He comes out of the water, then repeats the process, as I build a small fire in one of the pits. Watching the flames catch the kindling, I nod and point to his clothes in a pile far off in the distance. He walks over to grab them, the thin material of his gray boxers clinging to the outline of his perfectly shaped glutes. The fire grows in strength and I add some bigger pieces of wood. Returning to the fire pit, Nick tosses in his clothes.

"Careful, we don't want to smother the flames." I grab a long stick and poke around his garments to allow maximum oxygen. Then, grabbing the plastic bag with Caleb's and my clothes, I rip it open, adding them to the fire. There's a whiff of kerosene, which Red has soaked them in to help them burn better, and they go up with a *whoosh*. We watch the flames, Nick's arms folded across his body as he stands there dripping.

"It's too bad," I say, as fire dances along the fabric. "You looked really good in that shirt."

"I'm running out of clothes." Nick laughs. "I'm not sure if I'll make it till tomorrow."

"You're leaving tomorrow?" Carefully, I filter the desperation from my voice.

"After breakfast for Caleb. I have some important things to take care of. But I'll be back a few days before Wakestock to help get everything ready."

"We're still going through with that?"

Nick looks at me. "What do you mean?"

"Your dad has a contract. Isn't it pointless?"

"Unless there's a signature on the dotted line, contracts don't mean much. We're going through it tomorrow night with your mom and her lawyer. They'll give their suggestions and feedback and we'll take it back to the corporation."

"But it's the start of the process." I feel so powerless.

"Come here," he says. I oblige, walking toward him. He wraps his arms around me, and even though they're wet and cool, they make me feel safe and warm.

"Don't give up," he says. "Don't ever stop fighting for what you love."

There are so many things I want to say to that. To him. Tears come unbidden to the corners of my eyes, and I know they'll fall if I voice even just one of the frantic thoughts crowding my mind. Looking over at the clothes that have been reduced to black ashes, I settle for, "That was my only dress." Well, technically it was Paige's.

"Sssh," he says, rubbing my back in small circles as I lean my head against his chest. "You know, you never answered my question."

"Which one?"

"Right before the skunk episode. When I asked if I was forgiven for not coming out with the news of the contract straight away."

"I'm here with you now, aren't I?"

"Thank you." He bends and kisses my forehead. "Do you have to get back?"

"Yes, but …"

"But what?"

"I don't want to."

"What do you want?"

"To be with you."

He sighs. "I want that, too, but I have a feeling that your mom wouldn't be sending only Caleb out this time. It'd be a full-on search party. Her and Red with big flashlights. Come on. I'll walk you home."

"We have to put this out first." Grabbing the bowl that had held the de-skunking solution, I walk down to the water to scoop some up. The fire hisses in protest as I pour the liquid on, sizzling and spitting at the realization of its imminent demise. I know how it feels.

Chapter Twenty-Three

"Waffle bar!" Caleb jumps on my bed, jerking me out of restless dozing.

"Happy early birthday," I mutter into my pillow. "Five more minutes."

"People are coming now. We already let you sleep in." Last night's dreams had me tossing and turning. Most featured Nick saying he'd changed his mind and wasn't coming back. There was also a talking skunk that kept flicking cards at me and saying to put all my money on black. Sitting up, I rub my eyes and glance at my clock. People are arriving now? Meaning Nick will be here any minute. Meaning I need to wipe off the drool smeared across my face and brush away any nasty morning breath. Stumbling to the bathroom, I jump in the shower, sniffing for any lingering skunk scent. Throwing on a purple tank and white shorts, I run downstairs. Mom has set up the "bar" on the kitchen island. It's laden with the assorted candies; sprinkles; caramel, strawberry and chocolate sauces; and our favorite brand of Canadian maple syrup. T-Swift blares from the docking station. Mom's in the zone, pouring batter into the Belgian waffle maker, complete with a couple of black burn marks no scouring pads can remove, which may or may not have been from the one time I made waffles. Looking out the open window, I see a few kids, most of whom I don't recognize, milling about around the picnic tables. No Nick.

"Dude, what's that smell?" one of them says, waving a hand in front of his nose. My body tenses, ready to take on any snotty little kid that feels like dissing my family or my brother.

"It's skunk," James, looking — and smelling — none the worse for wear, informs them. His parents must have doused him in the antidote. "My man Caleb and I got assaulted last night by an evil little dude." He slaps Cale on the back.

The boys look suitably impressed as Caleb relays the story. You'd think they'd fought off bandits or something.

"Julia, can you help me pass out the drinks, please?"

"Sure." I take the tray of cups from Mom and bring them outside, placing them on the picnic table and snagging one for myself. Boys swarm around the OJ like wasps, and I escape back inside. "Is anyone else coming?"

"That's it for guests." She turns the oven on to keep the first batch of waffles warm. "I invited Red and the Schaeffers to drop by later this afternoon."

Perfect. Dan. That's not going to be comfortable.

"What about Mr. Constantine?" I wonder if she'll let me be there when he presents her with the contract.

"Him, too," she says.

"Nick!" I hear Caleb shout and look out the window.

"Hey, bud," he says, holding up his hands. "I feel bad for arriving empty-handed."

I walk out the back door, unable to wipe the silly smile from my face. "That's what happens when you get all your presents early."

"This is Nick," Caleb introduces him to his friends. "He's in a band. Like, a real one."

"Was," Nick clarifies.

"Cool!" the boys proclaim, crowding around to ask questions. I frown and go back inside.

"First batch ready to go," Mom confirms. Grabbing mitts, I open the oven and pull out the silver tray, lined with golden squares.

Marching outside I place the waffles on a table beside the tongs. "Breakfast! Grab a plate. The fixings are inside."

"We gotta go back inside then come out again?" This from the same kid who was complaining about the stench. There's one in every crowd.

"Beats getting stung by swarming wasps," I say, folding my arms and narrowing my eyes at him. The tray is empty in seconds and the kids filter indoors for the trimmings.

"Hey," Nick says when we're alone, eyes warm. "How are you this morning?"

I'm honest. "Okay."

"Just okay?"

"You're leaving."

"I'll be back." I know he's thinking of what I told him about my dad.

He walks over to me. "Julia, I …"

Boys burst out of the house, food in hand, like someone poured boiling water on an anthill. And here's Mom, carrying more waffles. We step apart.

"Do you want a waffle?" I ask.

"Sure." Picking up two plates, I hold them out to Mom, who tongs one on each.

Nick follows me inside and eyes the candy bar in all its cavity-causing glory. "My dentist would have an aneurism. What do you recommend?"

"Well, I'm an old-fashioned girl," I say, spearing a few Twizzlers with my fork. "I like to keep things simple." Using white plastic tongs, I pick up a few Sour Keys and Big Foots. "Some people get really crazy with their sauces." I nod at the chocolate, caramel and strawberry squeeze bottles. "But I like the plain stuff." Lifting the glass bottle containing thick, clear, Grade-A Amber syrup, I drizzle it over my waffle.

Nick watches me. "You're not making sure every square is filled with syrup, are you?"

"Of course not." I laugh, making sure each one is full to the brim. "That would be crazy."

He helps himself to some Jujubes, Fuzzy Peaches and Hot Lips. How appropriate. His hand wavers between the dark chocolate and strawberry sauces. "They mix well together," I say, and he smiles, criss-crossing one on top of the other on his waffle.

"They do."

"Cutlery?" I offer him a fork and knife.

"Thank you."

"Want to go back outside?"

"I do." He leads the way out the front door, into the sunshine. We walk over to sit on the swing.

"So what time are you leaving?"

"Around dinnertime. My flight's at eight."

"Oh." I pick up a Twizzler and take a bite. "Will you be working?"

"I have some stuff that needs my attention, yes. Also, I want to make sure everything's ready for Wakestock."

"What about the contract?"

"What do you want to know?" He pops a Fuzzy Peach in his mouth.

"What does it say?"

"The corporation looking to purchase the land made a fair offer." He hesitates, then, "I think you guys can get more out of them."

"If we were looking to sell." I look at him, putting my unfinished waffle down.

"If you were looking to sell," he agrees. Finished with the candy, Nick takes a bite of his waffle.

"If I ask you something, do you swear you'll be honest with me?"

"Cross my heart, stick a needle in my eye and all that." He makes an *X* over his chest with his plastic knife.

"Do you think we should sell?"

He thinks for a moment. "I don't know."

"You don't know?"

"Well, from a practical, rational perspective it would be the sensible thing to do. Your mom could pay off her debts and have enough money left over to set you all up nicely. You wouldn't have to worry about money for a long time. Maybe ever."

"I'm not very rational."

"No," he agrees. "That's why I like you so much."

"My mom works hard. We all do. But it's not really work, you know? My grandfather used to tell a story; I'm sure you've heard it. About a man who went out and caught just enough fish to feed him and his family. One day he met a businessman who told him he should catch more fish and take them to a market. With the extra money he could pay more workers, buy more boats and sell more fish. If he worked hard and kept expanding he would make a lot of money, and when he retired, he'd be able to do whatever he liked. The man looked at him and said, 'What do you think I'm doing now?'"

"I like that," he says.

"You said selling would be the sensible thing to do. What do you think will happen if we don't sell?"

"That depends," he says.

"On what?"

He smiles. "On whether Caleb finds his treasure or not."

"Come on, you don't believe there's something hidden on the property, do you?"

He shrugs. "What if it's not your typical treasure, but, like, a natural one?"

"What are you talking about?"

"'*Warm silver waters*,'" he quotes.

I raise a brow. "The hot springs?" We hadn't had time to take a look. There are so many things I still want to do with him.

"Maybe," he says, mopping up some strawberry sauce. "I got my dad to look into it."

"Are you serious?" I'm incredulous.

"Yeah, I told him it was part of the property assessment," he says, polishing off the last of his waffle.

"Why would you do that?"

"Well, your internet connection kinda sucks here, no offense." He grins, but I don't smile back and the smile slowly melts from his face. "What?"

"Don't you think that if your dad finds out there's something valuable on the property he won't be able to let it go?"

"What do you mean?"

"I mean, he'll probably tell the company and they'll want it even more." I stand up. "They'll make the offer irresistible to my mom."

"At this point, anything on the table is going to look pretty irresistible," Nick says.

My expression must scare him because he stands up immediately. "Tink, I'm sorry. That came out wrong."

"I think that came out exactly how you meant it."

Then Mr. Constantine is there, walking up our driveway. It's déjà vu, and I'm immediately brought back to the morning when I found out who Nick was and why he was here.

"Julia," Mr. Constantine's voice booms and the nearby birds scatter. "Both you and Nick are looking unusually dry this morning."

"Yes." My voice is strained, temper warring with common sense.

So, you know, a typical moment. Breathe.

"I hear there's a birthday today. I come bearing gifts." He looks over his Maui Jims.

I point. "The birthday boy is around back."

Mr. Constantine sniffs the air. "God. What died?"

"Nothing. Just good old-fashioned skunk," I say. "Still alive to spray another day."

"You might want to go through the house instead of around the side," Nick adds. Mr. Constantine takes his advice and walks up the porch steps, looking uncertain as to whether he should knock.

"Just go on in." I make an attempt to be somewhat hospitable to the father of the man I'm in love with. It's pretty tough to be friendly, all things considered. Which carries over into how I act around Nick. When his dad isn't around I can kind of forget about his day job. But seeing them together reminds me that they both just want to sell this place — *my* place — to the highest bidder. It must be done ethically, of course, according to him. But his words from the beach echo: *Business is business.*

"Skunk got your tongue?" Nick asks.

Only a few hours until he leaves. *Soak it up. Because you might not see him again.*

"Feel like seconds?" I ask.

*

"Dr. Plante is not going to be impressed." We walk up the porch steps into the house, holding our sticky plates.

"Who's he?"

"My dentist back home," he says, opening the door for me. "And he's a she."

I suddenly realize I don't even know where Nick lives. The image of him as some wandering pirate has been stuck in my head since the night we first met. Picturing him at the dentist's office in some fixed location is too weird.

"Where is home?" The smell of waffles inside is much better than the skunk stench outside. It reminds me of the fair.

"Home is Toronto. But I live in LA most of the time. We have a place in Greece we go to. Some of my parents' relatives still live there."

"I'd love to go to Greece." I've never traveled anywhere before.

"I'd love to take you."

Laughing, I open the oven door and tong another waffle onto his plate.

"What's so funny?"

"I'm sorry, that just seems pretty unrealistic."

"What does?" Nick just grabs the maple syrup this time.

"Me traveling. Us in Greece." I wave my hand, most likely not in the country's general direction.

"Why?"

"I don't know. How would I even get there?" I look out at Mom supervising the boys and chatting to Mr. Constantine.

"They have these really cool contraptions called planes ..."

I shove him. "I don't mean like that. I mean like money and stuff."

He raises an eyebrow. "I have a lot of frequent-flyer points."

"Quit it."

"What?"

"Kidding around."

"Who says I'm kidding?"

"Fine." My chin juts out. "When should we go?"

"When do things get less busy around here?"

"The fall."

"What about October?"

"I'll have to check my schedule." Not having enrolled in any school this year, I'm pretty sure it's clear. But still. A girl doesn't want to seem too eager.

"Fine. Get back to me." He looks at my empty plate. "No more?"

"Nah." I put my plate in the sink. There's a shout out the window, and I look up.

Caleb stands there, gesturing. I know that look on his face. He's upset. "But I need more time!"

I run outside. Mom stands there looking helpless as Caleb continues, "I've almost figured out all the clues." He sees me walking over. "Tell them, Jules."

"What's up?" I say.

"Your brother just overheard me telling your mother about the offer," Mr. Constantine says. "It's a great one."

"From what I hear we could do better," I say, folding my arms. He looks taken aback and turns to Nick.

"Any information about our client is confidential." His tone is cold and Nick flinches. "I thought you were professional enough to know better."

"I am professional."

"Maybe we can discuss this later?" Mom says, nodding at Caleb and his sticky-fingered crew.

"Of course." Mr. Constantine's face transforms back into a neutrally pleasant expression.

But the mood of the party has turned as sour as the candy keys. The other boys don't notice, but Caleb's preoccupied, not even perking up while opening his presents, though he puts on a brave face and thanks his friends for their gifts. How dare Nick's father ruin his birthday? I thought Mom said he was supposed to come later this afternoon.

Tight-lipped, I bring the plates into the house and start scraping them into the garbage. Nick follows me inside. I jerk open the dishwasher door and it bounces hard off its hinges. Nick grabs a food-free plate, rinses it under the tap and sticks it in the dishwasher. Through the open window I hear Mom announce that it's time to head down to the lake for some tubing and waterskiing. I look up to see Mr. Constantine shake her hand and tell her to have her lawyer look at the contract. Leaving, he pokes his head into the back door.

"Don't be late for the flight."

"I won't," Nick says, still loading plates.

"Good. Goodbye, Julia."

"Bye."

His hand rests on the inside of the doorframe. "I hope things work out for you and your family."

"I'm sure we'll be fine." Finished rinsing, I wipe my hands on the back of my shorts.

"Don't be late," he says again to Nick, rapping the doorframe, shirt cuff pulling back to expose a watch that looks like it costs more than our whole house. Nick nods and his father leaves, whistling.

"I don't think he realized that probably wasn't the best time or place to tell your family about the offer."

"Why are you defending him?" I close the dishwasher.

"He's just doing his job, Tink. No matter how much you hate it. He's not the bad guy." He takes a step closer and grabs my hand. "Neither am I. I know you're scared and you want someone to blame, but sometimes it's nobody's fault. It's just life." He pulls me closer and my cheek presses against his breastbone, his heart thumping steadily under my ear. "Want to go for a walk?"

"All right." My voice is partially muffled. We walk out the front door. Everyone's gone down to the lake. Other than the whirring of bird wings that sounds like the purring of a cat, it's quiet.

"What about a ride?" I nod at the quad. "You can drive."

"Won't say no to that."

We grab our helmets and I get on behind him. He starts the engine and we reverse onto the road. Hugging him tightly, I rest my forehead against his back, breathing in the scent of him and holding on for dear life.

Chapter Twenty-Four

As if by unspoken agreement, he heads for the trail leading to the cabin. Content just to be pressed up close behind him, I let my thoughts wander, surveying the forest through my bug-splattered visor. I feel an ache in my gut at the thought of losing it all. Every tree, every leaf, each intricate tangle of roots is familiar. It's not just my home, it's a part of me. The oxygen I breathe in from the trees, the water I swim in from the lake, the sunshine and starlight that infuse my pores; all have been absorbed by my body, so that my cells are made up of these things. What will happen if I am separated from them? When I am separated from them. Will I still be me?

Then I realize that some of the roots and trees are maybe not so familiar. The trail is completely grown over. Giving his waist a squeeze, I pull up my visor and shout over the engine, "I think we took a wrong turn."

Just then the quad hits something hard, and I'm flying through the air. Not in slow motion but so quickly that I'm flat on my back before I have time to process what happened. All breath knocked out of me, I sit up, gasping but undamaged. The quad's upside down, wheels spinning, and Nick is on the other side, also sitting, lifting his visor.

"That's the last time I let you drive," I shout. Good thing he wasn't going fast.

"Are you okay?" he asks, getting up and hurrying over to help me up.

"I'm fine. Can't say the same for the quad, though." I take off my helmet and walk up to it, bending down to turn off the engine. "I think the tie-rod is broken," I say, inspecting the vehicle. "Man, I wish I had a wrench."

"I also love it when you talk tools to me." Nick takes off his helmet and grins then sobers as he gets closer to the vehicle. "I'm an idiot. Sorry, Tink."

"I should've been paying attention to where we were going. What the heck did we hit, anyway?"

"Some kind of boulder or something. I didn't see it; it was hidden in the brush." Nick walks back to take a look. "So are we stuck out here?" He takes his phone from his back pocket. "No signal of course. Should we try flipping her?"

"We probably could, but then you'd ruin your last shirt," I say in mock horror. He smiles. "Besides, I don't think she's capable of going anywhere. We'll have to trek back."

"This does not look good for making my flight."

I allow myself a brief smile, thinking of Mr. Constantine's expression when he sees the empty seat on the plane. "I'll be able to get us back." But after looking around for a few minutes I realize that this is a part of the forest I don't recognize. How long was I daydreaming for? At least we have the quad tracks to follow back. "Let's go."

"Do you think your mom is going to be choked?" Nick asks as we trudge back along the path of crushed grasses and trampled shrubs. The air is humid and hot. "I'll pay to fix the quad, obviously."

"We'll just add it to the never-ending list of to-dos around here." I sigh. Then bring my hand to my nose, sidestepping around a big pile of relatively fresh bear poo. "Looks like Old Claw's been out this way."

"Should I be worried?" Nick says.

"Depends. How fast are you?" I tease. "Because all I need to do is outrun you."

That's when he goes back to the previous conversation. "You work too hard," he says, referring to the repairs. "You're young; you should be enjoying life."

"I do enjoy it. Besides, I don't really consider taking care of this place work. Well, aside from the odd toilet disaster," I amend, recalling his help. "But that trip to Greece does sound pretty tempting."

"I was serious. Actually, I think …"

"Listen." I stop walking, shushing him. "Can you hear that?"

"What?" Under the chirping of birds, buzzing of cicadas and scurrying of squirrels is a faint trickling.

"Water." I swallow, all that candy at breakfast intensifying my thirst.

"Nice." We walk through the forest toward the sound of the river. "It'll be safe to drink, right?"

I shrug. "Should be okay, but never a guarantee. I'd only drink it if you're severely dehydrated." The creek bed is a couple of feet wide, almost a river. I step from rock to rock to get closer to it. "And considering breakfast was only an hour or so ago, I think you can make it, tough guy." Crouching down, I cup my hands in the water and bring it up to my face. "But just 'cause we shouldn't drink it doesn't mean it can't cool us off." I splash the water on my face then do it again a second time. What the …? Looking down in surprise, I use an expression from my grandfather. "Well, I'll be damned."

"What?" Nick crouches beside me, putting a hand in the water. He looks up at me. "It's … warm."

"This must stem from the hot springs my mom was talking about."

"Seriously?"

"Can't you feel it?" I kick off my flip-flops and wade in. "It's like stepping into the bath."

"So cool."

"Let's see where it goes." Elated, I start walking barefoot across rocks, picking my way downstream.

"Tink, this is amazing, but I can't miss my flight."

"Right." Sinking back to earth with a thump, I look at the flip-flops in my hand.

"You should come back with your bro to explore it some more. He'll get a kick out of it."

"He will." I smile. "He'll love it. I think there's something in the journal that mentions it. It could be part of his treasure hunt."

Nick takes my hand as I jump down from a rock.

"He's lucky to have you."

"Who? Caleb?"

"Yes. Your whole family is."

"I'm lucky to have them." I look up at him. "And you. Even if it's just for a short time." Tell him, tell him now. "I …"

"I'm coming back," he says. "I know you don't think so, but I am."

I take the easy way out at the last minute. "… believe you."

"Good." Pulling me toward him, he wraps his arms around me, bending his head to kiss me. I feel small in his arms but powerful at the same time. I'm kissing him back with everything I have when he breaks away.

"I'm sorry, I …"

"Why are you apologizing?" he asks. I don't know. Why am I apologizing? For feeling too much? Wanting too much? "I'm the one who should be apologizing." He gestures around us then runs a frustrated hand through his hair, a mannerism I've grown very familiar with. "Attacking you in the woods."

"Just like the big bad wolf."

A wry expression crosses his face. "You got it. Except it was at her grandmother's cabin."

"Will her grandfather's do?" I look at him and lift a brow in a gesture Paige made me practice in the mirror for weeks. The expression on his face makes it all worth it.

"What are you saying?"

"I'm saying why don't we go and visit my grandfather's cabin? Make sure everything's in order?" Oh, my. Am I actually trying to seduce him?

"Tink." He groans. "You're killing me." I step toward him, hands encircling his waist, pressing myself up against him. They trail down. "There's nothing in the world I want more than to take you there right now." The "but" in his voice seems to reverberate around us. I pull my hands back, feeling the rejection wash over me like the water. But less warm.

"You have to catch your flight."

"My father expects me there."

"Well. You wouldn't want to disappoint him."

He's silent for a minute. "Please understand."

But I do. I understand that he doesn't want me as much as I want him and that he's leaving. "Let's go."

"Tink." His voice is pleading.

"It's fine. I'm fine." Pasting on a fake smile, I turn and follow the quad tracks. This is what happens. Nothing new to see here, folks. He'll be gone, and I'll be alone again. The realization hits me that my body has also absorbed Nick, and he is now a part of me as much as the elements I was reflecting on earlier. Briefly, I wonder ... if a heart breaks in the middle of a forest and nobody's around to hear it, does it make a sound?

Chapter Twenty-Five

Curled up on my bed, I wonder how people can survive long periods of intense pain without constantly wailing. When he was sick, my brother was so brave. He barely made a peep in the hospital. Even though I said I believed Nick when he said he'd be back, a small part still thinks that's the last time we'll see each other. Maybe even a medium part. *Thanks a lot, Dad.*

"Jules?" Lifting my head off a wet pillow, I see Caleb in the doorway. "Are you okay?"

"I'm fine," I say, wiping my cheeks. "How was the rest of the birthday?" He walks into the room.

"Good. Some of those guys are pretty cool." He walks over to sit at my desk. "Me and James are going to stay in touch."

"The McGregor kid?"

He nods.

"That's nice. He seems all right." Aside from getting us all sprayed by a skunk. I remember the hot springs. "Guess what Nick and I found today?"

His face lights up. "Treasure?"

"Not quite." I laugh, despite feeling bummed. "Remember how Gramps's journal talked about '*warm silver waters*'?"

"Yeah."

"Well, the other day Mom mentioned a hot spring, and I think we found it." I tell him about the wrong turn and the stream.

"That's awesome!" He runs out of the room and is back in two seconds with the book in his hand, flipping the pages. "Here it is: '*The moon is a wide band of gold on warm silver waters. Overhead, an infinity of diamonds sparkles just beyond fingertips.*'" He looks at me. "Do you think there's silver in the water? Or maybe it leads to diamonds or something?"

His face is alight with wonder and hope. I can't bear to snuff it out. There's been enough of that for one day.

"Maybe. Who knows? It could be anything. I didn't recognize where we were."

"I bet it totally leads to something."

"We'll have to check it out." I smile at him.

"Do you think Nick will come with us?"

I sit up, crossing my arms over my legs. I can barely say the words out loud. "He left."

"But he'll be back, right?"

"So he says." Even though it seemed easy for him to walk away.

"What about Wakestock?"

"As far as I know, it's still happening. I think that's one of the things he went to deal with."

"Good, because I've been practicing."

I smile. "You were really great last night. I can't even believe that it was you up there."

He ducks his head but not before I see the shy smile. "Did Mom tell you any more about the contract?" I ask.

"Not yet. Maybe we should go talk to her about it," he says as if he's about to get a splinter pulled.

"I'll do it," I say, getting up off the bed. "Why don't you go find James?"

Caleb follows me out of the room. "He has to help his family pack up. They're leaving today."

"I'm sorry, Cale, that sucks." I'm not the only one people leave.

"It's okay," he says, "I'll see him again. He's going to ask if he can come spend next summer with one of his cousins or something."

"That's awesome."

"Yeah," he says. "Nick'll come back, too, you know."

"I know."

*

Looking up at the stars, I realize it's been more than a week since I've had a chance to be alone with Astra. The Perseids will be starting soon. Always my favorite show, it's a dazzling star-fest, like the red carpet before the Oscars. I focus on slowing my breath as I look through the telescope. Mom went through the terms of the contract with us. Nick's dad is right; it's a pretty crazy offer. I still can't get over the sum written on it. But when I told her Nick thought we could get more, she seemed overwhelmed and said she'd call her lawyer tomorrow. Caleb just sat there, looking sad and not saying much. So much has happened since the summer started. I feel things shifting and changing around me and within me, and there is nothing I can do to stop it. My hand comes up to adjust a dial on Astra, bringing a stunning globular cluster, M13, into focus. It's breathtaking. Brilliant pinpricks of dazzling light, it's located in the constellation of Hercules, the Greek hero.

How fitting.

I wonder if that makes me Medusa, seeing as how on most days my hair does somewhat resemble the snake-headed Gorgon. I feel sympathy for the poor creature. It's not her fault she was so hideous. Maybe that's why she turned everyone into stone. To make them stay. Too bad I couldn't do the same with Nick. But then again, who wants someone who doesn't want to stay of their own free will? Something flutters against my cheek, and I pull away from the scope lens. There's a small piece of paper tucked into one of Astra's gears. How did that get there? Carefully plucking the paper from the telescope, I unfold it. It's Nick's writing.

Tink,
Thought you might like this quote from Neil deGrasse Tyson.

I smile. Carl Sagan's protégé and the world's most famous astrophysicist, he also hosted the *Cosmos* Netflix reboot Nick had mentioned. I read the sentence below.

"My view is that if your philosophy is not unsettled daily,
then you are blind to all the universe has to offer."

He knows me well. *Unsettled* is definitely how I'd describe myself. Does this mean that I'm actually really seeing the world around me?

"Julia."

I startle. "Hey, Dan."

"Checking out the lights?"

"Yes." Rolling up the paper and tucking it back into the scope, I look over at him. "I know this sounds rude, but I have a lot going on and kind of just want to be alone right now."

He holds up his hands in surrender, still looking gorgeous if you go for the blond Apollo thing. "I get it. Just wanted to say I'm sorry. For everything." I don't respond, and he continues. "I should've told you I was bringing Taylor. Heck, I shouldn't have brought her here."

"Dan." I stand up, crossing my arms over my chest. "You know what your problem is?"

"Are you going to tell me?"

"Yes. You always do what's easy. You take the path of least resistance. Me, Taylor. Why don't you think about what you really want and go after it?" I expect him to get angry with me, but he doesn't. So I keep talking. "Some people give up too easily. If something's hard they walk away." I think of my dad.

The globular cluster twinkles overhead and, in that millisecond, I see the people and the situations in my life in a different light. They say if something is not difficult, it's probably not worth it. Just like caring for your family can be difficult but worth it. A person's character determines if they fight through hard times or not. My dad didn't fight for us, but that's on him. I have fought for my family. I will fight for my home.

One of Mom's yoga maxims reverberates through me like one of her silly gongs: *If it doesn't challenge you, it doesn't change you.* I'm sure she'd get a kick out of it playing a part in my present epiphany. The fight is important, but so is the possibility of change. You don't win every fight, but you have to try anyway. The losses make you stronger for the next time. I could lose this place. I could lose Nick. But I will never lose what makes me me.

I look up to the stars, grateful for the clarity. They are part of me, now and always, and under their light I know my worth, with or without my home, with or without college, with or without Nick. I hear the echo of what Nick said the other night: *Deep thoughts, Tink.*

Dan takes another step toward me. "So you're saying I shouldn't let you walk away from me?"

"I'm saying at least make an effort. If that's what you really want."

I shake my head to clear it, looking at him. "But I don't think I'm what you really want. If I was, you wouldn't have brought Taylor here. And now she's gone. Maybe she wants you to go after her, maybe she doesn't. But if she's what you really want, don't you think you should at least try?"

"What about Nick? Don't you think he wants you to go after him?"

"Nick's coming back." As the words leave my lips, I finally believe them.

"How'd you get so smart?" he asks, eyes raking over me.

"It's the fresh air," I respond tartly. "Oxygen's good for your brain. Now, can I please have a few moments of peace?"

He smiles. "You're something, you know?"

"Thank you." I go back to the scope, not sure if he means it as a compliment. But not caring either. His footsteps echo down the bobbing dock as he hops back onto dry land. Finally.

"Julia?"

Mom? Now what? I lift my head and look back at the shore. "Julia!" she calls again, waving at me, voice laced with panic.

"What?"

"Have you seen Caleb?"

"No? Why?"

"He's gone."

Chapter Twenty-Six

"What?" I bound off the dock, Astra shoved haphazardly under my arm. Dan, who reaches Mom before me, grabs the scope. "What do you mean? He's probably around somewhere. Maybe he's saying goodbye to James?" Mom shakes her head.

"He left a note."

"Saying what?"

"That he figured out the clues to the treasure, and he's gone to get it."

"What?!" Oh, my God, is this my fault? "Why would he leave at night?"

"I don't know!" She's frantic. "The note said something about the moon showing the way?" *The moon is a wide band of gold on warm silver waters. Overhead, an infinity of diamonds sparkles just beyond fingertips.* Crap. "And both quads are gone." Double crap.

"Mom, it's okay. I know where he is." Alone in the middle of a forest. Where the other quad is. Leaving us with no vehicle to get out there. Triple crap.

Mom's wringing her hands. "And I know he says he's feeling better, but I think he's been overdoing it these past few days. He's not used to all this action."

"He'll be okay, Mrs. Ducharme." Dan's voice is reassuring. "I'm going to go get my parents. We'll get a few others to come help look for him."

"He knows the property well, but it's dark and getting cold, and he's not back to full strength. What if something happens to him ...?" Mom breaks off with a choked sob.

"Mom, Dan's right. He'll be okay." I swallow, thinking of the fresh bear dung we'd seen. Black bears aren't usually aggressive. Grizzlies, on the other hand ... Gramps had a sign that said, "In light of recent bear sightings we recommend the wearing of bells and carrying of pepper spray when out in the woods. Outdoorsmen should also be able to differentiate between black bear feces and grizzly bear feces. Black bear feces contain lots of berries and squirrel fur. Grizzly bear feces contain bells and smell like pepper." Despite the joke it's actually pretty tough to tell the difference.

Stop it. There hasn't been a grizzly sighting in months. Still. Quadruple crap.

"Mom, go get Red. Dan, come with me to the shed," I say. Mom flees in the direction of Red's cabin, neon orange sneakers reflecting in the dark. I unlock the shed and grab the pepper spray at the back, along with some flashlights and a few whistles we keep on hand to chirp at the occasional rogue swimmer. "Here." He takes them. "Let's go."

*

"Cale!" I shout. "Caaaaaaleb!"

"Caleb!" Dan shouts beside me, both of us shining our flashlights in different directions. Treetops block the light from the stars, and the night is black as pitch around us. After an hour of stumbling around in the dark, I'm finally able to locate the path that the quad went off earlier today. Everything takes that much longer when you can't see. I hear the others shouting my brother's name. Mom and Red, Mr. and Mrs. Schaeffer.

"The first forty-eight hours are crucial when someone goes missing," I say to Dan, mostly to distract myself. "Though I'm sure Caleb brought supplies with him. And hopefully pepper spray." I look down at the can at my side. Here's hoping we won't have to use it.

"So he thinks there's buried treasure out here or something? What gave him that idea?"

"We found a journal of my grandfather's at his old cabin." And we all encouraged him.

"Thought you guys weren't allowed to play out there." Dan used to try to convince me to go there to make out. That seems like a lifetime ago.

"We made it into a clubhouse for him." I shine my light over a clump of trees, though presumably he'd respond if he heard us.

"You and Nick?"

"Caleb helped." I don't know why a defensive tone has crept into my voice.

"Neat." His posture is stiff.

"You're really gonna pull the jealousy thing when you brought your girlfriend here?" I say. How have I never noticed how immature Dan is? "And while we're searching for my brother, who's probably lost, alone and possibly very frightened right now?"

"I'm sure he's going to be fine. He's a smart kid. Decision to come out here alone at night notwithstanding."

"He wouldn't have done it if he'd thought we had more time." Mr. Constantine showing up with an actual contract must have made things feel a lot more real.

"Do you think your mom is going to sell, then?"

"I don't know." My voice is grim. "Looks that way." Unless Nick can pull off a miracle and make Wakestock the event of the century. Even then, I don't see how the numbers would add up to compete with the ones on Mr. C's contract. "Caaaaleb!" I shout again. Where is he?

Dan shines his light over the ground in front of him, and something metallic gleams back. "What's that?" he asks. I point my light in the same direction.

"The quad." We walk up to the machine, still flipped on its back.

"You trashed your quad?"

"Nick was driving." I squat beside the quad, looking for footprints to see if Caleb's been this way, but the ground's hard and offers no signs. Sliding my hand underneath, I can feel that the seat's been pulled up. The Gatorade and granola bar stored in the compartment for emergencies are gone.

"Mom!" I shout, then look at Dan. "Call your parents over."

Dan yells for his dad and mom, and the adults gather round. "Caleb's been this way."

"How do you know that?" Dan asks.

"We keep a snack in that compartment." I point. "It's gone." My heart beats faster.

"So where do you think he went from here?"

"Maybe to the stream?" I say, "Mom, we found the hot springs you were talking about. Or not the spring itself, but the water that must come from it, it's warm. He thought it might lead to treasure or something."

"Where is it?" Mom asks, voice urgent.

"This way." I gesture with my flashlight. "I think. Can you hear it?"

Everyone strains to listen. Red says, "I remember that old stream." Relieved to have someone else in charge, we follow Red to the banks of the running water, our lights beacons in the dark.

"Where does it lead, Red?" Mom asks. "I presume it ends up in the lake, but what about the other end?"

"The water starts from some falls way back, not even sure if they're within the property line."

"Do you think he knew which way to go?" Mom asks, shining her light up and down the river.

"I don't know," Red says. "Why don't we split up? It's a big area; we're going to need more help. Someone ought to go back to the campground and rustle up some more people."

"The authorities have been called?" Mrs. Schaeffer asks, putting an arm around Mom.

"Yes, I called them, but he hasn't been missing for very long." Mom's voice breaks.

"It doesn't matter, Anna; he's alone in the woods, they'll come." She looks at her husband. "Call them, Eric."

"You won't get a signal out here." Mom's pacing. "It'll take too long to get back."

"Why don't we flip the quad?" I ask. "It might still work."

Red looks at me. "Good thinking." We walk back to the quad. Red, Dan, Mr. Schaeffer and I gather round the back end. "Ready?" he yells. "One, two, three." We grunt and strain, pushing and heaving, as the quad slowly lifts, up, up and over, crashing down with a leaden bounce.

"Now to see if it runs." Red shines his light over the quad.

"I think the tie-rod is broken," I say. Shoot, why didn't I bring my wrench?

"Not broken, just bent." Red bends down and whacks at it with his Maglite. "We might be able to limp out of here. It's the engine being flooded I'm worried about." He hops onto the back with the agility of someone fifty years younger. "Keys?" I hand them to him. He turns the engine over. It sputters then dies. He tries again and it makes a coughing sound, like it's trying to clear something from its throat and failing. He tries a third time; the cough morphs into a purr. Red pats the ATV. "Attagirl."

"You're not leaving, are you, Red?" Mom looks crushed. Like how she looked when Caleb was in the hospital.

"I'm staying," he says.

I'm not going anywhere.

"I'll go get some more help." Mr. Schaeffer looks at his wife. "Alison, you stay here with Anna." He gets on the quad, flicking on the headlights and reversing out slowly. "I'll be back with reinforcements."

"All right," Red says, thumping on the front of the ATV. "Drive safe, it's dark out there."

Mr. Schaeffer nods, lifts his hand in farewell and is gone.

"Alison, why don't you and Anna head down toward the lake," Red says. "I'll take Julia and Dan up the other way."

She nods and they start out, following the creek bed, their lights bobbing off in the distance. The temperature is dropping. I hope Cale is snuggled warm in some sleeping bag somewhere. We walk in silence, waving our lights back and forth over the rugged terrain.

"Caleb!" I shout. No answer.

"I didn't know about the waterfalls," Dan says. "Did you?"

Red grunts. "We don't go around advertising them because they're dangerous. All we need's a coupla dumb kids jumping off the cliffs and hurting themselves. That'd only open us up to lawsuits — nothing but trouble."

"So, Red, you knew about the hot springs?"

"'Course I did," he says. "Your grandfather used to talk about harnessing them into pools. He said the water had therapeutic antiaging properties from all them minerals in there."

"Really?"

"Well, they haven't hurt this old body none."

"You've swum in the pools?" I'm incredulous.

"I used to hike out every once in a while." He grins and gestures to his body. "How else do you think I look so young? That, and your mother works me to the bone, which helps keep up my trim physique." He says it with the utmost fondness in his voice.

"Exactly how old are you, Red?" Dan asks. I, myself, have no idea.

"Sixty-seven," he says, stroking his beard. "I'll be sixty-eight next month."

"Sixty-seven?" Dan says. "I thought you were in your fifties."

"I can't believe I never knew about this," I say.

"You knew, Julia, you just forgot," Red says. "You've had a lot on your mind these past few years. In fact, your grandfather even took you swimming there when you were little." I try to recall it but come up with nothing. A longing for Nick sweeps my body. I wish he were here now, even just to hold me and tell me it's all going to be all right. We are going to find my brother. "Caleb!" Red bellows.

"Look!" I shine my light. "There's a cave."

"Careful," Red cautions. "Stay here. Let me make sure there's nothing else squatting in there." I shiver, hoping Old Claw has found another spot for the night. Red grabs the whistle around his neck and gives it a few short blasts. Nothing. I'm sure if Caleb was in there he would've come out. There's no reason for him to hide from us. Unless he thinks our finding him will stop him from finding the treasure?

"Caleb," I yell. "This isn't funny. Come out if you're here. We're worried!" Red gets closer to the cave, shining his flashlight in. A flurry of bats fly out and I scream, ducking and throwing my arms up to protect my face.

"It's okay, Julia, they're gone," Dan says.

Trembling, I stand up, but still ducking my head. "All the adrenaline," I say, embarrassed, "has me on edge." I effing hate bats.

"Totally understandable," he says, patting my shoulder. And I forgive him for everything, just like that.

"Caleb?" Dan calls, shining his light over the cave. It's set back into a solid wall of mountain. Water runs down over the face of it. There's a valley between two of the larger peaks that looks somewhat accessible. It's also where most of the water is coming from. Red comes back. "I'm going up through there to look," he says. "You guys stick around here."

"I'm going with you," I say. "Dan, you wait here for the others."

Red doesn't argue. That's one of the things I love about him: he treats me like an equal. We walk to the foot of the hills. "What makes you think he came this way?" I ask. And how would he be strong enough to climb over?

"If I were a kid looking for treasure, this is where I'd go," Red says. "There's a plateau on the other side. That's where the main waterfall is. It feeds into a large pool, which is where this water runs off from." We start climbing, and I grasp at roots and tree branches, anything to help me up. It's not straight up and down, but it's steep. I can't see how he would make it over here. Dan's shining the lights on us so we can see where we're going. At last we reach the top of the plateau. Red takes the Maglite out of his back pocket and shines it all around. Up here there are fewer trees, and light from the stars shines down brightly, reflecting off the large pool in front of us.

"An infinity of diamonds," I breathe. It's the most magical thing I've ever seen without help from the lens of a telescope. The falls gush down a higher, steeper rock face that stretches around the pool in a wide arc. Steam rises from the pool, vapor in the moonlight. Walking over to the edge, I put my hands in the water. Not surprisingly, it's hot. "This is amazing."

"Yeah. And now that everyone knows about it, ruined."

"What do you mean?"

"Once word gets out about the hot springs, you think you're going to have only one party interested in the land? This is the icing on the cake," Red grumbles. "So much for my private baths."

I can't believe he doesn't see it.

"But, Red, this could save us. We won't have to sell to the casino developers. Mom herself said she's always dreamed about something like this. We could turn it into a natural eco-spa or, or so many things!" My brain's exploding with possibilities. "We could put into any contract that we'd be able to stay on and run it — or maybe we'd only need to sell some of the land or lease it or …" I know Nick will help me with this, I know it. "This is a treasure. Caleb was right." Thinking of my brother I yell again, "Caleb?!"

"Julia?" a tiny voice squeaks.

"Caleb!" Ripping the flashlight out of Red's hands I start running in the direction of his voice, swinging the light around like a drunken firefly. "Where are you?"

"Over here!" he shouts. "I'm stuck." I follow his voice, still not seeing him. I stumble on some rocks, sliding a bit, then trip over a log.

"Oomph." The log squawks.

"Caleb!" Pure relief floods my body. "Are you okay? Are you hurt?" He brings a hand in front of his face, wincing at my bright beam.

"I'm okay, but my ankle's stuck. And possibly broken." His voice is apologetic. I shine the light on his foot. It's wedged into a crevice between two large rocks. His pant leg is pulled up and there's a bluish-purple tinge already spreading up his swollen leg.

"Red," I shout. "Over here." Red scrambles down.

"What did you get yourself into, boy?" His tone is gruff but I see the relief in his face as he shoves Caleb's head into his chest.

"Just a little accident."

"A little accident?" I snap. "Do you know what could've happened if we hadn't found you? It's getting close to freezing out here and you're stuck. What if some animal came, or, or, or …?" Cutting myself off, I see his teeth chattering. Probably from cold or shock. Most likely a combination of the two. I take off my sweater. "Sorry, I was just so worried." Tears spring to my eyes as I wrap it around his thin frame.

"Okay, Caleb, this might hurt. Look away now." Red's tone brooks no argument. I hold his hand, and Red wrenches the foot out with all his strength. Caleb screams, a high-pitched unearthly sound and I wrap my arms around him tight.

"Breathe, try to breathe."

Caleb gasps at the pain but doesn't cry.

Red shines the light on his ankle. It's enormously distended, and blood oozes from several spots where dirt mixes with exposed tissue. "You're not going to be able to walk on that," he says, sitting back on his haunches. Shoot. How are we going to get him down?

Just then there's a whirring of chopper blades in the distance. From below, Dan starts flashing the Maglite. On, off, on, off. Signaling like a homing device. Could it be coming for us? Red adds his light to the sky, crisscrossing Dan's beam. The helicopter closes in overhead, its blades causing me to shield my eyes as gale-force winds stir up the water and dirt. The chopper lowers as much as it can on the far side of the open cliff. Bright lights blast down and a ladder is thrown out the side of the chopper. Caleb and I look at each other in amazement.

"Is this seriously happening right now?" I murmur. A head pops out of the side of the Medvac chopper, dark hair blowing every which way under protective headphones.

"Hey!" An arm waves as the person shouts down over the chopper noise. "Need a lift, Tink?"

Chapter Twenty-Seven

"I can't believe you got a chopper to come get us." Still completely floored by the evening's events, I sit dumbly in the hospital waiting room. Red insisted on going back down the mountainside with Dan to get Mom, who is on her way. The search and rescue attendant, Kevin, loaded my brother into the rescue basket, which was really more like a mini-stretcher. After Caleb's frantic insistence that I come along, I was quickly winched up, wire cable smoothly retracting with the flick of a switch. It was one of the most frightening and thrilling experiences of my life. "How did you even know Caleb was missing?"

"Well, after all that rushing to the airport, my flight ended up being delayed." Nick smiles, dark eyes crinkling. "Then Dan called."

"Dan called?" It must have been right before we went into the woods. I wonder why he never told me.

"Yeah. He said something about your brother going off to search for buried treasure and being missing." His brow creases. "It was getting dark, and I didn't have a good feeling. Then I saw these guys here finishing up their training on the tarmac. When they came into the terminal I explained the situation. They were hesitant to go out without being formally called in but I offered to pay for everything up front. Just as we were taking off, the call came from emergency services and off we went."

"Thank you." I blink back tears. "I still can't believe it." The drama of the night has me shaking a bit. That and being back in the hospital where we'd lived all winter long.

Nick checks me over. "Do you want some water? I think you might be in shock yourself."

"I'm fine." He goes to get me some anyway, coming back with a little Styrofoam cup. "I just saw the nurse. Sounds like they're almost done operating on Caleb's ankle."

"That was fast."

"I guess the staff knows him pretty well around here?"

"Yeah, they take good care of us," I say. "What about your meetings? Don't you have somewhere important to be?"

"I do." He sits down beside me and passes me the cup. I take a small sip. "Right here." He puts his hand on my knee and I lean my head on his shoulder.

*

When Caleb gets out of surgery, Mom is there. So is Mr. Constantine. The doctor explains to us that the surgery went well, though it will be a few weeks before Caleb can bear weight on the ankle. He'll have to be in a wheelchair, then on crutches.

"Oh, man," he groans, face pale. "I'm going to be stuck inside all summer?"

I hide a smile. A few weeks ago nothing would've made him happier. "Don't be silly," I say. "You can still hang out down at the beach, practice your guitar."

He brightens. "That's true. And the treasure's still out there somewhere."

I look at Nick. "I think you already found it."

"I did?"

"Yeah. The hot springs."

Mr. Constantine looks up from his phone sharply. "The hot springs have been confirmed?"

"Dad, about that ..." Nick leads his father from the room. I filled him in during the helicopter ride. We both agree that harnessing the springs would create a whole other world of possibilities for us and the campground. Nick's going to talk to his father about the potential for other kinds of developments and garnering other interest aside from the casino developers.

"So there's no treasure?" Caleb looks crestfallen.

"Caleb, what you found adds so much value to the land. It could actually save our home, especially if we get investors involved."

Mom's eyes fill with tears. "I never even thought that something like that could be possible. It was right in front of me the whole time."

"Mom, go easy on yourself. After Dad left you had other things to worry about, like caring for the property and us. Though we are model children," I tease. "And when Caleb got sick, I'm sure some random pool way back on the property was the last thing you were thinking of." I wrap my arms around her in a big hug.

"I'm so lucky to have you." She kisses the top of my head. "Both of you."

*

I stand with Nick at the airport, saying goodbye as people stroll by with their suitcases, kids in tow, some on their phones, some with coffees in their hands. Nick has a million meetings lined up in the next week, most to do with the campground. "I can't believe how much you're doing for us."

"As much as I love to be painted with the good-guy brush, don't forget my father and I do stand to make a profit," he says drily.

"But you didn't have to care. You didn't have to listen to me. You could've just come in and taken what you wanted." And I would've given it to him. As it was, he already had my heart. "Then you helicopter in from out of nowhere like in some ridiculous movie. And you're coming back to help us with Wakestock."

"Hmm," he says, a teasing glint in his ebony eyes. "I never really thought about it like that. I do sound pretty great, don't I?"

"That or just plain crazy."

"Well. Being in love can make you do crazy things."

Wait. What. Did. He. Just. Say.

"What?" I stare up at him.

"The second I saw you trip on the dock I knew. It happened for my mom and dad like that. Without the literal falling, of course."

"You love me?" I repeat, dumbfounded.

He grins. "Hey, you were the one just listing off the evidence."

"Despite the fact I can be an anxious, hot-tempered mess?" I say, then immediately wish I hadn't.

He shrugs. "Who isn't? It keeps things interesting." He looks down at me, one hand coming to my cheek. "You're beautiful, Julia. Inside and out."

They announce his flight and that everyone should now be through security. He just stays standing there, looking at me. Is this really happening? Nick loves me?

"I'll miss you," I say, mouth dry.

"I'll miss you, too," he says, bending his head to kiss me, right there in the middle of the airport with everyone around. Which doesn't help me process his declaration any faster. He picks up his bag and takes my hands, kissing each one. "See you soon?" Those dark eyes, so beautiful in his equally beautiful face, seem to absorb every last inch of me, and reflect back someone I've never seen before.

"See you soon." I lift my hand in farewell.

He smiles, shrugging his bag over his shoulder. "Bye, Tink." Turning, he starts walking to the security gate. I stand there, eyes devouring every last second of him before he disappears behind the opaque walls. He shows the woman his ticket, and she directs him on through.

"Wait!" I shout, heart suddenly in harmony with the entire universe. He turns, brow lifted, gaze inquiring. Balling together all the emotion in the pit of my stomach, I let it explode out of me. "I love you, too."

He grins, an affable smile I'd recognize on any starless night. "I know, Tink." And then he's gone, through the doors.

Chapter Twenty-Eight

"This is unbelievable," Paige says, eyeing the stage and sound equipment. Hundreds of people mill around, laughing and talking on the beach and waiting for the band to warm up.

"I know." I look around, unable to take it all in. "Nick handled most of it. The man should be an event planner."

"He can just add that on to real-estate mogul, handyman, talented musician and, oh, your boyfriend," Paige says, and I blush, still so crazy happy it feels like my heart is permanently about to burst.

"I think I said the same thing to him once, minus the boyfriend part."

"And he's really found an investor for the property?"

"Yeah, apparently they're an eco-tourism company with a great reputation. We're talking about it more later with Mom and Mr. C." Nick just flew in last night, and he's been so busy I've barely had a chance to talk to him. Cheers go up as he and the rest of the band take the stage, getting ready to open for Discarded Unicorns. He looks incredible. Tight blue shirt and jeans, red kicks and that hint of scruff that makes him appear dangerous and very, very sexy. So, you know, his usual look.

Paige and I scream as loud as we can as the crowd claps and whistles. The energy in the air is palpable as diehard fans begin to lose their minds at this impromptu reunion.

"Hey, everyone," Nick says into the mic, voice low and upbeat. "Thanks for coming out to the Wakestock benefit and to all our corporate sponsors. It's great to see so many people here." More whistles, screams and cheering. "You all are doing an amazing thing supporting the campground. It's a fantastic place owned by a lovely family, and this is going to give them a little boost before they make some changes around here that y'all should stay tuned for." He looks over at one of the crew who in turn is looking at his phone, walking around trying to get a signal. "What are we at, Kev?"

Kevin looks up in disbelief. "The date with Alex is currently at $45,400," he says. "Some bidder from Vancouver." My mouth drops in shock as the audience roars. I catch a glimpse of Alex's stunned face offstage as his Unicorns bandmates slap their lead singer on the back with teasing catcalls and whistles.

"Well, then." Nick turns and winks at Alex "You better make sure you show whoever it is a good time." He picks up his guitar, throwing the strap around his neck, and strums it, leaning forward into the mic again. "Almost as good as the one we're about to show you right now. This is a new song I wrote for a very special someone. She's here in the audience, as a matter of fact."

"Oh, my God, he's talking about you," Paige breathes, staring up saucer-eyed at the stage. "Shinto and Haru are going to completely freak when I tell them."

"Her name's Julia, but I like to call her Tink. 'Cause, you know …" He grins, looking straight at me. "… she makes me feel like I can fly.

This one's called 'An Infinity of Diamonds.' One, two, three, four!" The band launches into the song. It's our story, about a girl he "fell" for on the dock. Ha. Super catchy and fun, it's one of those songs that has everyone jumping up and down and waving their arms. I have no doubt it's going to be on the radio.

"I can't believe this," Paige hollers.

"I know." We dance crazily beside each other, Nick holding my gaze through the whole song. Girls all around scream his name, but I don't mind sharing because I know when he gets off that stage, he's all mine. The band finishes the song to pandemonium before launching into their next one. I see Caleb making his way up the side steps for his number with the band. He looks like a mini-Nick rock star on crutches, his hair half-spiked. He even has a small solo in the next song. Mom, standing beside the stage with Mr. Constantine, sticks two fingers in her mouth and lets out a piercing whistle. The band finishes their set, comes back with one more song for an epic encore and then before I know it, Nick is standing beside me, sweating and exhilarated, giving me an out-of-this-world kiss on the mouth. Paige melts away into the background.

"You were amazing," I say, when I finally have my breath back.

"You have to say that; you're my girlfriend."

"Have you ever known me not to say exactly what I think?"

"True." He gives me another kiss.

"And that song … about us. It's amazing."

"Alex wants it."

"Alex, the lead singer of Unicorns Alex?" I look up at the band who are coming onstage now to more screaming and fanfare, their lead singer looking somewhat recovered from his auction news.

"Yeah, he wants me to co-write some stuff for him. Maybe I'll even get a publishing contract. That's where my heart is, the writing and composing." He looks down at me, tracing the outline of my own heart, beating like a hummingbird's. "One of the places, anyway."

"Did I ever tell you how incredible you are?" I say as Discarded Unicorns break into their latest single.

"Yes, but it never gets old." He leads me out of the crowd, holding my hand. I catch Paige's eye and wave. She's dancing with Dan and Taylor. Dan listened to my advice and got Taylor to come back for the concert. I hope it works out for them. Down at the shore, Nick looks out at the lake.

"I can't wait until you hear the proposal from the eco-tourism company. It's perfect; they have this whole natural-hot-springs-spa thing all worked out. They want to make it like a holistic getaway retreat, yoga, your mom's health food, massages, the whole shebang. And the best part is we've worked out a leasing deal where you guys retain ownership of the property. They even want your input planning and running it."

"I still can't believe it," I shake my head. "But I'm so happy other people will get to enjoy this." I gesture around. "I just couldn't bear the thought of some poor sap, slack-jawed at a slot machine, pumping in their life savings."

"Casinos aren't all bad." He grins. "But I do feel this arrangement is much better for the parties involved."

"Way better." We stand there holding hands, and I look up at him, smiling.

"There's something else."

"What else could there be?" *You love me, you helped rescue my brother and the campground and you just wrote me the most kick-ass song.*

"These." He holds up two pieces of paper that look like tickets. Airline tickets. I squint and grab the papers. Airline tickets to Greece.

"Are you kidding me?" I shriek. "Greece?" Feeling like I'm going to pass out, I fan myself with the papers.

"Your Mom and I figure you deserve a vacation. We'll go in the fall when things slow down around here." Nick eyes me. "We don't need to make a quick stop at the Sugar Shack to stabilize that blood pressure, do we?"

"I'm pretty sure you're getting that confused with blood sugar." I throw my arms around him and kiss him. "Thank you."

"Well, you're not with me for my knowledge of medical terms. Or lack thereof."

"So there is something you don't know everything about," I tease, feeling light-headed from all the exciting possibilities my life is currently brimming with.

"I know one thing, Tink," he murmurs, bending his head down to mine as we sway to the Unicorns.

"What's that?" I say, gazing up at my pirate.

"I'm crazy about you."

"How crazy?" I look at him from under lowered lashes. The whole coy thing really does get easier with practice.

"More than all the stars in the sky."

I resist the urge to tell him that makes no grammatical sense and smile. "That's a lot."

"I know."

We kiss one of those ridiculous end-of-movie kisses, with the crowd around us, the band in the throes of an amazing melody, illuminated by the celestial bodies overhead. Only it's not ridiculous, it's real life. And it's mine.

About the Author

Alisha Sevigny holds a degree in professional writing and sociology from the University of Victoria. She is also a film school graduate, former literary agent and hot yoga lover. She really does love sunsets on the beach and has traveled the world, finding inspiration in different cultures with her first book, *Kissing Frogs*, set in Panama. For *Summer Constellations* she decided to bring things a little closer to home and drew on her experiences from her family's campground adventures during summer vacations. Now a Toronto-based writer, she grew up roaming barefoot through the wilds of the Pacific Northwest, which accounts for her strong connection to the earth as well as for the sorry state of her feet. She gets pedicures when she can.

Connect with Alisha on social media and her website:
alishasevigny.com
Instagram: @alisha7e
Facebook: facebook.com/alisha.sevigny
Twitter: @alisha7e

Acknowledgments

This is always the hardest part of the book to write! How to express the rib-shattering love and gratitude I feel for all the people who have even slightly aided me in writing this book? I most likely won't remember everyone and apologize in advance, but if you are reading this, know that you are one of them.

I'll start by saying how thrilled I am to have *Summer Constellations* come out with the wonderful Kids Can Press, as a representative of their recent Loft imprint. A heartfelt thank you to my incredible editor Kate Egan for coaxing out many delightful offshoots of inspiration from this story; it's been an effortless partnership. Thank you to Michaela Cornell, one of SC's first champions and my go-to, and to the lovely Lisa Lyons Johnston, KCP's fabulous president, as well as the rest of the bright stars there, including Jennifer Grimbleby and the rights team who champion SC around the world!

I'd like to thank my brilliant agent, Ali McDonald, for her belief and encouragement and for always being there to talk me through the crazy, and to the rest of the team at TRF, including Lydia Moëd, Kelvin Kong and Sam Hiyate.

To Pierre-Louis Beranek for my lovely author photo and to Kaythe (pronounced Katie) who helped me choose the correct colour of foundation for said photo. To the extremely talented Emma Dolan who designed not only this gorgeous cover but also, highly coincidentally, the cover for my first book, *Kissing Frogs*, and whom I horrifyingly forgot to mention in those acknowledgements, though the universe is giving me a second chance to make it right. THANK YOU, EMMA! There.

I'd also very much like to thank my mom and dad for being the best parents a girl could ask for, who always gave us everything they had, not the least of all heaps of love. Thank you to my siblings, Ashley,

Angela and Aaron, for being my companions and friends, not only on those endless road trips but through this too-short life trip. To my extended family: aunts, uncles, cousins, nieces and nephews, not least of all my sweet and spunky grandmother, Flo! You are all very much adored and appreciated and, of course, constant fodder for my characters.

So much love for my hometown, both the physical environment itself and the people I grew up knowing, who continue to support me. Each interaction, each relationship has shaped me into the person I am today.

To Tim Rice for his knowledge on Search and Rescue (that scene is legit, I promise), my cousins Aveanna and Brandt for assuring me that kids still say "sick" when they mean "cool" (or at least the ones in this book do) and to Emily Rondel for her time in sharing her vast birding knowledge (most of which, unfortunately, didn't make it in as the story evolved, but valued nonetheless).

To my children, my hearts, my sweet, sweet babes. You make it so difficult for your mother to write, she knows these precious years are far too short. And to my husband, where words quickly become inadequate when describing the amaranthine love and appreciation I have for all that you do and everything you are.

Lastly, thank you, dear reader, for picking up this book and spending some time with me. I now consider us friends and feel comfortable imparting some big sister advice: Never forget to see the beauty of a sunset from a sandy beach or the hundreds of variations of green in a fragrant forest. When you look up at the stars, notice the breath enter and leave your body and be happy for it. This is your life. Open your eyes, your mind, your hearts, and go live it.

Dream Wildly,
Alisha